MW01278162

RESCUED BY THE WOODSMAN

M. S. PARKER

BELMONTE PUBLISHING, LLC

This book is a work of fiction. The names, characters, places and incidents are products of the writer's imagination or have been used fictitiously and are not to be construed as real. Any resemblance to persons, living or dead, actual events, locales or organizations is entirely coincidental.

Published by Belmonte Publishing LLC

ISBN-13: 978-1983783982

ISBN-10: 1983783986

1

If there was one thing my family knew how to do, it was throw a party.

Actually, there were a *lot* of things my family knew how to do...throw a party for a small gathering of two hundred, run a non-profit, rub elbows with the rich and famous, and elegantly ask for a check for five hundred grand to help fund the arts, or perhaps alleviate the suffering in the Sudan.

All while sipping champagne and nibbling on canapes that looked more like tiny works of art than something edible.

I shouldn't have sounded so cynical – this was *my* party, after all. No less than three or four dozen people had come up to greet me, hugging me tightly or shaking my hand as they said, "Congratulations, Stella...so what's next for the youngest Best?"

Stella Best, that was me.

And what was next?

I had no idea.

Normally at those times, one of my sisters or my longtime boyfriend, Aaron, would speak up to fill the void, but my sisters were off playing hostess along with my mother and father. Aaron was still on his way here. He was late, but we'd forgive him that. After all, he was coming across the country to attend my party.

Flattering, right?

I mean...it should've been.

Yet, I wasn't overjoyed at the thought of seeing him, and when people asked about him, I had to force a smile to come off as enthusiastic as I replied something along the lines of, "Oh, he's on his way...I can't *wait* to see him. It's been too long."

Aaron lived in Denver while I'd been going to college in Michigan and spending my breaks back here at home in New York City. We met up over holidays or for long weekends, but ever since he'd taken the job in Denver, our relationship had become...tricky, at best.

I told myself it was the stress of trying to keep the love alive over the miles, but it was getting to the point that I didn't quite believe it.

"Honey, I'm so proud of you," a familiar voice said from my elbow.

I turned, and with a real smile, threw my arms around the diminutive frame of the woman at my side. "Aunt Millie!" Millicent Royce was my mother's great-aunt, a great dame of sorts among New York society, and she'd been thumbing her nose at conventional thinking since before it was cool to do so.

She was, in short, my idol.

Standing five-four in a pair of three-inch heels she wore despite being eighty-four years old, the woman was nothing short of an icon in my eyes. Born in the early part of the Great Depression, she told me stories of how her brother had gone off to fight in World War II, and even though her toes had been cramped and twisted inside her worn-out shoes, her brother had been over in Germany in a pair of boots that had long since worn through, so her mother had sent Millie's shoe ration ticket off to her brother. It was insane to think about, shoes being *rationed*. It was even more insane when I thought about it happening to Aunt Millie because the woman now owned over *a hundred pair* in various styles.

She told me stories about living in the fifties, a time where she worked in a typing pool and had watched, with awe, the beginning of the Civil Rights Movement, and how she'd felt drawn to get involved herself. She'd ended up jailed, more than once, and had almost gotten disowned by her father. But in the end, her mother had put her foot down.

Aunt Millie was everything strong and brave in my eyes. As she wrapped her arms around my neck, I hugged her back and breathed in the scent of perfume – Chanel No. 5. She wore nothing else.

"I'm so proud of you." She pulled back, beaming at me. But the bright light faded more and more as she studied my face. "You don't look quite as pleased with yourself as I would have thought. Graduating with honors, a dual major. What's the matter, love? Why aren't you walking on the moon?"

"Oh, I'm happy," I told her with a small smile. And I was. Mostly. But Aunt Millie made it possible to be open about things I wasn't always open about. "I'm just...I don't know. I'm feeling at loose ends, I guess. Out of sorts. I've had my plate full for so long and now, I'm...*done*."

"You're far from done." She tapped my chin. "You're just getting started."

"Hello, my lovelies..."

A low, warm voice came from behind us, and I spun around to find Aaron standing just a couple feet away.

"Aaron!" I hugged him, but felt uneasy that I was less happy to see him than I was to see my aunt – and I'd seen her two weeks ago. I hadn't seen Aaron in a little over a month. "Did you just get here?"

"Yes." He dropped a quick kiss on my cheek. "I saw your parents as I was making my way over here and said hello, of course, but I haven't been here more than ten minutes. Aunt Millie..."

"You can call me Millicent," she said, although her voice was warm, almost friendly.

Still, it was a reminder of something I realized some time back. Aunt Millie didn't like Aaron. *Millie* was for friends and family. She didn't see him as either.

"Of course." He took her hand, and I had the feeling he was about to bend over and kiss it, but she gave him a quick squeeze and pump before turning back to me.

"I'll let you have a few minutes with your beaux," she said, smiling as she cupped my face with both hands. She drew me in for a Chanel-scented hug. "Find your happy, darling."

❄

THOSE WORDS WERE STILL HAUNTING me a little while later as Aaron and I spoke with my parents.

"It took some doing, shuffling my workload, but I wouldn't have missed Stella's party for anything," Aaron was saying.

It was the third time I'd heard the story.

"If the red-eye hadn't been overbooked, I would have already been here, but since I had to get my ticket last minute, I wasn't able to get in business class that first flight." He paused, then added with a mock shudder, "And you know how deplorable the main cabin is."

"Of course." My father nodded, clearly appreciating the sacrifice Aaron had made to come to my party.

I wanted to yawn.

I also wanted to point out that flying in the main cabin should be an easy enough thing if he'd wanted to actually make it out to see me *on time*, but I didn't. I couldn't explain why I felt so out of sorts, but I wasn't going to take it out on him.

"Darling..."

Turning my face up to Aaron's, I smiled, hoping I was hiding my apathy well enough. "Yes?"

"I have a surprise for you." He gestured to my parents. "I was hoping to make the announcement to all of your family, but your sisters are such excellent hostesses we'll never get anybody in one place." He gave me a wide grin. "My boss has agreed to give you a job at my company. It's an entry-level position in my department, but that's where everybody starts out."

I blinked, not quite comprehending.

I hadn't even started looking for a job yet, hadn't figured out where or how I wanted to put my marketing degree to work. I'd been thinking about finding a non-profit or something like that, and not just because eventually, my parents would want me to come on board with the family business. I wanted to *help* people, not just make money. I had enough of that.

Everybody was staring at me. "Does this mean..." I glanced around, then back at Aaron. "You'd be like...my boss?"

"Yes." He chucked me under the chin as if I were five. "But don't think that means you can slack off. I know what you're capable of." As he spoke, he reached into the interior pocket of his suit coat and pulled out a small box. "And one more thing..."

Dread settled over my shoulders like a wet cloak, and all the air left my lungs.

No. No, no, no.

He wasn't...

"Don't worry." He flashed his grin at me. "It's not a ring. Yet."

I nearly sagged to the floor in relief when he flipped it open to display a key, polished to a high shine. "A key to your new home. Have I told you about my new apartment? I'm renovating it so you'll have your own office space. My office is a little bigger, of course, but it's hard trying to find the perfect space in a city like Denver, and this is probably just temporary. We'll look for a house soon..."

As he continued to speak, blood roared in my ears. Aaron tucked away his 'gift.' A key that was a copy of the one he'd already given me when he took me to the new apartment just a month ago. This 'gift' was all for show.

I gritted my teeth. He'd offhandedly mentioned that the

second walk-in closet in the bedroom was actually ideal for a small home office, with just a few minor adjustments. I bet *that* was my new office.

"A new job already," Mom said, resting her hands on my shoulders.

Her touch tugged me out of the daze, and I managed a half-hearted smile. "Yeah, great news, huh?"

"You still look shell-shocked. Of course, Denver is very far away." She pressed her lips together, looked a little teary for a moment. "Oh, my baby is growing up."

"Mom," I said weakly. "Come on."

❄

"COME ON, BABY...THAT'S IT..." Aaron panted above me, his hips pistoning against mine, our flesh slapping together. "I'm gonna come soon...are you there?"

I tugged his face to mine, wanting desperately not to answer that. "Come here," I said instead.

He ignored me, working a hand between us where he proceeded to mash his fingers against my clitoris like it responded to the *amount* of pressure. I gasped, although not entirely out of pleasure. He didn't notice, but when I covered his hand with mine, he laughed shakily. "That's it...I love it when you play with yourself. It's even better than when I do it."

It figured–

I cut the thought off and concentrated on the feel of my fingers slipping around those sensitive nerves. Aaron kissed me, and I sighed into his mouth. I did like kissing him, and with his weight pressing me into the bed while my fingers worked my clitoris, my pleasure seemed to ignite and catch up to his.

"That's it, baby," he muttered against my mouth. "I'm gonna...yeah..."

I tuned him out, focusing on the gathering tension between my thighs as a cry slipped out of me.

Aaron shifted and moved higher, hips driving against mine harder and faster.

Not yet, not yet...

"I'm going to come, Stella..."

Finally, I felt the tightening begin in my belly, and I gasped, arching up into him, moving against my hand and him.

Just as he climaxed, I came too. I was still in the middle of it when he dropped down on top of me. He grunted and rubbed against me a couple of times, and as soon as the tremors faded, he rolled off. "That was good. Missed you, Stell."

He pulled me against him, and it wasn't more than five minutes before he was asleep.

Me, I just laid there, still wet from him and myself, staring into the darkness.

Find your happy, Aunt Millie had said.

I eased away from Aaron and slid from the bed, grabbing my nightshirt on my way from the bedroom. In the bathroom, I closed the door before turning on the lights. I had to squint as my eyes adjusted, but I stood in the mirror and stared at my reflection.

How was I supposed to find my *happy*...whatever that meant?

I'd graduated. I had a good boyfriend. Now, apparently, I had a job – which I'd be starting in two weeks. Aaron had informed me of that bit of information on the way to my apartment. At twenty-two years old, was there something more that I was supposed to *have* or be doing?

Was I missing something?

I had absolutely no idea.

But if this was what life was supposed to be about...then I didn't know, but surely there was something *more*.

2

Six days later, I was wishing for a do-over of the entire week.

Maybe even longer.

I was supposed to have had two weeks to get things in order, plus have a little bit of time to spend with my family, but on Wednesday, my new employer had called me out of the blue and asked if I'd be available to start on Monday.

Now, instead of doing some shopping with friends or maybe going to one more show on Broadway with Aunt Millie, I was in an airplane hurtling toward Denver.

The clouds were thick.

We'd left behind blue skies and sunlight in New York, but about halfway through the flight, the clouds had started to appear, first white and puffy, then thicker and darker, ominously so.

The pilot had mentioned some rough weather ahead, but this was a little more than I'd expected.

A sudden jolt, followed by a cry, jerked me from my perusal of the clouds, and I looked back into the main cabin where the noise had come from. I saw nothing but the curtain. A few seconds later, the curtain was hurriedly pushed back as one of the flight attendants came through. The plane shuddered and bucked, and I gasped, grabbing for the armrests and holding on, like that would do any good.

"Somebody back there got hurt...bleeding..." someone said.

That had me jerking my head up, and I saw the man in the seat across from mine looking back. He sighed and lifted a hand to flag the airline attendant down, but she had her back to him, so he just undid his seatbelt. He caught my eye, and I said, "I don't know if that's a good idea."

"I'm a doctor. Supposed to be heading to my son's wedding then out to Hawaii for some R&R." He shrugged deprecatingly. "I'll be careful, but I want to check on that injured passenger."

I'll be careful, I thought. Famous last words.

My grim thoughts might have been a harbinger. I kept glancing behind me, macabrely fascinated by the hustle going on in the main cabin. The flight attendant had hung up the phone and hurried back into the main cabin not even a minute after the good doctor had headed back there and I'd watched, wishing I could hear.

A woman rose to get something from an overhead compartment, blocking my view of what was going on, and another attendant approached her, gestured toward the seat, and I heard enough to know that the pilot wanted everybody buckled up. There was no way I was leaving *my* seat. The plane bucked again, and I had some miserable image of the damn thing bucking and kicking like a rodeo horse or something equally fierce.

The pilot came on the overhead speaker, and over the pounding in my ears, I heard his low, garbled voice. His words were cut off halfway through by another shuddering jolt that rocked the cabin of the plane – then there was a crashing noise behind us.

A few more voices rose, followed by swears and a woman sobbing.

Slowly, I looked back and saw the door to the overhead bin was open – and everything in it had come tumbling out.

A man in a seat right below it sat with his head in his hands, a thin trickle of blood running from his temple.

The good doctor, I believed, was going to be busy.

❄

I WAS IN CHEYENNE.

My head was killing me, and I didn't think all of it was from stress, although the flight from hell definitely hadn't helped.

Granted, my headache wasn't anything compared to the guy who'd gotten whacked with a wooden cane earlier. While the airline attendants wouldn't say what actually happened, the passengers were speculating quite a bit. One of the women I'd spoken with while emergency medical personnel boarded to get the two injured passengers off first said she imagined the passenger who'd gotten into the overhead bin hadn't closed it well.

It will be the airline's fault, of course. She rolled her eyes.

One of the attendants had checked the bin after the woman closed it – at least I thought that was what she was doing, but maybe she'd been scolding the woman about getting out of her seat. I didn't know.

I was too busy being torn between being glad I was out of the air – that flight had been rough – and getting more and more frustrated that I wasn't in Denver.

And I wasn't going to *make* it to Denver anytime soon.

"The plane has to be cleaned, I'm afraid," the attendant told the man in front of me. "A passenger was injured, and our policy dictates–"

"I don't care about the policy!" He thumped his fist on the desk. "I was supposed to be landing in Denver *now*. Why did we divert to Cheyenne?"

A couple of people behind me murmured in agreement, while others stirred restlessly.

I flicked my eyes to the digital screen overhead and watched with dismay as our flight went from *delayed* to *canceled.*

Others noticed, and the cacophony around me grew until I stepped out of line. They weren't going to be getting us to Denver anytime today. I knew that much. I could tell by the strained look in the woman's eyes as she tried to appease one unhappy passenger after another.

My headache increased, the pounding so severe I thought it might make me sick. Slowing down by one of the vendors, I bought a soft drink and some over the counter painkillers, chasing the pills with the liquid caffeine. Maybe that would help.

The fact that I was in *Cheyenne* instead of Denver *definitely* wasn't helping. The flight had been diverted here although we hadn't been given a clear explanation why. The two cities were less than two hours apart. I wouldn't think that the weather would be *that* different...would it?

As I stood in line waiting to rent a car, I googled the Denver airport on my phone. A groan escaped me the second I saw the headlines. A small fire on a plane had temporarily closed one of the runways, and several flights had been diverted, the article informed me. It had nothing to do with the weather after all.

Hell.

No wonder the harried woman in the airline uniform behind the counter had looked like she was in need of a spa day – or ten.

I didn't *need* to be flown anywhere though. With Denver being less than two hours away, I realized I could just drive the distance instead.

Less than ten minutes later, I found out just how wrong I was. I could have driven if I'd had the foresight to book a car, but since this day hadn't gone as planned, I had no idea I'd need one.

"All the cars?" I asked, echoing the words the counter agent had just told me.

"Yes, I'm afraid so." She gave me a sympathetic smile. "I'd tell you to try one of the other agencies, but with such a large flight being diverted because of that fire…" She shrugged.

Groaning, I covered my eyes while the couple behind me started to murmur about finding a hotel room before all of *those* were gone.

"Maybe we should go back to the airline counter," the woman said.

"The airline will cover a night's hotel," the car rental agent offered, clearly having overheard.

I groaned. "I need to be in Denver today."

I'd already tried calling Aaron to let him know what was going on, but he wasn't answering. I'd sent a text, but so far, I hadn't heard back. I didn't want him to get to the airport and me not *be* there. I should be landing and ready to greet him. I should be happy about starting this new phase in my life. I should be a lot of things…not standing here.

"What's this?" I picked up a brochure that showed an aerial view of the Rockies and the nose of a small plane.

"Oh, that's the sightseeing flight company my boyfriend owns." She beamed at me, looking like a proud mama. Then she waggled her eyesbrows. "Actually… he's going to Denver in an hour or so."

I waggled my eyebrows back at her. Perfect.

❄

IT'S A VERY different thing flying in a commercial jet compared to the small plane in which I currently sat.

Hank Jackson's little outfit boasted several small engine planes, and this one here, he'd told me, was his baby. His first craft and his personal favorite was "as sound as could possibly be."

It better be, because I was paying him double his normal rate to allow me to ride with him. He'd initially said no, said he was thinking about not going, but I think he'd done that just to make more money.

Got some rough weather coming through. Going to get rougher in the next couple of days too. Best just to get yourself a hotel room and wait it out, honey.

I'd persisted, and after offering double, plus a hefty tip, he'd agreed, but I had a very limited amount of time to get my keister to his place because he wanted to leave before the weather got bad again.

In truth, I didn't know why I was so desperate to get to Denver, but something was pushing me, driving me, to get there as soon as possible, by whatever means I could manage.

If I could have gotten a hold of Aaron, I might have waited out the next storm, but so far, he hadn't answered any of my texts or returned any of my calls – so yes, I was that determined.

"You ever been up in a small plane before?" Hank asked, his voice friendly. He'd told me he would have pointed out some of the sights – if I liked – but I told him it wasn't necessary. I wasn't there to check out the mountains. I'd be living here. I had all the time in the world to do that.

A heavy jolt shook the plane, and I couldn't help but feel like somebody had thrown me into a large tin can and was rattling it. It hadn't been like this on the jet.

"Ma'am?"

Belatedly, I realized he'd asked me a question, and I glanced over. "Pardon?"

He had his eyes focused on the plane's controls and was looking outside. "I was asking if you'd ever been on a small plane before?"

"No, Mr. Jackson. I can't say that I have." I managed a weak laugh. "I'm assuming it's not always this entertaining."

"Oh, we're doing well enough, all things considered.

Bouncing a bit, but that's the wind. Everything going right as rain." He laughed a little. "What's right as rain mean anyway?"

"I couldn't tell you."

Maybe if I closed my eyes, it would be better, I thought. So I tried – for all of two seconds. The heavy bump and rolling sensation of the plane only seemed to intensify when I couldn't see. *Definitely not trying that again.*

"It won't be much longer, sweetie. Good thing I'd already planned on tucking into Denver for a day or two," he mused. "Won't be a good idea to try and fly back home with the way things are getting worse."

My hands tightened on the armrests. "Are they getting worse?"

"Oh, just a bit." He sounded unconcerned, his round face still set in a smile. "Don't you worry, honey. I've been flying planes since I was sixteen years old."

He sounded so calm, so self-assured, and I tried to take comfort in that. It might have even worked. But barely a second after he said those words, there was another tremendous shudder of the plane, followed almost immediately by the sound of something ripping.

I shot Hank a look.

That was the last clear thought before panic took over as the plane dropped from the sky like a stone from a giant's hand.

3

I don't know what woke me, the pounding in my head or the cold. At first, I just shivered and tried to pull the blankets around me, but there weren't any blankets.

There was something else holding me down, digging into my chest. I fingered the material.

Straps!

That really brought me out of the semi-fugue state I'd been in.

Jolting upright – or trying to – I looked around. The instinctive, jerking movement sent pain crashing through my head, and I groaned, reaching up to rub at my skull.

"You okay over there?"

The sound of the voice, only vaguely familiar, had me stirring in the seat as a memory tried to come back. A name floated to the surface of my thoughts, and I grabbed at it. "Hank?"

"Yes, ma'am. You okay?"

It all came flooding back, and I groaned as I looked around. "We crashed, didn't we?"

"Yes, ma'am. We did. Are you okay?"

He was going to keep asking that until I answered. I gave him the most honest answer I could at the moment. "I'm not entirely sure. My head hurts. I'm still taking stock."

"You just keep on doing that. I've already sent word about the crash, but that storm we were trying to outrun seems to have it in for us because it's gotten bigger and meaner. I don't think they'll be sending out anybody until it passes."

I shivered, the words not really making sense as I wiggled all my body parts and gingerly felt for injuries. I didn't think there was much of anything, which was a miracle considering we'd just been in a freaking *plane* crash. Then, abruptly, Hank's words made perfect sense. "What do you mean they won't be sending anybody out?"

"They can't, not with the storm that's moved in. Now don't go fretting, okay? I radioed the crash in, and they know we're out here. We just have to wait this storm out." There was a note of strain in his voice I hadn't heard earlier, and I realized I hadn't asked how he was.

"Hank, were you hurt when we...um..." How did one phrase it? When we crashed the plane? When we fell? "Are you hurt?"

Please don't let him be hurt, I thought desperately. I'd bribed him with double the money to bring me up here–

No. We weren't up in the sky anymore.

We'd crashed. Crashed, and I needed to calm the *fuck* down and think.

"Well, I'm not too bad all things considered, but I do believe I got a broken leg." He delivered the words with the same implacable calm he'd used throughout that hellish flight.

"I...what?" He hadn't just said what I thought he said, had he? Scrambling at the safety belt that had protected me through the flight – and crash – I finally managed to free myself. The light was fading, clouds rushing overhead like mad. Just as I took notice of them, I saw something fat and white floating down.

Snow.

It couldn't be snowing. It was September.

In the Rocky Mountains, I reminded myself. It could very well be snowing.

"Okay...I'm just going to..." Swinging my legs out of the seat, I eased myself off of it, intending only to take a look at Hank and see if maybe I could do something to help.

But I made the mistake of looking back toward the plane.

Or what was left of it.

"Aw, hell," I whispered.

"Don't go thinking about it, Miss...Stella, right? Look at me right now," Hank said, voice still gentle but firm.

It helped. I swung my head around and met his gaze.

"I think if you gimme a hand, I can get myself loose and we can make camp in what's left of my bird here." As he spoke, he wrapped his hands around his right leg, and that was when the odd angle of his lower leg became apparent.

"I do believe you're right," I told him, echoing his *aww shucks* manner of speaking. "I think that leg is broken."

He grinned at me, a pained sort of smile, but a smile nonetheless. "We'll stabilize it before I try to move. Think you're up to helping me with that?"

I swallowed, then nodded. "I'm game if you are."

❄

By the time we'd managed to rough out what Hank had decided was just as fine a camp as any he'd ever seen, the rest of the daylight was gone. I'd spent the past half hour searching for my phone, but since there might have been another twenty minutes left of sunlight, I gave up until tomorrow.

"How far do you think we are from the nearest town?" I asked as I watched him add to the fire he'd built.

We were in the hull of the plane, or what remained of it, and he'd used the emergency supplies he always kept on hand to build said fire and make some beef stew for us to eat. "It's dehydrated stuff, but not bad, really," he'd told me.

I was just glad to have water and something to eat.

Earlier, I'd damn near frozen my butt off so I could pee.

Hank had made himself a crutch out of a length of wood I'd found while out scavenging for firewood. It was just barely tall enough to suit him, and he'd disappeared for just a few seconds, but he hadn't frozen *his* tail off just to tend to his bladder.

His rather miraculous emergency kit had everything in it we could need for a few days here, plus fishing line, a knife, and other odd items that I was sure he could put to use – if he could walk.

"Nearest town..." He shrugged and scratched at the scruff growing on his face. "Hell...I don't know. Denver or Fort Collins is probably a couple of days walk away. A few smaller towns are closer, I think, but still twenty miles..." He named one and looked around with a squinty-eyed look and pointed. "That's as the crow flies. If I'm right about where we are, there's a road about five miles away, but I'm afraid I'm not up to walking five miles."

I gulped. I didn't know how anyone could walk that far in this weather, bad leg or not.

He gave me a pained look. "We'll be okay, though. I know they heard my relay, and I called ahead to the county airport. I've got all the doodads on my bird that they need to find me."

"Just...not tonight." I managed a weak smile. "You know, I could walk five miles. Which way–"

"Not happening." He pointed a finger at me, shotgun style. "We stay together, and we stay with the bird. It's the easiest thing to see from the sky, and that's how they'll come looking for us. Besides, we'll be fine. It's going to get chilly but nothing we can't tough out." He laughed as the wind whipped a few snow flurries in. "It's a good thing it's not winter yet!"

❄

WAKING UP WAS PURE HELL.

I'd been in a car crash when I was seventeen. There were reasons some parents didn't like their kids riding with friends who only recently gotten their driver's licenses. That wreck was one of those reasons. Teenagers could be very easily distracted, as I'd learned.

None of us had been hurt, thankfully, but the first few days after the accident, I'd been stiff and sore, like somebody had worked me over with a baseball bat – or at least that was how I imagined I might feel after such an ordeal.

This was even worse.

Now, I felt like somebody had worked me over with a giant-sized bat – a studded one.

Taking a few minutes to stretch and try to ease the various aches, pains, and kinks from my body, I drew in a few breaths and smelled something that bothered me. A lot.

Last night, after we'd eaten, Hank had mentioned we were higher up in the mountains and that it probably wasn't even snowing down in Denver, but the higher altitude up here changed the equation. I had a feeling the equation was about to be changed again. There was a faint dusting of flurries outside that I could see, but there was more coming, I could smell it. One thing about living in New York City and Michigan was that you got a good idea of what it smelled like when snow was in the near future.

And it was most definitely in the very near future.

Shit.

I remembered what Hank had said about a rescue team not being able to look for us in the storm. Was another storm moving in or was the worst of it over?

I had no idea, but the thought of being trapped up there with nothing but the wreckage of the plane for shelter had terror welling inside me. I had been so *stupid*, being so determined to get to Denver, I couldn't even wait for a damn storm to pass.

I inhaled a long breath. It would be okay.

Hank hadn't seemed too worried.

Okay, he'd seemed concerned, yes, but panicked?

No. He certainly hadn't seemed panicked.

It's not good business ethics to panic around the customers, I thought sourly. But then again, the plane was wrecked. Then again, I was alive. Would it matter if I saw him panicking?

I wasn't sure.

Casting Hank a look, I eased myself upright and gazed around. He had some of those emergency lights in his kit – the kind that glowed green once you snapped them – but he hadn't wanted to use those, and we'd decided to save the batteries in the flashlight as well. He did, however, have a light that was powered by wind-up, so I took that and felt my way out of the plane. Once I was farther away from Hank, I started to wind up the battery, hoping the noise wouldn't wake him. He had slept restlessly, his leg hurting him, no doubt.

Once the light was powered up, I used my hand to cover most of the beam and slid back inside, angling the tool so that it swept over the floor. I needed to find my phone. I had a dim hope that it might still be in one piece.

Before, I'd focused my search near the storage compartment where I'd stored it and my purse. The compartment had been busted during the wreck, scattering everything inside. Now, with the beam of light forcing me to look at only one small place at a time, I might get lucky…

Fives minutes past. Then fifteen. Then thirty.

I was about to give up when… there!

I found my purse underneath a piece of the wreckage. Excited, I pulled up other pieces until… I nearly cried out in joy. My phone.

I examined it closely. I'd started buying the more rugged cases for my phones after a few hard drops had sent me to the store twice to buy a new phones. To my relief, the case had protected it from most of the damage. There was a crack in the screen, but I could still *see* the screen, and the crack was down near the bottom left-hand corner. I didn't care about cosmetic damage as long as I could *use* the thing.

Holding my breath, I pushed the power button. It powered on just fine, but my hopes were dashed when I saw there was no signal.

I bit my lip as I shot Hank another look. He was still snoring softly, his injured leg tucked against the wall of the plane.

We needed to get help.

It was beginning to get light outside, just enough for me to make out my surrounding. I'd just hike a little bit. I'd pick out a landmark and walk toward it, a straight line. That would be safe enough, surely.

I started to walk, keeping one eye on the phone, hoping for at least *one* bar, another on the skyline. There was a tree in front of me, maybe a few hundred yards away that looked like it had been struck by lightning or something. I decided to walk toward it. It wasn't that far, and surely I could see the plane from there.

I stopped every few hundred feet to look back and make sure, getting a little more nervous as the plane shrank, growing smaller and smaller, while the tree didn't seem to get much bigger.

Still, I kept walking. I was going downhill. We'd been on a more level area, and going downhill...that had to be good, right? Hank had mentioned a road, and a small town...it would be *down* the mountain. At least I thought so.

I glanced back, looking for the plane.

Fuck. I couldn't see it.

And there were still no bars on the phone.

"Time to go back," I muttered to myself, discouraged at not finding a signal. I'd last seen the plane no more than a hundred steps back so I'd be okay, but I didn't dare go any farther. Turning, I started to retrace my steps.

From the corner of my eye, something moved. My heart leapt. Was it a rescue party?

"Hello?" I called out, staring in that direction. "Is—"

The next words froze in my throat as something slunk out from behind a tree trunk, revealing its body.

Its very big body.

A wolf.

My heart was pounding so hard in my throat that I almost couldn't swallow. Very slowly, I took a step backward, praying with everything inside me that it was just a dog. A nice, lost little dog. But I knew I was fooling myself.

Shit.

Shit.

Shit. I took another step back, trying to remember what the right thing to do was. I was a nut for those *"What to do if"* scenarios, and if that had been a bear, I knew I should have raised my arms and made a lot of noise. But what did I do with a snarling wolf?

Don't run, a voice whispered in the back of my head. *If you run, it's going to chase you.*

Another movement off to the side had me sliding my eyes to the left.

It was another wolf.

And another...

And another...

"You...wolves don't eat people, right?" Maybe just me talking would make them go away. My sisters always told me that I could be *that* annoying.

The big one – the one I'd seen first – took a step toward me, lips peeled back from his teeth as he made a menacing growl.

"You don't want to eat me," I said, lifting a hand. It shook. My voice shook. Every part of me was probably shaking, from my voice straight down to my toes. Why the *hell* had I left the plane? "I eat too much junk food. I'd be bad for your heart."

I was babbling now. Babbling to a wolf that had just taken another menacing step toward me.

Panic bubbled up in my throat as he took one more. Time seemed to slow down, his body tightening like a coiled spring.

This is it...

I tensed, preparing for the pain of its teeth sinking into my skin, and I threw myself backward as he lunged, knowing it was pointless.

I fell.

And I kept falling, head over heels before my butt hit hard cold earth, and I started to slide down, down, down.

There was a huge *crrracck* that echoed through the air – possibly my skull because I hit something – hard. And I kept falling.

But sharp teeth didn't sink into me, and I was glad of that.

That was my last coherent thought before darkness swam up to grab me.

4

I had woken up hurting the last time and this time was no different.

Once more, my body ached – *all* over, and my head was killing me.

Groaning, I reached up to touch my temple, and even that slight movement was enough to send agony crashing through me. Lowering my hand, I closed my eyes and waited for the pain to recede. It did, slowly, but awareness didn't come with it.

I felt like my entire head had been swathed in cotton.

Where was the plane?

Shouldn't I be in the plane?

It had crashed, right?

I reached back into the void of memories, trying to think. That made my head hurt worse, but I persisted because something didn't seem right.

I was *inside*, and I was *warm*.

The scent of woodsmoke filled the air, not at all unpleasant, but it was another indication that I was in some kind of shelter.

Give it a minute, Stella. Maybe you're sick. Maybe you hallucinated the whole plane crash thing – wouldn't that be fantastic?

It would, because that would mean I hadn't come this close to being wolf food.

Wolf food.

The wolves.

Bile welled up in my throat as the memory came crashing back.

Oh, shit.

The wolves.

I wasn't sick because there was no way in hell I would have hallucinated *that*.

So the plane crash had happened. I had walked away from the plane, trying to get a signal on my phone...and I had ended up surrounded by wolves.

And now I was inside. Somewhere.

Time to figure out where, and what was going on.

I cracked one eye open. When nothing swam in front of my vision like last time, I decided to try the other.

Okay. This was progress. I wasn't seeing double, and the pain in my head didn't get any worse. Without moving my head around, I took in as much of the room as I could.

I thought I was in a cabin. I saw wooden planks overhead. A lodge, maybe. Had there been a rescue team? I'd heard a noise...a gunshot, I thought. Maybe the rescue team had scared the wolves away, and I was in a lodge or something. That would explain the woodsmoke, the wooden planks that made up the ceiling. Slanting my eyes left, I saw a table, a few other things I couldn't make out without really moving my head.

No people, though. At least not to the left. There was a wall to my right. I couldn't see it, but I sensed it. If I wanted to see anything else in the cabin, I was going to have to sit up.

I really didn't want to. Moving was going to suck.

But move I did, in slow, slow increments, easing my elbows underneath me and curling my abdominal muscles, trying to avoid any actual *head* or *neck* movement because, oh, *mama*, was my head hurting. A noise caught my ears, and only sheer instinct kept me from turning to seek it out.

Even that slight change in position allowed me to take in more of the cabin. It was small. Definitely not much of a lodge, if it was one at all. A door and a massive coat hung from a hook on the nearby wall, along with a pair of boots lined up underneath.

There was a dampness under the boots that made me think somebody had been wearing them – recently.

I heard that noise again.

Breathing.

It sounded like somebody breathing.

"Hello?" I called out.

"Hello," a low, smooth voice responded.

I jerked the rest of the way upright and yelped – because that voice was a lot closer than I expected. Whipping my head around, forgetting the pain it was going to cause, I found myself staring at a shadow.

That shadow stood by the fireplace I had yet to take it – that's because it was to the left of the door, at an angle I couldn't have seen until I was either upright or moving my head with a lot more freedom than I really wanted.

The sudden movement had my head swimming, and I moaned, cradling my skull in my hands as I waited for the pain to subside.

"Easy," that low voice said. "You hit your head when you fell. You've got a concussion at the very least. You don't want to be moving so suddenly."

"I was trying not to," I snapped without thinking about how it would sound. Even as it dawned on me just how bitchy I *did* sound, I decided I didn't care. I hurt too much *to* care, and I groaned once more, that pain so all-consuming, I almost wished it would just swallow me and get it over with. Finally, it eased back, and I dared to lift my head a bit, then a bit more, but doing it so slowly, it must have appeared comical to the man who watched me.

And it *was* a man – the voice I'd heard earlier could never belong to a woman.

It had been a nice voice, I thought. It would have been even nicer if I'd had some idea he was standing less than ten feet away, so he hadn't scared me so much, but still...a nice voice.

"Any better?" he asked, moving away from the fire and drawing closer to the edge of the bed.

The ability to answer was momentarily gone, mostly because the ability to speak was momentarily gone. He'd robbed me of the ability to speak. Just looking at him.

He was...impressive.

I'd heard the phrase *'he was a mountain of a man,'* but until that moment, I'd never really seen any particular male who could fit said phrase. Not only did this guy *fit* it – he seemed to define it. From where I sat on the bed, he looked...massive. I had no idea how tall he was, but I could tell he was inches taller than me, with wide shoulders and a chest to match. They were covered by red and black checked flannel, and under the flannel, he wore a black thermal shirt. Jeans covered thick, strong thighs. He wore no shoes, only socks. The sight seemed oddly incongruous with his massive, powerful appearance,

His hair fell in a straight, thick line to his chin – or roughly to his chin. I was having a hard time determining where his chin was because it was covered by a thick beard just a little darker than his brown hair.

His eyes were a piercing pale grayish-blue, and he stared at me with the same intensity that I must be watching him with.

The beard framed a mouth that looked too soft for him, and that mouth, just as I noticed it, turned down in a frown. "Well?"

I blinked. "Well, what?"

"Is your head any better?" he asked.

I had the feeling he'd asked it once or twice before.

"As long as I'm not moving, the pain is only mildly horrible," I said, swallowing back the nervousness the sight of him brought on. "What am I doing here? Who are you?"

"My name is Lukas." Under the shaggy fall of his bangs, I thought maybe he arched an eyebrow at me. "Do you remember what happened?"

"There was a plane crash…" Licking my lips, I looked around – carefully. "My pilot…where's my pilot?"

"I didn't see the pilot with you. There were wolves."

Gorge rose up to choke me once more, and I battled it back. If I started to puke, my head would split wide open, I knew it. "I know," I said, my voice barely above a whisper. "I remember. I…I think I fell. I thought they were going to attack me."

"They would have. I was in the right place at the right time, with the right kind of firearm." That brow was still arched. "I scared them off. You went down a pretty steep embankment and hit your head. What else do you remember?"

"I remember my pilot was left alone at the plane," I replied. "We need to go get him."

"We can't." Lukas shook his head. "The storm has moved back in, and there's snow and freezing rain moving in. Once it clears, I can go out and look for him, but until that happens, this kind of storm is a death trap for anybody moving around in it."

"He's hurt!" Panic welled inside me. Hank was hurt, and it was *my* fault, and I'd left him alone out there.

"And it won't do him any good if you or I were to go out there and end up hurt – or worse – because of the storm," he said implacably. "You said your plane crashed. Did you radio for help?"

The question caught me off guard. Had Hank radioed for help? Hank's voice came back to me on a wave of memory. *Don't you go fretting…they know we're out here…*

"I didn't, but Hank did. My pilot," I clarified. He was still watching me intently, and it was so *unnerving*. I would have inched back on the bed if it hadn't been so conspicuous and painful just to move. "My pilot radioed out after the crash. They…" Whoever *they* were. "They know about the crash and who we are, about where we are."

I added that last part in, because *hello*, big, scary-looking stranger who kept watching me almost the same way the wolf had. Incongruously, I found myself thinking...*do you want to eat me*? Almost an echo of the same thought I'd had with the wolves.

But while the idea sparked a sort of terror inside me, it wasn't *entirely* unpleasant.

Heat suffused my face, and I hurriedly looked away, forgetting about my head until it was too late. "Aw, shit," I groaned, reaching up to cradle my throbbing skull.

The good news was that the pain chased away any hint of that lingering, borderline erotic thought.

Borderline hell, my libido whispered.

My libido could get stuffed.

"There's no way we can help Hank tonight?" I asked stiffly. My eyes drifted to the window, mostly covered by thick, heavy curtains.

Lukas moved toward it and pushed the curtains aside, revealing a maw of darkness, unrelieved by moonlight or stars. It was then that I heard the roar of the wind and the odd *plinking* sound of icy rain. "I'm not going out in that. While I can't stop you, I don't suggest you do it either." He looked outside for a long moment before shifting his attention to me.

We studied each other while my heart beat a chaotic rhythm in my chest, then I nodded. "Okay. Um...is there a bathroom?"

He gestured to a door on the opposite side of the room, and I eased myself upright. I took note of my clothes then and sighed. They were covered in dirt, mud...and blood, I realized. Sucking in a breath, I reached up to touch my head once more but found no wounds there.

"You've got scrapes on your face and hands. I cleaned them as best as I could without waking you. There's a first aid kit on the sink you can use," he said, clearly following my thoughts.

It was unsettling how well he did it.

"Can you handle cleaning up on your own?"

I glanced at him. He had gone back to staring out the window.

"I...yes," I managed to say, staring down at my hands. The backs were covered in small scratches, and my belly decided right then to pitch and heave. Twice, I realized. I'd come this close to death twice in one day.

Dimly, I heard him moving around, and when I looked up, I found him standing in front of me. "Something for you to put on," he said gruffly. "I'll try to get your clothes clean."

I took the clothes and nodded in thanks, then, before the panicked emotions could take hold, I hurried into the bathroom. Fuck the throbbing in my skull. I needed a few minutes of privacy.

❄

THOUGHTS of the wolf and Lukas kept intertwining as I lay in bed sometime later. He'd had chicken soup waiting when I got out of the bathroom, and although I'd only been able to eat about half of what he'd given me, my belly felt so much better for having food in it.

I didn't feel much better.

I was warm, relatively safe – I thought – and had food.

Hank was out there in the cold, in another storm. I knew he had food and could build the fire back up. We'd dragged firewood close but how long would it last?

The guilt kept me from being too comfortable as I lay tucked in the cocoon of blankets, the warmth of the fire filling the cabin.

Lukas sat in a chair near the fire silently. He hadn't said much of anything since offering me the soup, and he'd barely looked at me either.

Still, I kept thinking of the intense way he'd watched me earlier.

The same way that wolf had.

You don't want to eat me...do you?

That was the thought in my mind as I fell asleep.

Maybe that was why I ended up dreaming about Little Red Riding Hood and the Big Bad Wolf...and I was Little Red.

Only I didn't end up going to Grandma's house.

Rather, I was in this very cabin, lying in this very bed as the wolf prowled around my bed and looked at me with Lukas's pale, gray-blue eyes. And he didn't growl at me. Instead, he spoke with Lukas's low, smooth voice.

"What are you doing out here alone in the woods, Little Red?"

5

"I'm getting tired of waking up cold and sore," I grumbled. At least today I was able to ease my body upright without everything in me screaming in agony. It just moaned instead. I considered that progress.

It was cold in the cabin, and although I hadn't looked around, I had a feeling I was alone in there.

"Lukas?" I called out.

There was no answer.

Shivering, I climbed from the fading warmth of the bed and went over to the fire. It was down to coals, and I jabbed at them with the poker a bit, then added one of the logs from the stack nearby. I hovered there, watching until flames began to lick up the sides of the dried wood then I hurried back over to the bed, diving back into the blankets.

I wrapped them around me, shivering as I waited to warm back up and wondered where Lukas was. The fire had died down so low, I knew he hadn't been in here in a little while, but where was he?

The question nagged at me until I clambered out of bed, keeping one of the thicker blankets wrapped around me as I moved over to the window. Watery sunlight filtered down through the clouds, and while the snow and rain had stopped, I couldn't tell if the storms were done or just taking a timeout.

For a few minutes, I paced, casting looks at the window, then the door as I wondered where Lukas could have gone. What was I going to do if he had just...*left*?

"Why would he do that?" I muttered.

It wasn't like he *had* to go and save me from the wolves.

"You don't know that he did, though."

Talking to myself, arguing with myself was going to drive me insane.

My bladder ended up driving me to the bathroom, and after I'd taken care of that, I took a better look at the scratches on my face and hands. They weren't deep, and they already looked better, save for one along my jawline that would probably take a few days to heal. Head cocked to the side, I eyed it. I'd probably hit a rock or something.

I wondered if it would scar, then imagined what my mother and sisters would think about all of this.

I could just see them all shaking their heads in despair.

Of course, it would happen to Stella.

Not that they wouldn't be worried about me. I had no doubt that they were, but out of my perfect family, I was the one who had things...happen. And if somebody was going to be in a plane crash, it would be me. If somebody was going to escape a near-wolf attack, it would be me. If somebody would end up trapped in a cabin with a mountain man...

A door opened.

I rushed from the bathroom and came out just in time to see Lukas stepping out of his boots. He glanced my way, then went back to what he was doing. He took off his coat, and I felt my breath hitch in my chest as the material of his flannel stretched tight across wide shoulders as he hung the heavy outerwear up.

He really was a rather fine specimen of manflesh, I had to admit.

"Hi," I said nervously.

He gave me a short nod.

"You...um...were you out looking for Hank by any chance?" I asked.

"I found the crash site." He moved over to the fire and poked at the log I'd added, then tossed on another one. "It's cold in here."

"I know...I just woke up a little while ago. I put that log on, but I'm sort of used to central heat, not fireplaces." It was a lame attempt at a quip.

He didn't even smile.

"Was Hank there?" I asked when he offered nothing else beyond the fact that he'd found the crash site.

"No." He shot me another look. "There were a lot of footprints – looks like a helicopter landed close by. I'd say he was rescued not long after the storm broke. If you hadn't gone off chasing wolves, you'd be tucked up some place nice and warm right now."

"I wasn't chasing wolves," I snapped.

The only sound he made was a low snort.

"I was *trying* to get to a spot that I could get bars on my cell phone," I informed him. "My cell phone..."

Abruptly, I realized I hadn't seen it since I took my tumble right after the encounter with the wolves. Shit. "I don't have my phone. Do you have a phone?"

"No landline." He jabbed at the fire again, then made a satisfied grunt, rising to his full height. He had to be close to six and a half feet. "No cell phone is going to work up here. I found a suitcase in the airplane. Is it yours?"

The question distracted me from the idea of trying to call for help – briefly. Turning my head, I spied the carryon I'd been lugging around since I'd left New York and a thankful sigh escaped my lips. I always packed a couple days worth of clothes in my carryon, thanks to the airlines losing my luggage a time or two. Most of my stuff was being shipped out, but at least I had a change of clothes. "Thank you," I said, moving to get it.

He brought it to me and hefted it up onto the bed. I went to touch his arm.

He moved back – fast.

Feeling slightly stung, I turned my back on him and sat down, unzipping the carryon. Everything inside it was stilled neatly tucked into place thanks to the straps and the fact that I had it crammed tight. "I can clean up and change now."

He didn't respond.

"Was there a note? Any kind of message Hank might have left?" I asked. "Are they out there looking for me?"

"Not right now." He glanced toward the window. "There's a break in the storm, but it's already starting back up. Look."

I groaned at the sight of flurries swirling outside the window. I'd just seen the sun not even ten minutes ago. Tearing my mind away from the weather, I went back to the topic of Hank. "You're sure he was rescued?"

"I didn't see it happen personally," he replied, his voice short. "But it looked like it. There were footprints inside the fuselage of the plane, and more than a few."

Anxious, I got up to pace. "I need to call my family. If Hank gets into town and nobody knows where I am, they are going to be frantic. Is there anybody near here that has a phone?"

"No." He blew out a breath and turned away. "I can't get you to a phone, but I've got a shortwave radio that we can use to contact emergency services. They can figure out a way to get word to your parents."

"Oh, thank God." Relief flooded me. "And my boyfriend. Somebody needs to call my boyfriend," I added.

His lips twisted into a sardonic smile, and abruptly, the dream from the past night flashed through my mind. *You don't want to eat me, do you*?

The wolf had licked his lips as he looked me over.

Now, as Lukas turned his head and met my eyes, he gave me another penetrating glance. It was quick, over in a blink, but I felt like that look had seen clear through me.

"And your boyfriend," he repeated in a monotone.

❄

TEN MINUTES LATER, I had assurances from the nearest sheriff's department that they'd get word to my parents and Aaron that I was safe. It sounded like the sheriff knew Lukas, judging by the rapport the two of them shared and I felt better with every passing moment.

After he'd put the shortwave radio away, I looked at him with a thankful smile. "Thank you."

He just shrugged and went about making lunch.

I offered to help, but he brushed it aside. "Rest. You're still injured."

"It's just a headache," I said and offered my help once more.

"No."

It was delivered so curtly, I backed off, retreating to the bed I'd used since I'd woken here. I didn't lay down though. I unzipped my suitcase and went through it, finding the warmest clothes I had. "Do you need to use the bathroom?"

He made a *go-ahead* gesture, and I tucked myself into the small bathroom, away from the somewhat terse silence.

Maybe Lukas just didn't know how to interact around people. If he lived here, then he probably didn't run into a lot of people. How long *had* he lived here? Did he just not like human beings?

I could understand that.

Sometimes I didn't like them myself.

But there was no reason for the two of us to barely speak or dance on eggshells as we waited for me to be rescued. Right?

So...we could talk.

Or at least I could – I'd ask questions, and we'd sort of get to know each other.

It wasn't like I had anything better to do.

❄

"Do you know *how* to have a conversation?" I snapped at him.

It was probably four or five hours later. I'd lost track of time, and he didn't exactly have a clock hanging on the wall of his sparsely furnished cabin. He wore a watch, but I think he'd grown tired of having me ask, "What time is it," after about the third or fourth time.

Over the meal he'd prepared for dinner – venison steaks with baked potatoes...*soooo* good – he looked up and met my eyes. "I know how to have conversations," he said, his tone pleasant enough. Then he added coolly, "I just don't like having them."

Aggravated, I shot to my feet, grabbing my mostly empty plate and carrying it to the sink. I could have eaten more of the steak – there was a piece left on the serving platter, but it was really hard to sit and eat across from somebody who didn't want to speak to you.

So I just wasn't going to bother.

"I'll take care of the dishes," Lukas said when I started to fill the sink with water.

"I'm not helpless," I responded, my tone as short as his was.

When he didn't respond, I went about washing my plate and flatware, then the small baking tray he'd used for the potatoes. When I was done, I dried the dishes and put them away.

He was still sitting at the table eating.

I had a feeling he was taking his time to avoid me.

It was enough to give me a complex.

Tempted to just go and lie down, I wondered how much longer I'd have to deal with this – then something occurred to me. "I've been sleeping in your bed."

He tensed.

It was so minute, I might have missed it, but I was watching him closely – looking for a reaction, I guess.

I finally got one.

He slid me a look from the corner of his eye, then shrugged, the movement almost too casual. "There's only one, and you're hurt. I'm fine in the chair."

"But I can–"

My attempt to tell him that I'd do fine in the chair – and hey, it was closer to the fire – was cut short but a heavy crashing noise, and the tinkling sound of shattering glass.

I jumped, a startled yelp leaving my lips, as a huge tree branch came crashing through the window just beyond Lukas's right side.

He swore and twisted away, although it was maybe a foot shy of hitting him.

Heart pounding, I rushed to his side – or tried to. He caught me around the waist and scooped me up onto the table. "Shoes," he said shortly.

The word made no sense. "What?"

"There's glass all over the floor. You need more than socks on your feet."

He brought me the hiking boots I'd been wearing on the plane, and I dutifully pulled them on, lacing them up halfway before I leaped off the table. He pulled his coat on, and I shifted nervously from one foot to the other. "What are you doing?"

He gave me an *are you fucking kidding me* look. "I need to get that out of the window so we can get it covered up."

"Oh." Clearing my throat, I looked from the heavy branch back to him. "Should I help?"

He shook his head, and a moment later, he disappeared out the door.

I sighed, then looked around.

Well, he'd said there was glass all over the floor. I could work on that.

❄

IT WAS FREEZING in the cabin by the time we were done. Lukas had boarded the window up from the outside, then come back inside with a sheet of plastic from somewhere. He nailed that into place, then rummaged up more blankets and added those to the window as well.

"It's still going to be cold," he said, not looking at me.

I dumped the last of the glass into the garbage can.

"It's better than nothing though."

Nervously, I glanced back at one of the other windows. "And what do we do if the storm gets worse and it gets a *lot* colder?"

Lukas didn't answer, but his face was grim.

6

A hand glided up my side.

Aaron murmured my name. "I missed you," he said against my lips.

Sighing into his kiss, I wrapped my arms around him and wiggled closer. He was so warm. Everything about him was warm and solid, and I felt cold and empty.

His mouth skimmed down my jawline, my neck, pressed against the pulse he found there.

"Aaron..."

One hand tangled in my hair, twisting it. The other slid between my thighs, and I gasped as he sought out my clitoris, rubbing against it, toying with it until I arched up, desperate for more.

Clothes fell away.

We kicked the blankets aside.

Curling my arms around the wide shelf of his shoulders, I tugged his mouth to mine, but he had begun a meandering path lower down my body. When he caught one swollen nipple between his teeth, I groaned. He tugged on it, stretching it out with his teeth before drawing it back into his mouth.

The sensations arrowed straight down into my core, heat

licking at me until I was certain the flames from the fire had managed to reach us.

Flames...the fire...the fireplace...

His beard rasped along my skin, and that tickled another memory.

Aaron didn't have a beard. I shoved him upright and found myself staring into slate-blue eyes. "Lukas," I whispered.

He reached up to touch my mouth. "I want to kiss you again." That was all he said, then he was kissing me, and it was a kiss that shook me to my toes.

Was this real?

It had been Aaron before–

Dream, I thought. I'm dreaming.

Then I stopped thinking because after Lukas kissed my mouth, he began to move lower on me, pausing to kiss the tip of each breast. That was when I realized that I was naked, and so was he. The fire burned in the fireplace like an inferno, and it was so warm in the cabin. I didn't feel chilled at all. How could I with his hands and mouth roaming over me?

"I want to kiss you again," Lukas said, but this time, he said it between my thighs. I was too caught up, too lost in the pleasure to be embarrassed, further proof it was a dream, I'd think later on. I'd never been comfortable with Aaron doing this, and he didn't seem to mind that I didn't like it.

But not liking it didn't seem to be an option right now.

Lukas licked me, and my entire body lit up like the sky on the Fourth of July.

He licked me and pleasure flared inside, so hot, so bright, so all-consuming, I might have forgotten how to breathe.

Did it matter?

What did breathing matter when something felt this good?

He thrust two fingers into my cunt and twisted them. I came hard and fast, moaning, and then Lukas was on top of me, his mouth slamming down on mine as he drove inside me.

I cried out and wrapped my legs around his hips.

"I want to eat you up," he growled against my lips.

And I thought of the wolf.

If this was what it was like when Lukas feasted on me, then I couldn't think of anything I wanted more.

❄

I WOKE UP, panting.

I woke up with the dream clear as crystal, vivid as life, pulsing in my brain.

I woke up with my entire body clenched, right on the verge of orgasm, and it didn't help that Lukas was pressed against me. I was lying on my side, and he had me tucked up into the cradle of his body – his cock was against my butt, and it was thick, heavy, and hard. It took everything I had not to press back against him.

He grumbled under his breath, and I squeezed my eyes closed.

Please don't let him be awake, I thought desperately.

If he was awake, I just might die of embarrassment.

But he made no noise. His breath stirred my hair, and I continued to lay there, so aroused I hurt with it, but I was afraid to move for fear that he'd wake up.

Seconds crept by, turning into minutes. I counted a full two of them before I dared to move. He hadn't so much as moved a muscle and other than that one sleepy grumble, he hadn't made a sound either.

He was still asleep.

Carefully, I started to slip out of the bed. The second I stuck a toe out from under the covers, I almost changed my mind.

Lukas sighed and shifted, thrusting his hips against my ass.

I bolted out of bed.

I had no choice. It was either that or turn around and climb on top of him.

I wasn't sure I was ready to handle the consequences of that

– no matter what they might be.

I darted into the bathroom as the bed squeaked behind me and shut the door. I just barely managed to keep from slamming it, and once it was closed, I turned around and pressed my back against it.

What the hell?

What the *hell...*

❄

"Is it *always* like this?" I demanded. Turning away from the window – one of the *unbroken* ones – I found Lukas staring at me. But the minute I met his eyes, he looked away. A few seconds of uncomfortable silence passed. "Well?" I prodded him.

"What?" he asked, sounding irritated. "Cold? It's the Rocky Mountains. Yes, it gets cold up here."

"I'm talking about the storm. How much longer is this going to last? I want to get *out* of here." Realizing how rude that sounded, I hurried to explain. "It's not that I don't appreciate you saving me, or the hospitality..." Such as it was. He barely spoke to me. "But I've got a life to get back to. A job I'm supposed to be starting. My boyfriend must be worried, my parents."

"The sheriff is getting word to your family," Lukas said, not offering anything about Aaron. "And there's nothing we can do about the storm. It's out of your control, and mine."

I'd gathered *that* much. It had stormed all day, the snow piling up outside while frozen rain turned the windows to sheets of ice. There was one good side to the weather – I think all the ice had frozen over the boards outside, and at some point, we stopped hearing the window whistling through the plastic and blankets. Maybe snow had plugged whatever gaps and the fluffy white stuff that held me prisoner was offering some insulation against the cold.

And it *was* cold.

Lukas had ended up giving me one of his flannel shirts and a pair of socks to wear over my own. My jeans did a good enough job of keeping my legs warm, and I spent most of the time by the fire, but my arms were freezing. Or they had been, up until he held out the black and gray checked flannel shirt.

"It'll break soon," Lukas said, and I thought I heard a note of reassurance in his voice. "These storms never last more than a few days."

A few days. Closing my eyes, I dropped my forehead onto the mantle and stared down into the flames until it was too warm to stay so close.

A few days.

If I had to stay this close to this odd, compelling man who barely spoke to me, I just might go crazy.

❄

I WOKE TO AN ODD SILENCE.

It took me a while to understand what was so odd about it, but finally, I realized the wind had died down.

It had roared and wailed like a grieving, angry woman for the past few days and finally, it had calmed. I could still hear it out there, but it was more of a whistle than a wail, and I hurriedly climbed from the bed. I didn't see Lukas anywhere, so I swapped out the sweats he'd given me to sleep in for my blue jeans and hurriedly changed into one of my other shirts as well. While it had a plaid design, it was made of challis and had as much warmth as a dress made of tissue paper, so I pulled on the flannel Lukas had given me yesterday, and the socks too.

I'm a stunning work of art, I decided, staring into the mirror in the bathroom. It only showed my head and shoulders, but that was enough to see the two clashing plaid designs of my shirts, but I was at the point to where comfort and warmth were far more important than fashion. Once I was dressed and somewhat warm, I went over one of the windows – an unbroken one – and peered outside, gaping when I saw the sun trying to cut through the cloud layer.

I didn't even think twice. I grabbed my tennis shoes and pulled them on, then took the extra coat from a hook by the door and headed outside. If I didn't get some fresh air, I was going to go crazy.

I didn't see Lukas anywhere outside, but more importantly, I saw no wolves.

I kept an eye out for both as I circled around the cabin, coming to a halt at the back where I saw a smaller, separate building tucked off between two towering pines. The tree branch that had crashed through the window was lying a few yards in front of the small shed, an ax buried in the trunk. Guess he didn't lack for firewood around here. That was a good thing.

Curious about the shed, I started toward it. "It's probably where he keeps the bodies of all the women he's rescued," I muttered morbidly. Not that I really believed it. He was...weird, but not creepy weird. Just...weird. And I wished he'd talk to me more.

The door was padlocked. Yet more proof of the weird. Somehow I didn't think he had a lot of trouble with people breaking into his home around here. Annoyed, mostly because poking around in the shed would have given me something to do, I reached out to tug on the padlock.

I never managed to get my hand on it, because Lukas's hand caught my wrist.

"You're nosy," he said right in my ear.

I shrieked, startled by his sudden and silent appearance.

Jerking back, I tried to pull away, but he hadn't let go of my wrist.

"Good grief," I snapped. "Make some noise next time."

"What are you doing?" he asked, ignoring me. "Any reason you've got trying to dig around in my personal business?"

"I..." Huffing out a breath, I glared at him. "Yes," I snapped. "I'm bored."

"That's no reason." He gestured to the house. "There's stuff in there. Go nose around in there."

"Why? You afraid I'm going to find skeletons of the bodies you've got tucked in there?" I demanded.

A grin crooked his lips, momentarily lighting his eyes. "If you actually think I've got skeletons in my shed, how smart is it of you to let me in on the fact?"

"I don't think that." Sniffing, I tugged on my wrist again. He finally let go.

Backing away from him, I resisted the urge to rub the area where he'd been touching me. He hadn't hurt me, but my skin *burned* where he'd touched. I could feel my pulse pounding against my skin, and there were other things pulsing as well. Abruptly, the dream from the other night came back to the fore of my mind, and that just pissed me off. "I just don't see what the big deal is if I kill time looking around in the tool shed."

"Because it's *my* shed," Lukas said, jutting his chin out at me. "Go on. Get back inside...or maybe you want to go chase down wolves again."

"I didn't chase down wolves," I snapped.

"Could have fooled me." But his voice softened a little. "Go on. Get inside, Stella. It's safer in there. Look...the weather is clearing. Tomorrow, if you don't drive me absolutely insane, I should be able to take you into the nearest town, okay?"

❄

If I didn't drive *him* insane?

A few hours later, his words were echoing inside my head, and I was hard-pressed not to sulk in a silent snit in the corner. Not that *he* would have noticed. Once he'd come in, hauling another armful of firewood, he'd prepared some food then retreated to his chair with a battered book.

He was clearly as talkative as ever.

I don't know how much time passed or even what time it

was, but finally, that silence, his refusal to look at me, even the memories of that dream were driving me *crazy*. I wasn't sure how much longer I could put up with it, and at some point, after he turned what seemed like the gazillionth page in his endless book, I snapped.

"You know, I can't *wait* to get to Denver. My boyfriend must be worried sick, and I've got admit, I miss him like crazy," I said.

Over the top of his book, Lukas cast me a look, his brow arched.

"We've been dating practically since I started college," I told him. What in the *hell* was I doing? He didn't give a damn about Aaron and me.

His eyes drifted back to the page, and he slumped deeper in the chair. Clearly, his attention was *not* on me.

"I think he's going to propose at Christmas." The words popped out of me with no conscious thought of my own. "It's been terrible being away from him all this time. He helped me get this job, you know. Well, it's not like I'm not qualified for it – I am. I totally am."

I kept rambling.

Lukas barely glanced at me or acknowledged anything I said.

Did that shut me up?

No.

It did have one positive benefit, though.

That night, he elected to sleep on a pallet of blankets in front of the fireplace instead of in the bed with me.

It probably had more to do with the fact that I hadn't been able to shut my mouth up than anything, although would it have *killed* him to...I dunno, chat a little? Be nice? Talk to me?

He had to be one of the most anti-social people I'd ever met.

I was *so* ready to get back to town.

Get back to Aaron and away from Lukas, and how unsettling he was.

How attractive he was.

How...*everything* he was.

7

This time, it wasn't pain that woke me, nor was it the absence of noise, but rather bright, almost blinding light. For a moment, I couldn't even figure out what the light was. And then, I was so excited, I got out of bed in such a rush, I tangled myself in the sheets and comforter and ended up on my ass on the floor.

Sunlight. That was sunlight.

And not just a little bit of sunlight, but a lot of sunlight. The kind that blinded you on a bright, sunny day. Especially when it reflected off the snow.

I had known a lot of days like that. Clambering to my feet, I hurried to the window and peered outside, ignoring the chill that had settled in the cabin. The fire had died down again which meant Lukas had gone out.

That was okay.

It was okay because the sun was shining and the sky was blue.

It was so blue it hurt to look at it.

Pressing my hand to the clear pane of glass, I sighed happily. I could go home.

So what if Lukas had been taunting me about not taking me

to the nearest town if I drove him crazy? That was some faulty logic there. If I was driving him crazy, didn't it make more sense to take me to town where I *wouldn't* drive him crazy?

With another sigh, I rested my head against the frame of the window and wondered how long it would take to get to Denver. Hank had said it would take days walking but I had no idea how long it would take driving the distance from here.

It didn't matter. I was going home today. And heaven help Lukas if he thought he might keep me here any longer. I'd get my hands on the fireplace poker and threaten to beat him bloody.

I hurriedly got dressed, my cabin fever now at an all-time high. After I shoved my feet into my shoes, I hurried outside, hoping to find him out there, shoveling out the Jeep.

No such luck. The Jeep wasn't even there. He *had* dug it out – I could see the snow piled up where he'd worked, and the churned mess where he'd been walking, as well as tracks that led around to the back, but I didn't know where he was.

"What the hell?" I grumbled.

There was no answer. Not that I had expected one. Who was going to talk back to me? The birds? Lukas? Even if he had been here, the birds were more likely to speak to me than he was.

Groaning in frustration, I spun on my heel and looked around. But there was no answer to his whereabouts other than the tracks that disappeared behind the cabin.

"Fine," I said out loud. "I'll just follow those."

For a little ways, at least. I definitely *wasn't* going out of sight of the cabin – we weren't doing the dance with the wolves again. Besides, it wasn't like I could get to town on my own, but at least I could get an idea of where he might have gone. Maybe he had some secret stash of firewood that he wanted to replenish before he left. A secret stash that he kept somewhere other than at the cabin. Because of course, that made perfect sense.

I came up short at the sight of the Jeep located right behind the cabin. I wouldn't have seen it if I hadn't walked back here, but it was arrowed off, pointing to the east, and I could see beyond it where he had cleared some more of the road.

There was also a snow-plow attachment affixed to the front.

Now I felt silly. It had been snowing off and on for the past two days. Of course, he needed to do some work to clear the way so we could get off the mountain.

Feeling relieved, knowing that he was somewhere close by, I started to turn around, but a low, pulsing noise caught my ears. Music. It was music.

Curious, I cocked my head as I looked around. The Jeep was off, the engine quiet, so it wasn't coming from there...I didn't think. The shed, I realized. It was coming from the shed.

Now, I was more curious than ever.

The door was shut, but the music was playing loud enough that I could hear it despite the muffling effects of the snow piled inches thick on the roof, on the windows.

The snow around the shed itself was packed down, and I could see where he'd been adding to a woodpile outside the door.

His secret stash, I thought, amused.

I wondered what he did in there.

Maybe he was an artist. There wasn't any way a lot of natural light could shine in there unless he had skylights, but that didn't mean he couldn't do something artsy in there.

It could explain why he was so temperamental and so private. Knowing I shouldn't but unable to resist, I eased closer. I had no doubt that he had some way of locking the door from the inside. He just seemed like that kind of guy. But there were the windows...and I was so curious.

As I got closer, I could make out the strains of what sounded like metal music. Death metal, possibly. One of my friends from college had been in a death metal band, and I had learned far more than I wanted to know about the differences between screamo, death metal, and regular old heavy metal.

I never would have pegged Lukas for being a lover of metal, much less death metal.

The window up ahead beckoned me, the music like a siren song but not because I enjoyed it so much as because I just had to look.

I had some whimsical idea that I would find him at a potter's wheel or maybe carving something. I could see him sitting under a beam of light, a block of wood in one hand and a knife in the other.

It was that whimsical thought, I decided later, that made what I saw that much more shocking.

A foot from the window, inside that packed space by the woodpile, I stood frozen in my tracks, my brain struggling to process what was happening.

It was Lukas. He was stripped down to the waist, and his back was covered in ugly, angry welts. And there was no doubt how those welts had come to be on his back because, as I watched, hypnotized by the scene playing out in front of me, a heavy leather belt came flying over his shoulder and landed on his back, leaving yet another dark, angry mark in its wake.

I sucked in a breath, horrified.

What was he doing? I wanted to rush in there and grab that belt, make him stop. But my feet wouldn't move, and I couldn't get my brain to engage either.

What was he doing?

He hit himself again, his entire body shuddering.

It happened a third time.

He stopped, swaying for a moment, and I stood there, still immobilized and horrified. What was this? Some crazed sex fetish?

But that didn't make sense. I had a friend who had confessed to me her senior year of college that she was a sub and her boyfriend, one of the quietest, shyest boys I had ever met, was her Dom. I never would have guessed it from either of them, but I'd gone to a BDSM club with them once, and some of the stuff I had seen had almost clicked. And what Michelle had with her boyfriend Clay...it had clicked. It made sense in my head, for the two of them.

This...it didn't make sense.

Nothing I saw in front of me made sense, and I had the surreal impression that Lukas was not enjoying what he was doing to himself.

Then why is he doing it? a small voice inside me whispered. *Nobody is making him. He has to be enjoying it.*

No, he doesn't, another part of me whispered. People did things they didn't like all the time. They felt compelled to. But it still didn't make sense. And Lukas became more inexplicable to me with every passing second.

There was a break in the music, and I panicked, terrified he'd turn or that I'd make some noise and he'd know I was out there.

That fear was what broke my paralysis, and *finally,* I was able to make my legs move. Quicker than I would have thought possible, I rushed into the cabin, kicking off my shoes before cleaning up the snow I tracked inside.

Then, still feeling unsettled, I paced back and forth, struggling to make sense of what I had seen. Fifteen minutes later, I was still struggling when Lukas appeared in the doorway. He dumped an armful of firewood on the pile, and I swallowed back a hysterical laugh as I remembered my silly thought that maybe he had a top-secret woodpile stash tucked away somewhere.

"Are you ready to go?" Lukas asked shortly.

The sound of his voice made me jump.

His voice was ragged, almost husky. I wondered if it was because of pain.

Don't wonder. Don't think about it. It's better that way, I told myself.

I needed to forget what I had seen.

But I didn't trust myself to speak. As he continued to watch me, I gave a quick nod and turned to start gathering my things.

He disappeared into the bathroom and emerged almost ten minutes later.

He hadn't showered, so that left me to wonder just what he had been doing. *Don't wonder!* I reminded myself. I didn't need to think about what he had been doing.

He went to pick up my suitcase, and I grabbed it before he could. "I've got it," I said the words coming out shrill, almost panicked.

He gave me a strange look, and I flashed him a bright smile. "Sorry," I said. "I'm nervous about the drive. It can't be easy driving in this stuff. Do we need to clear the driveway?"

I didn't think about the fact that he might have seen some of my footprints out in the snow. Yet he gave no sign that he suspected I'd seen him.

So I wasn't going to let on that I knew.

"I already took care of clearing most of the snow around the cabin." He continued to eye me strangely, so I turned away from him, determined not to let him pick up on anything from me.

"What about down the mountain? I don't guess the street department comes up here to clear the roads." I strived, and I think I succeeded, at keeping my voice light.

"I've got a plow attachment on the Jeep. Come on. Let's get going."

❄

IT TOOK MORE than an hour to get to the nearest town. We had to drive at a crawl. If the roads were clear, it might have only taken twenty minutes. All this time and the nearest town was a few twists and bends in the road away.

But I understood why Lukas hadn't wanted to drive these roads in the storm. There were drop-offs that made my heart thud in my chest even though the day was clear and he was a good driver.

The beauty of the mountains was enough to make my breath

catch in my throat, and for a little while, I was able to forget about the past few days, even my uneasiness about what I had seen in the shed. But as we reached the outskirts of the small town, it was harder to brush all of that aside.

It was getting hard to brush *anything* aside.

"We'll stop and eat breakfast," Lukas said.

"Okay." I forced the word out. I managed to bite back, *And then what*?

Because I honestly had no clue. I didn't have my cell phone. I could call Aaron because I had his number memorized and I could call the house back in New York, but my sisters? And were my parents *home*? I kept their numbers stored on my cell phone – I didn't have their cell or work phones memorized.

What about my job?

What about a lot of things?

The diner we stopped at was a hole in the wall, but it seemed that was about all this town had. We placed our order and then I went to use the restroom. That was where I saw the payphone. They actually had a payphone here. I hurried to the restroom, then rushed out to get my purse and dig out the change needed to call Aaron.

Excitement burned in me as I dialed the number – *finally*, a connection back to my life.

The excitement fizzled out after ring number three as the phone clicked over to his voice mail and I had to leave a message. I sat down with Lukas after hanging up the phone and gave him a wan smile. "No answer. I had to leave a message on his voice mail. Hope nobody needs to use that phone."

Lukas didn't offer any response, staying bent over his coffee like it held all the answers in the universe.

Our food came, and we ate in an awkward silence made even more awkward – for me – by memories of what I'd seen him doing in the shed, memories of ugly marks on his broad, muscled back.

He took care of the ticket before I even had a chance to dig out my credit card. I'd told him I'd pay for the food as a thank you, but apparently, he had other plans. "I wanted to buy your breakfast," I said as the waitress walked away, glowing over the ten dollar tip he'd given her.

He simply grunted an unintelligible response, and I rolled my eyes as I reached for my purse. "Fine, just leave me more cash to make phone calls. Wonder if they'll swap me out a ten for a roll of quarters." Loose change jangled in the bottom of my Michael Kors bag, but I wasn't sure how many calls I could make with that handful of coins. "Man, I miss my cell phone right now."

"Here." Lukas dumped a handful of quarters on the table in front of me. "Use that. I figured there was a chance you wouldn't get ahold of him on the first call."

"That ready to get rid of me, huh?" I shot him a smile, hoping to get some sort of response.

I did.

He stood up.

"What are you doing?"

"I got you to town." He shrugged. "You can call your boyfriend and work something out."

"You..." Blinking at him in realization, I tried to battle down the odd spurt of panic. "You're just leaving me here?"

After relying on him for the past several days, it seemed surreal that he would just suddenly not be there.

"Wasn't my plan to hang around. You needed a lift, I got you one." He jerked a shoulder in a shrug as he pulled his jacket on. The day was a lot warmer than the past few had been. I hadn't even needed the coat he'd offered me, but he'd put it in the truck all the same. Maybe he'd been a Boy Scout. *Be prepared*...wasn't that the motto?

"I know, and thank you...but I didn't realize you were just going to just...leave me here." It was what I wanted – being somewhere other than trapped in that cabin. I had to remind myself of that. Trying to cover my lapse, I gave him a cocky smile. "I can always just stick out my thumb and hitch a ride."

He studied me with those slate blue eyes for a long moment before shrugging. "Do what you need to do."

Then he turned around, and I watched that broad, strong back as he strolled right out the door and climbed into the Jeep parked in front of the diner.

He left. He really just *left*.

It wasn't until that moment that I realized I didn't even know his last name.

8

I wanted to go back to New York.

Hell, I'd even go back to Michigan, and I'd been so ready to leave that state behind, it was laughable.

It wasn't that there was anything wrong with Denver – I didn't think. I hadn't had much chance to go out and get around much, despite the fact that my new employer had given me an extra week off after the ordeal. The *ordeal.* That's what everybody was calling it.

The ordeal.

The plane crash, my days with Lukas, all of it was called *the ordeal.*

Unless it was Aaron. He barely talked about it. When I tried to talk about how uncomfortable it had been, how scared I'd been, he brushed it all off like it was an everyday event.

Now, as he led me around the office building of the advertising firm where I would be working with him, he had his hand on my waist, and I had the weirdest feeling I was there as more of a prop than anything else.

"Aren't you excited?" Aaron asked as he led me from the area where the cubicles were to the stairs. The stairs, clearly, were the gateway to the upper echelon here at the firm. While my cubicle was nice, bigger than what I'd expected, it was still a cubicle.

Offering him a polite smile, I looked back over my shoulder. "Shouldn't I get to work?" I asked.

"This is part of it," Aaron answered. "You've got to get to know everybody, know who is who, babe." He gave me a broad smile as he slid his hand from the small of my back to my elbow, squeezing lightly. "Come on. Let's go meet the bosses. Don't be nervous about it."

"I'm not nervous." Frowning at him, I told myself not to get annoyed about his arrogant attitude, but it was getting hard. He'd been acting like a prick almost since the time I'd arrived.

I hardly even recognized him.

"You don't have to pretend around me, you know." He stopped at the top of the steps and turned toward me, smoothing his hands up and down my arms. The weather had returned to something I considered closer to normal for fall, although it was cooler. I had on a lightweight knit sweater, and through it, I felt the heavy, almost hot weight of his hands, and I had the irrational urge to knock them aside. "It's a different world out here, outside of college, without Mom and Dad's influence to help."

"Mom and Dad's influence haven't helped me do jack shit," I said. This time, I did step away, and I made sure to take an extra step so that he couldn't reach out and touch me again as I finished speaking. "They didn't get me into college, they didn't earn my grades."

"They didn't get you this job either." He cocked a brow, eyes resting coolly on my face. His expression was telling. *I got you the job.*

"I hardly asked for your help." Then, realizing we were about two steps from devolving into a fight, I gestured toward the offices. "Did you want to finish up the meet and greet?" I offered him a conciliatory smile and held out my hand.

After a long moment, he accepted.

Still, he was cool toward me as he led me to the first office. "This is the assistant head of marketing – Terri Lubatti." He knocked on a partially open door and stepped inside, his cool expression replaced by a warm, open smile. "Terri, darling...are you ready to meet that brilliant friend of mine?"

Darling? I slid him a look from the corner of my eye. And I was his *brilliant friend* now?

A woman rose from behind the desk as I stepped inside and she barely glanced at me, her blue eyes focused on Aaron. "Aaron...are we still on for our meeting this afternoon?"

"Of course, of course." He leaned his hands on the table. "Stella is anxious to get to work, but I wanted to show her around and make sure she knew everybody. You know, help with those first day jitters."

Finally, Terri glanced at me.

She was pretty, a fact that didn't go unnoticed by me. I wasn't too concerned about her being pretty, but I was somewhat annoyed by the fact that she looked at me as though she was staring down her nose at me – or maybe she was trying to decide if I smelled bad.

Since she wasn't making an attempt to hide her immediate dislike, I didn't bother wasting a smile on her. "Hello."

She inclined her head. "Try not to take too long learning your way around. We've got some big things in the pipeline, and we need all hands on deck."

Once we were out in the hall, I slid Aaron a look. He still had that smile on his face, so I decided not to make a pithy comment about how friendly the assistant head of marketing had been with him – but man, I wanted to.

"Come on. The boss isn't in right now so you'll have to meet him some other time. I want to introduce you to Breanna."

❄

BREANNA WAS a breath of fresh air.

She was short, slender with long dark hair and eyes that took in everything. Something about the way she looked at Aaron had me curious, but since Aaron lingered in the cubicle even after he made the introductions made it impossible for me to ask her anything, and by the time he left, I completely forgot.

Breanna was going to 'mentor' me for the next few weeks, which was welcome news. When Aaron mentioned that I'd be working under a mentor the first few weeks, I'd worried it would be him. And had immediately felt guilty.

We were living together, we were lovers. It wasn't a good idea for him to even be my boss, but it wasn't like I was going to walk away from the job over it. Having some distance between us was a good thing.

It was almost lunchtime before Aaron told us he had important meetings to get to so he'd have to leave us.

Once he was gone, Breanna spun around in her seat and smiled at me. "Finally! Daddy's gone!" She laughed, the sound bright and irresistible. "You can't tell me he doesn't come off like a hovering parent sometimes, watching everything you do."

"Well...I get the hovering," I said with a reluctant smile. "But I'm going to avoid thinking about any sort of parental similarities."

"Good idea." She wrinkled her nose then scooted her chair down and gestured to the wider space she'd cleared at her desk. "Why don't you come join me? I'm working on an ad campaign for a new club that's opening up soon, and we're trying to come up with a logo. Maybe some new eyes will help."

We worked for a good hour before we decided to break for lunch, and by that time, Breanna was more than happy with what we'd accomplished. "You've got a great eye for design, Stella. This logo is far and away better than what we were coming up with, but it still holds true to what the owner wanted to do."

"It's not that much different from what you were aiming at," I said, shrugging. "Like you said…new eyes. Sometimes, that makes all the difference."

We ended up walking across the street to an Asian Fusion restaurant, and I gorged on sushi and salad. One look at the cocktail menu told me I'd be back at a time when drinking was allowed.

"I desperately want to try that ginger drink," I told Breanna as she scooped up noodles with a pair of chopsticks.

"We should come out here on the weekend." She winked at me. "Assuming Aaron doesn't keep you glued to his side. I imagine the two of you spent enough time apart, what with you being in Michigan and him being here."

"Oh, I think we'll manage to make time for you and me to hang out." I was already planning on it.

As we finished up and paid, a familiar form outside the window caught my eye, and I frowned as I realized it was Aaron. He was standing outside the restaurant next door talking to Terri. Remembering how she'd looked down her nose at me, I eyed them closely. The discussion seemed…heated.

But before I could decide if I wanted to say hi to Aaron or anything, Breanna caught my arm in hers. "Come on. We've still got almost twenty minutes. We can walk by some of the shops, and I can tell you about the fun stuff you need to make time for." She tugged me on down the sidewalk in the opposite direction where I'd seen Aaron. "So…serious, and important, question. Do you ski?"

❄

THE THANK *you* card fell out of my purse as I rushed into my cubicle just a few minutes before my scheduled start time. I was on salary so it wouldn't matter if I was a few minutes late, but I personally hated not being on time.

That was one of the big bones of contention between Aaron and me at the moment and the reason behind the fight we'd had that morning. He didn't see what it mattered if I didn't get there until nine-thirty. Since I was scheduled to start at nine, I insisted it was a big deal.

My parents were having my car shipped out, but so far, it hadn't gotten here, and when I'd texted them last night – because there had been another fight yesterday – Dad told me Mom was taking care of it. He reminded me that she'd been caught up in the charity gala she was handling, and it might have slipped her mind.

So at lunch today, I was picking up a rental.

I didn't care if I had to rent for the next month, I wasn't relying on Aaron anymore for rides. If we lived closer to the bus line, I'd be riding the bus to get here, but that was too much of a hassle. I should feel bad that I wasn't showing much environmental concern, but right now, I was concerned about conserving my sanity more than anything else.

"Wow. You look mad." Breanna appeared at the opening of my cubicle, her eyes wide as she took in the sharp, jerking movements of my hands as I shoved in all the odds and ends that had fallen out of my purse.

The *thank you* card was already buried. I'd bought it on a whim, thinking maybe I could somehow track him down and mail the card, but I had no idea how I'd go about doing it. Why hadn't I at least asked for his last name?

That was yet one more thing that annoyed me because I'd spent way too much time the past few weeks thinking about him. First I hadn't been able to get away from him soon enough, and now I couldn't get away from him in my own thoughts. He was *always* there.

"How is the solo project going?" Breanna eased a little farther into the cubicle, her eyes flicking to the whiteboard I'd left propped up in the one empty corner of my work area. She grinned at the notes. "You're a mad scientist when it comes to work, Stella. I can't make heads or tails of that yet."

The comment drew a laugh from me. "Thanks...I think."

Turning, I eyed the shorthand I'd developed in college and thought a little about the ideas I'd had for the project last night. I'd made a few more notes but hadn't had time to add them. I was actually a little excited about this project – we were donating our services to a gala fundraiser to help raise money for a children's home. The home was specially geared for at risk and medically fragile children, some of the most vulnerable youth out there. Aaron had given the project to our team, and when they'd ask who wanted it, I'd all but grabbed it.

"It's going pretty well, I think." I didn't go into detail about any of the work I'd done at home, and she didn't ask. I took that to be a good sign since I was still technically mentoring under her.

The phone in the cubicle next door rang, and she popped up, rushing over to answer it. "Umm...uh-huh. Absolutely, yes. I'll let them know!"

As this one-sided conversation carried on next to me, I sat down and flexed my hands. I was going to let the argument with Aaron go. We were just getting used to living with each other. That had to be it.

"We need to go upstairs," Breanna said from behind me.

I spun around, meeting her eyes. "What?"

"Big meeting. Everybody is being called in. We've got ten minutes."

"Did you say everybody?" I asked, arching my brows. Aaron wasn't...

Just as the thought crossed my brain, he came striding by, his tie hanging loose around his neck, head bowed. It was something that happened when you'd been with somebody for a while, but I could tell by his body language, by the way he held his shoulders, by the very way he cut through the room that he was still pissed off.

So I didn't call out to him.

Maybe it was the coward's way out, but I preferred to think of it as the wise woman's course. When Aaron was in a mood, he was likely to fire off at anybody or everybody, and he wouldn't take into account where he was either.

Since I doubted anybody here wanted to witness him in one of his tantrums, the wise woman's course wasn't just *wise*...it was kind too.

That was what I told myself as I turned back to my desk. Breanna was watching me closely, but she proved her own wisdom by saying nothing. "When are we supposed to head upstairs? Did you say ten minutes?"

❄

WE ONLY WAITED FIVE.

Since we weren't among the bigwigs, if we wanted to have a seat, we'd have to fight for one.

The strategy worked, and we ended up in two of the remaining three seats.

Aaron got there just in time to slide into the one last seat. It was next to Breanna, not me, a fact that made me more than a little grateful.

"Daddy...you can't–"

"Terri, enough."

At the head of the room, Terri was having a heated discussion with her father, the head of the company. Cal Labutti was in his sixties, and if it wasn't for the bad spray tan, he probably would have still been a good looking man. He had a full head of black hair, which I suspected he dyed, and had passed his blue eyes onto his daughter.

Now, as the two of them shared a terse silence, somebody at the back of the room cleared a throat.

Yeah, like that didn't make things more awkward.

Mr. Lubatti turned from his daughter to face the room, clapping his hands together sharply.

"I imagine all of you want to know why I called you here together," he said, smiling broadly. "I thought it would be best to tell you in person...I've made the decision to sell the company. It's been bought by Grayson Investments, and he'll be taking over, starting next week." He paused, looking pleased with himself. "And I will be in Hawaii...getting married."

A smattering of congratulations broke out, but it was half-hearted at best.

Everybody, including me, was eying the boss with speculation and more than a little concern.

The company had just been *sold*?

"Now, don't look so glum," Mr. Labutti said, still giving us that shark's smile. "I didn't build this company from the ground up just to see everything outsourced and dismantled. That was part of the agreement when I sold. All of you will keep your jobs, assuming your performance is up to snuff. But I told Mr. Grayson it would be. We didn't become the best advertising firm in the state by having kids around who half-ass everything now, did we?"

This comment was met with more enthusiasm, even a scattering of applause.

"That's more like it. So..." He gestured to his administrative assistant, a sturdy woman with hair dyed the most brilliant shade of red I'd ever seen. "Helen is going to pass out some information. Mr. Grayson has ordered a mandatory company retreat coming up next week. You'll meet him at the retreat. You'll love it...beautiful lodge, up in the Rockies."

"The Rockies?" I said involuntarily, and I couldn't suppress the shudder. I wasn't so certain I wanted to go back into those mountains...ever.

Showing he wasn't a total douche, Mr. Labutti gave me a smile. "You'll be driving, of course, Stella. Don't worry...this trip will go as planned."

The meeting dismissed a few minutes later, and I hesitated out in the hall, feeling the odd urge to talk to Aaron, despite my frustration with him. Maybe it was the unease caused by having to go back into the mountains. Maybe it was because the company I'd just started working for was already being sold.

I didn't know but I was uneasy, and I needed the familiar.

However, long after the last person trickled out, Aaron still didn't appear.

I started to go back inside and froze in the door.

Aaron was talking to Terri, their heads bent and close together. He had a hand on her shoulder, and something about the way they stood together seemed...intimate.

But I had to be imagining things.

That's all it was.

I was imagining things.

❄

"Is THERE something between you and Terri?"

Aaron had been ignoring me for most of the evening, and finally tired of being ignored, I'd given voice to the question that had lurked inside me ever since I had seen them together after the meeting.

Aaron jerked his head up, staring at me across the coffee table where we were eating.

Tonight, it was Chinese takeout.

I'd asked if he wanted to go to the Asian Fusion place by the office, but he told me he wasn't in the mood for that sort of thing. And here we were eating Chinese takeout. Again.

I was getting tired of takeout, but Aaron's kitchen was sort of lacking on things like pots and pans. I'd told him I'd take care of buying what we needed, and he'd been all affronted, assuring me he could handle buying some fucking kitchen wear.

Lately, it seemed like he was affronted by everything.

Including the question I'd just put before him.

"What's that supposed to mean?" he demanded, eyes narrowing.

"Just that." I dumped the last bite of moo-goo gai pan into

the box and gestured abstractedly with my hand. "I saw you talking after the meeting. Looked...kind of cozy. And you're *always* having these important meetings, but she seems to be the only one you're ever leaving the office with. If it's so important, why isn't Brendan there? Isn't he the head of marketing?"

"I don't think I like what you're implying," he said, biting the words off.

As he threw his chopsticks down, I resisted the urge to apologize. I didn't like the fact that I felt I *had* to imply it, but the fact was, something didn't seem right with him and Terri, and I wasn't going to ignore it.

"Should I start bringing itemized receipts so you can see who I'm meeting with, darling?" His tone was snide and cool, enough to make me want to smack him.

Before I could answer, he waved a hand and got to his feet. "I'm going to my office to finish up. Clearly, you're not in the mood for my company if those are the thoughts you're having about me."

It wasn't until he was closed up in his office that I realized he'd managed to avoid answering me...*completely*.

9

The trip into the mountains was beautiful although I couldn't help but notice that the snow was pretty much gone. At least at this elevation. The caps of the mountains were still snowy white, but we hadn't been near the peaks when we crashed.

Why couldn't there have been weather like this when the plane went down? Then I wouldn't have had to spend days trapped with Lukas, and maybe I wouldn't still be thinking about him, even now.

I immediately had to quash those thoughts, because if I let myself, I'd find myself thinking about him too *much* and in very much the wrong way.

I was still carrying that *thank you* card, although it was getting more and more ragged by the day. I didn't know why I was even bothering anymore. It was obvious I'd never see him again, but for some reason, having it made me feel better.

"Wow, check out the lodge," Breanna murmured, poking me in the shoulder from the seat where she sat behind me.

I perked up and leaned into the aisle, craning my neck to see.

Huge log buildings jutted into the sky, glass windows sparkling in the sunshine, taking up large expanses of the walls.

It would make for great views, I thought idly. I might even enjoy it, as long as there was no snow. Or wolves.

As we drew nearer, more details came into view, and it became pretty clear that this was a top-notch sort of place, the kind of retreat my dad might take some bigwigs he was trying to woo money from. It seemed the deeper the pocket, the more you had to do to impress them.

A place like this would certainly do the trick. I'd have to remember to pick up a card and send it to him, or email him. Dad was always looking for new ways to court sponsors for the non-profit the family ran, or to help support this cause or that... he was good at it. Gifted, even. And he knew exactly what he needed to do to charm the money from the right hands.

Places like this charmed all sorts of people.

Once the buses parked and we climbed out, people with clipboards were waiting for us, gesturing to the largest building – the main lodge, we quickly learned.

As we filed inside, Breanna fell into step on my right while Aaron lagged along a few steps behind me. He'd been quiet the entire trip up, but when I asked him if everything was okay, he'd just nodded.

Now, though, I had to wonder.

Once we were given the key to our room, I waved bye to Breanna and caught my bag in one hand. "You ready?" I asked him.

He gave me only the vaguest nod, and we walked silently to the room we'd been assigned. It was lush and opulent, done in a rustic style suiting the lodge itself. "I was kind of wanting to take a walk around, stretch my legs," I said, turning toward him after I'd put my suitcase on the stand by the dresser. "Come with?"

"I've got a headache." He offered me a tight smile and shrugged. "Maybe we can take a walk around after dinner."

I didn't bother pointing out it would be dark then, just nodded. "Sure. But I'll go ahead, give you some peace and quiet."

"Great."

On my way out of the room, I noticed Breanna walking out of hers. I smiled at her hopefully. "I don't suppose you're in the mood to go for a walk, are you?"

"Please." She glanced back at her room and then smiled back at me. "The room is gorgeous and all, but I've never been one to enjoy just lying around on vacation. I need to be doing something all the time."

I grinned at her. "Somehow, that doesn't surprise me."

She made a face at me, and we both laughed as we fell into step and headed toward one of the paths branching off to the right.

"What do you want to do?" she asked.

"Just walk around. I'm the same as you," I confessed. "I want to be doing something, not just sitting in a hotel room watching TV." I wouldn't have minded cuddling with Aaron, not that I was going to tell her that. That wasn't going to happen, though. Aaron had been standoffish ever since the confrontation about Terri, and nothing I said or did was changing the distance between us. I was starting to think that distance might be permanent. Which didn't fill me with heartache the way I would have expected.

It did give me a weird twist in my chest, but if that's what heartache was, then I didn't understand why people wrote songs about it. It was more annoying than anything else. The fact that it didn't really *hurt* made me sadder than the actual fact that we just might be drifting apart.

I brooded over that as I walked with Breanna. We stayed within the confines of the lodge's grounds. I'd told Breanna about my encounter with the wolves, and while she was more of an outdoors person than I was, she understood my reluctance to embrace the wilderness quite so openly just yet. She asked more about Lukas, and I told her only vague details. It wasn't like I could tell her much more.

I suppose I could have told her about the fact that he was hot in a weird, wild, mountain man sort of way. Or I could have talked about the crazy episode in the shed, where he'd strapped himself with a belt. But I was reluctant to do that.

So I kept the details vague…he was grouchy and bossy and didn't like to talk.

She hooked her arm through mine. "Speaking of bossy, I've a confession to make. Our new boss, I googled him and...wow." Breanna grinned at me as we circled one of the saunas set up on the grounds. This was the third one we'd seen. People in the Rockies must love their saunas.

"How wow?" I asked dutifully.

"I'm talking *melt your panties* wow. And there's more," Breanna said without losing a beat. "I heard these crazy rumors flying around that he's not exactly...vanilla."

It took me a second to catch on to what she meant, and then my face flamed red.

"Are you talking about our boss's sex life, Breanna, seriously?"

"Wait until you look at him, and he melts your panties. I'm just hoping mine don't turn to fire the second I see him." Breanna laughed a little.

"You're a tramp," I said with a laugh.

"Somebody has to do it. Somebody's going to have to do him." She sighed lustily. "Might as well be me."

Almost an hour had gone by and we'd ended up back at the lodge. I was about to thank her for the walk when her hands shot up, gripping my elbow.

"He's here." She stared past me, wide-eyed. "Honey, he's here. Brace yourself...and grab hold of your panties."

"What?" I asked, half a laugh forming in my throat.

Breanna squeezed my elbow tighter. "The new owner. Our boss. *Pay attention*. That's him over there at the cabin." She bit her lip, glancing from me back in the direction over my shoulder. "He's by the large private cabin. That's reserved for him. It's not like he's going to sleep in a regular room like us peons."

I slid a look in the direction Breanna was looking.

"No!" She grabbed my arm. "You've got to be subtle!"

She started to walk, dragging me along a few steps. "There... look now. And again...hold onto your panties."

It wasn't my panties I needed to hold onto. Well, the man was definitely panty-melting.

Still, it was my jaw that I needed to catch hold of, because as I swept my gaze in the direction of the panty-melter, my mouth dropped open.

No way.

I was seeing things.

I had to be.

And...okay, maybe I was wrong. He was missing the beard, but those shoulders, the way he walked. The mouth.

Oh, fuck.

The new owner was Lukas.

10

I still hadn't managed to make sense of this new twist of events when Aaron joined Breanna and me outside our room less than ten minutes later. We were expected to meet at the main building for dinner. It had been made clear in the materials provided that part of the *team building* was sharing dinner. Missing the evening meal was not acceptable. Neither was skipping breakfast. Lunch could be solo or in groups, but the first and last meals of the day were to be a 'team' thing.

The autocracy of it annoyed me.

What if I didn't want to eat with everybody else? What if I had a phobia of people watching me eat? What if the sound of other people eating drove me or somebody else here nuts?

I doubted Lukas would care. He'd already made it damn clear he was more interested in throwing his weight around than anything else. That's what this retreat was about. I had no doubt of that.

Lukas had been *alllll* about telling me what to do.

I huffed out an annoyed breath, and it was loud enough that Breanna glanced over at me. "Are you okay?" she asked.

I was tempted to confess the whole mess to her. If Aaron

hadn't been there, I probably would have, just to get it off my chest.

But Aaron *was* there, and I wasn't about to let him in on the fact that our new boss was also my reluctant savior.

Giving her a weak smile, I said, "I think I'm just hungry." Once inside, we all headed straight for the buffet. It seemed like lunch had been ages ago and everything smelled *amazing*.

To my surprise, I *was* starving. I hadn't had much of an appetite ever since the plane crash. I told myself it was the change in altitude, but more likely it was the adjustment in learning to live with somebody. Somebody who mostly only ate Chinese takeout.

Now, though, I was starving, and I filled my plate until it almost overflowed.

Breanna joined Aaron at me at our table along with a couple of others I didn't know particularly well. We made idle chatter for several minutes when we noticed abruptly that we were the only ones talking. A chill raced down my spine, and I had to resist the urge to close my eyes and shake my head.

Not yet. I thought. *Not yet*. But in the next moment, I heard Lukas's voice boom out over the room.

"Good evening," he said, his voice sending a shiver down my spine. "I'm Lukas Grayson. I've recently acquired your firm." He paused a moment. I sat with my back to him so I had no idea what he was doing, and I refused to turn around and look at him. Others were craning in their seats or had half-turned them so they could see him. I was doing everything I could to *not* see him. Aaron glanced over at me with a frown on his face and did a little *turn around* motion with his finger.

I stubbornly remained as I was.

"This firm is just one of several I've purchased, and once I'm assured that it runs smoothly, I'll be around less and less. That's part of the reason for this weekend. I want to see how you work together, your strengths, your weaknesses."

As he spoke, I had the odd feeling he was staring right at me, all but compelling me to turn and look at him.

Don't be stupid. He doesn't even know you work for the company. You know how big business works...this purchase was probably months in the making.

"We'll be working on a project while we're here, and I want to tackle it in a different manner. I've broken you into teams, and each team will prepare a marketing tactic for this project. I'll be the judge of which team has the best approach, but I'm not just looking for creativity. I'm looking for teamwork, initiative."

As he continued to speak, Aaron reached over and touched my hand. "We got this, babe," he said in a low voice.

"I've already selected the team leaders," Lukas announced. "Aaron and...Stella."

I jerked at the sound of my name on his lips, and unable to resist, I finally turned and faced him.

He was staring out at the small sea of faces watching him.

He did glance our way, though, because Aaron had just risen to his feet, his charming smile fixed firmly in place. "Mr. Grayson, appointing Stella as a team captain hardly seems fair. She's the least experienced employee, and she just graduated–"

"I've seen several of her current projects," Lukas said, dismissing Aaron. "What she might lack in experience, she makes up for with creativity. And her co-captain will be Breanna. I believe Breanna does have the experience."

My face flaming, I turned back around in my seat and reached for my glass of water. My hand was shaking slightly, but I didn't know if it was because of what Aaron had just done...or because I was still trying to process Lukas's appearance.

11

"You know, just because we're on different teams doesn't mean I can't help a little bit."

Aaron had joined me at the water cooler, and now as I sipped my water, I tried not to roll my eyes. This was the second or third time he had made such an offer, but there was something in his tone that kept rubbing me the wrong way. Of course, I could still be annoyed with him for how he'd embarrassed me in front of everybody, calling me inexperienced.

I wasn't too concerned about the rules for this goofy game. But I was getting annoyed at Aaron's insistence that I needed his help to come up with an ad campaign for charity.

I had been cutting my teeth on this sort of thing since high school.

"No, thanks." I manage to smile. "I think I can handle this one on my own." I glanced past him and saw Terri was watching us. There was a possessiveness in her eyes that was getting harder and harder to ignore, but now wasn't the time. "I think your co-captain is looking for you."

I refilled my water bottle, ready to get back to work, but as I turned to go, Aaron touched my shoulder. "You know, we should at least bounce our ideas off each other. We worked so closely together, with me helping you with your school projects and bouncing ideas off your head over the past couple of years, we think a lot alike now. I'd hate for our projects to sound similar."

Speculation started to hum in the back of my head, but I squashed it. I didn't know where he had gotten the idea he had helped me with my projects for school. Maybe I'd mention them from time to time, but that was it.

With another bright smile, I said, "I think we'll be okay. There are enough unique voices in each of our groups that we should be just fine."

Striding back to the table, I tried to shove aside the idea brewing inside my skull, but it didn't want to be shoved off to the side at all.

"You look annoyed."

Huffing out a breath, I said, "I was trying to hide that fact."

"Oh?" Breanna arched her eyebrows. "From who? Me?"

"No." I slid a glance toward Aaron's group, gathered on the far side of the conference room. But I said nothing.

"Ohhhhh..." She clicked her tongue, then shrugged. "I don't think he noticed. You didn't really start looking like you wanted to chew nails until you started back over here."

"Good." The rest of our group had yet to wander back from the break we had just taken, so I sat down and let my head fall back, one of my favorite positions to think. But I wasn't thinking. At least not about the competition. How often had I told Aaron about things I was working on?

Enough, I realized. I'd told him enough.

And he would later tell me about the inspiration he had for one of his projects.

Sometimes, that inspiration had sounded oddly...familiar. I hadn't let myself think about it. I'd done it on purpose too. Now, despite the fact that I didn't really want to consider it, I couldn't help but do just that. Was my boyfriend *using* me?

You're imagining things, I told myself. But I didn't think I was.

"Are we having a nice break?" a cool voice asked.

I lifted my head to see slate blue eyes studying me.

I batted my lashes at him, unable to resist the urge to try getting a rise out of him. "Oh, so nice." If I had to keep faking smiles at people, my face was going to crack, but I summoned up one more for Lukas as he glanced from me to Breanna. Before she could comment, I said, "Research shows that people who take frequent breaks tend to be more productive. We've made progress."

"I'm sure you have." The corner of his mouth tucked up into a smile, and then he turned to go. He had been in the corner of my eye almost every time I turned around, but this was the first time he had said anything to me. It was actually the first time he had come within ten feet of me the entire time.

I wish he hadn't bothered. When he was at a distance, I could pretend, but when he came close, it was harder. There was an ache down low in my belly, and it was unsettling and unwanted.

I did not want to be attracted to him. I did not want to find myself thinking about what might be going on behind those unusual, compelling slate blue eyes. And yet...here I was.

More of our group finally returned to the table, and I shoved thoughts of Lukas and Aaron aside. I was going to get to work. I was going to stop thinking about both of them and do what I had been hired to do.

"So, who has ideas?"

❄

I HAD my shirt halfway off, arms over my head when a pair of arms slid around me. Blame it on the fact that I was still unsettled from the crash and maybe on lingering cabin fever, but I didn't react well.

Shrieking, I slammed my head backward in a panic and twisted away from the restraining arms.

It didn't dawn on me until I heard Aaron's voice that the arms were not restraining but embracing.

It was Aaron. He had come up behind me and wrap his arms around me. That was all.

"What the hell, Stella?" he demanded.

I hurriedly yanked my shirt back down and turned to look at him, feeling embarrassed.

"Sorry. You startled me."

"Who did you think it was?" he demanded.

"That's the problem. I wasn't thinking. I'm still off balance from the plane crash, from being trapped in the mountains for so long. And now here I am again – in the mountains – and not because I want to be." I glared at him.

He rolled his eyes. "Stella, you have got to get over that plane crash. It's not like you were hurt. You barely had any bruises from it, for crying out loud."

"Get *over* it?" My jaw dropped open. "I could have died. You know how many nightmares I've had about it?" I paused and then added, "You should. You sleep right next to me."

His face softened, and he came up to me, reaching out to touch my cheek. "Oh, come on, baby. I didn't come in here to fight."

I jerked back from him. "That's just too bad because I'm not in the mood to do anything else. You want me to get over something that just happened a few weeks ago, and I'm supposed to just be over it already? Something that could have killed me? Let's see you drop out of a tin can and just be over it in a couple of weeks. Get surrounded by wolves and brush it all off in no time."

His face tightened. "Do we have to have this discussion again?"

"No. We could talk about Terri." I was just looking for things to be annoyed about now, but she was as good a reason as any. I didn't like that the woman had spent half the day glaring at me, and more than once, I'd see her muttering to somebody, and both of them would be looking at me. "What's her problem with me anyway?"

"I don't know what you mean." But his eyes slid off to the side for a fraction of a second before he looked back at me.

"Bullshit," I said.

"This isn't about Terri," he snapped. "This is about you and me. Sometimes I wonder if there even is a you and me. You don't seem to want me touching you anymore. I thought maybe we could fix that coming up here into the mountains–"

"The mountains." I broke out into a laugh. "After what happened to me the last time I was in the mountains, you think this is my idea of a romantic spot?"

Aaron pointed a finger at me. "Don't start that shit again. I'm so sick and tired of hearing about your fucking plane crash."

I smacked his hand out of my face, outraged.

His eyes narrowed, but he continued to speak, unfazed. "Just stop feeling sorry for yourself. You survived. You're lucky. You ought to act like you appreciate that fact instead of whining all the time."

I gaped at him. "You think I don't feel lucky? Do you think I wish I had died?"

"I don't know. Do you? You certainly didn't come rushing back into my arms like you were happy to see me!"

Insult flared. "You were so busy talking on the phone when you picked me up at the diner, you hardly noticed me. Wheeling-and-dealing, sweetheart," I said, throwing his own words back at him. I felt sick to my stomach. Turning away from him, I covered my face with my hands. "Would you just leave me alone? I don't even want to talk to you right now."

"Leave you alone? Yeah, maybe I'll do that. Maybe I'll just spend the night somewhere else."

"What? With Terri?" I couldn't cover the sneer in my voice. "It's pretty obvious she wouldn't mind, although I don't know why in the hell she's so enamored."

The next thing I heard was the sound of a slamming door.

12

"All right." Lukas stood in front of the room and nodded once we finished turning in the projects. Ours was done in PowerPoint, so all I had to give him was a thumb drive. When I passed it over to him, sparks seemed to flare as my fingers brushed his palm. I had to resist the urge to rub my hand down the side of my jeans as I returned to the table I shared with the rest of my group.

Both Terri and Aaron carried their presentation up to him in a series of project boards, although a large portfolio, which I knew Aaron had, would have done the trick. Terri walked so that her board had been facing toward me, and I had to fight back a disgusting snort when I saw the logo centered on the white surface. It looked almost like a dead replica of my current project back at the firm.

Breanna nudged me.

"Holy shit," she whispered into my ear. "Do you see what I'm seeing?"

I simply held up my hand. But I was glad somebody else had noticed it.

"I'll spend the weekend looking these over. I'll announce the winners on Monday. The winning team, of course, will receive a prize. There's not much use in a contest if there is no impetus for winning." Lukas spoke to the group at large, his eyes roaming over each of us.

From his table, Aaron said, "I'm a competitive man. Simply competing is impetus enough for me."

A couple others at his table smiled, and a few of them made similar comments. Eyes slid our way. I guess they wondered if we had anything to add.

We didn't.

"Go on," Lukas said. "Enjoy the rest of your weekend. The buses will be here at noon on Sunday to take everybody home."

From my table, I heard a comment Aaron made about hitting the sauna as Brianna leaned in. "That skank totally ripped off your logo," she said.

I nodded. "I know. But these aren't for a real work project."

"Still, everything has to go through the head of marketing before being signed off on. And the head of marketing is in their group. They're going to think you stole the idea." She gave me a pained look.

My face flamed at the very idea of that, and I sucked in a breath. "I guess I'll redo my logo."

"Why don't you talk to the marketing head instead? I'll go with you. I've been working with you on that or watching you work on that as part of my mentor job. I can vouch for you."

"I appreciate the offer–"

"Don't you dare say no to me. She's a bully. You give a bully one inch, they're going to take up more than a mile. They'll take up your entire life."

Finally, I smiled. "Those are some wise words. Sounds like you speak from experience."

Breanna fluffed her hair, her eyes sliding away from mine. "I do." After a moment, she looked back at me. "I was not always this fabulous and confident creature you see standing before you. I had to deal with my own special bully off and on throughout school. We all have to find our own ways of dealing, but let me tell you, ignoring her is not going to do the trick."

❄

IT WAS those words that sent me on the path to the sauna nearest to the building where Aaron and I were staying.

Terri might not fit the textbook definition of a bully, but she'd been hassling me since day one, in quiet ways. And she was moving in on Aaron. If I let some silly fight drive us even further apart, she would just love that.

So maybe it was a petty reason to seek my boyfriend out, but I could be petty from time to time.

Besides, I missed him. I missed what we'd shared, and I wanted it back.

I couldn't get it back if I let this...whatever it was between us fester.

He wasn't in the sauna I first checked, so I started down the path to another one farther away on the property. I had to check the map to make sure I was heading in the right direction, and the gathering darkness made me nervous, although I told myself it was silly to be worried. I couldn't help it, though. Even though the sun had been up when those wolves came after me, I'd developed an odd phobia of the shadows. I jumped at weird sounds now. I hated it, but I didn't know how to get over it.

I was glad when I saw the low building in the pool of light ahead growing closer, and I put an extra step in my stride, although I tried to be quiet. I wanted to surprise him – I hoped he hadn't gotten any friends to go with him. The two of us needed some one-on-one time.

He was right, I had been more standoffish since the wreck.

It wasn't that I didn't want to be with him or anything. He'd just seemed...not too into me. Women pick up on that. It's hard not to.

But he'd clearly been into me earlier until...things got in the way. We'd fix it. Whatever the problem was, we'd fix it.

Feeling more optimistic than I had in a while, I reached the door and eased it open carefully. Unlike the first sauna, though, the doors on this one didn't creak like they were dying. This one was smaller, clearly designed to be more private.

If I'd been thinking, maybe I would have wondered why my so very social boyfriend had chosen this sauna.

But I wasn't wondering about anything but being alone with him.

As I entered, I wished I'd taken the time to put something sexy on. But I'd work with what I had. Fluffing my hair, I reached up to unbutton my jacket as I looked around. Like the other saunas I'd seen, this one had an anteroom with hooks for coats and the like and two dressing rooms.

I saw Aaron's coat, and another one hanging next to it. I managed not to frown and dealt with the disappointment. Maybe whoever it was would be quick on the uptake, and if not...hopefully, Aaron would be.

I was halfway across the floor when I caught sight of the shoes on the ground.

Heels.

There were high heels on the floor next to Aaron's gleaming Italian loafers.

I swallowed around the knot that had suddenly formed in my throat and lifted my eyes to the door. It was privacy tinted, and there was a discreet sign to please knock before entering.

Yeah. I'd knock.

A husky voice came from inside. "Occupied," Aaron called out.

I knocked again.

"Didn't you hear me?" he called out again.

I knocked harder.

Aaron appeared in the doorway a few seconds later. "Look..."

"Oh, I am." I stared at him hard. He had a towel around his waist, the ends gripped in his fist. Terri hadn't bothered. She was leaning back against the bench, naked as the day she was born and the look on her face when she saw me was so smug. My hand curled into a fist, ready to knock the smug right off her.

I'd never hit anybody in my life, but I wanted to then.

Aaron gaped at me. I stared at him for a long moment and then turned away.

13

I was so done. I had come out to Denver because Aaron wanted me to and look what happened.

I was in a plane crash. I almost got eaten by wolves. And now I find out my boyfriend has been cheating on me.

And I had no doubt he was cheating. That was not just some one-time interlude I just witnessed.

I knew it wasn't.

My head was pounding.

I was so furious I was almost sick with it. Part of me was tempted to figure out a way to get off this stupid mountain right this second and get to Denver, pack my clothes and fly back to New York City on the first flight available.

But I didn't. I was going to think through what I did next because some part of me sort of liked it here.

Not in the mountains *here* but Denver here.

I wasn't living in the shadow of my excellent family, my parents who knew everybody and were known by everybody or my sisters who weren't just good at everything, they *excelled*.

I could carve out a place for myself here. Maybe. But one thing was clear, I was done living for other people. Maybe I would quit my job. Maybe I wouldn't. But I wasn't going to keep working at the firm just because Aaron seemed to think I should. Or because he had gotten me the job. I was going to pack up first thing when I got home, and whatever I couldn't fit in my car, I would get later. I'd stay in a hotel for a few days until I found someplace to stay on my own.

But I sure as hell was not going to try to make things work with Aaron anymore. Behind me, I heard somebody shout my name, but I ignored it.

Part of me wanted to go back and tell him he should hurry back to Terri. She was probably lonely without him.

But I didn't. If I saw Aaron anytime in the next twenty-four hours, I might belt him. I kept walking, not paying much attention to where I was going or what was going on around me.

One might think that my time in the mountains would have taught me better than that.

One would be wrong.

I almost crashed head-first into Lukas, and if it wasn't for his hands coming up to steady me, I probably would have bounced right off his hard chest and ended up on my ass on the path.

"You should pay attention," he said, that low, whiskey-smooth voice a caress on my jagged nerves.

I'm done, I thought again. Done living for other people and I was going to do what I want for a change.

It was odd, but that thought circled through my mind right then. Standing there with his hands on my arms and his eyes resting on my face, I went and did something I never would have done ten minutes earlier. Reaching up, I hooked my hand around the back of his neck and pulled his mouth down to meet mine.

I gave into the secret urge that had haunted me since that dream, and I kissed him.

I couldn't believe I was doing this – *kissing* him. I was kissing Lukas.

He kissed me back after a few seconds of utter stillness, and it was the most erotic thing I had ever experienced in my life. I slid my tongue into his mouth, and I whimpered as he began to suck on me. He bit me lightly. Hunger hit me hard and fast like a punch in the gut only there was no pain, just pleasure.

He slid a hand up my spine from the small of my back all the way up to my neck, pressing our bodies together.

The kiss seemed to last forever and no time at all, and then he lifted his mouth away. Whimpering, I tried to follow, but he held me in place. "This isn't a good idea," he said gruffly.

"I'm tired of thinking about whether or not something is a good idea. I'm tired of thinking. I just want to feel." I met his eyes boldly.

"Are you sure about that?"

"I've never been more sure of anything in my life."

A moment later, he had me plastered back against him, and I shuddered as he sealed his mouth over mine with a kiss so decadent, so deep, so wet and torrid, it was almost to intimate for people who were still dressed and still upright. This was a kiss that belonged in bed. This was a kiss that belonged to two people who were naked and entwined around each other. And then we *were* entwined, my legs wrapping around his hips as he boosted me up. "Hold on," he said, his voice practically a growl.

I clung to him, not having much choice because the world was spinning around me.

It wasn't just that he was moving, either. The very earth seemed to be spinning. I had never known anything like his kiss. Then my back was pressed up against something hard, and he pulled away again. I groaned and reached for him. He caught my hands and pinned them to the wall next to my head. It was then that I realized we were inside. I hadn't even noticed when we had left the path. I didn't recognize our surroundings, and dimly, I heard myself asking, "Where are we?"

"My cabin. Look at me, Stella." His hand cupped my face, guiding my gaze to his. "Look at me."

Where else was I going to look? I didn't say that though. I

merely met his eyes and found myself caught up in that hypnotic, alluring gaze.

"You realize what's going to happen if we keep this up?" he asked.

"I sure as hell hope so." I couldn't stop the smile from spreading across my face.

"What about your boyfriend?"

"I don't have a boyfriend," I simply replied.

He continued to study me for a long, pensive moment and then slowly, he nodded. It was as if he was debating something that required a great deal of thought, a great deal of concentration, and he'd finally made his decision.

Then he fully lowered his head and pressed his mouth to my neck. "You better be sure." That was all he said, and then he slid his hands under my shirt. A moment later, it was gone so quick, it was almost like magic. Poof. Just gone.

I gasped as he took my breasts in his hands, my bra suddenly a barrier that was just intolerable. I wiggled against him, wanting to take it off but not daring to move. I had the insane idea that if I moved, this would all shatter and fall apart like a dream.

It didn't, but I almost did, especially when he freed the front clasp of my bra and cupped both breasts in his hands, plumping them together and circling my nipples with his thumbs.

"You're beautiful," he said, voice gruff.

Heat exploded inside me as he studied me, hunger naked and raw in his eyes.

After my dream, I had wondered, even when I didn't want to acknowledge it, I had wondered if he wanted me at all.

Now that I had my answer, I couldn't help but wonder something else. How had I not seen it? How had I not seen this hunger?

He boosted me higher, and I whimpered as he closed his mouth around my right nipple. With teeth and tongue, he tasted me. It was like he had found some delicious treat and was determined to enjoy it thoroughly.

He stripped my bra away, and as it fell to the floor, he switched to my left nipple and treated it to the same attention he had bestowed to the right.

I kneaded his shoulders with my fingers, moaning under the onslaught of pleasure, so decadent and intense, I couldn't even begin to process it.

His hips moved against mine, and once more, the pleasure that exploded inside me was too intense, too real, too much.

I was already so wet that my panties began to slide over me, back and forth, with every move of his hips.

He tugged at the button on my jeans, freeing it. I almost wanted to cry when he dragged the zipper down because I had no doubt that he'd strip them away and then be inside me. While part of me wanted that, another part of me wasn't ready for all of this to end.

But instead of dragging my jeans down, he slid his fingers along the lacy band atop my panties. His voice was husky as he murmured, "Are you as wet as I think you are?"

I shivered at the sound of his voice.

"I don't know."

He slid his fingers inside just passed the band of the panties before slowly moving lower. The sound that escaped him with something caught between a growl and a moan, and I stared at him through my lashes as his head fell back. "Fuck, you are."

His fingers slid across me, circled my clit, dipped lower and circled my entrance, but he didn't enter me. He toyed with me. I was whimpering and ready to beg by the time he actually went just a little lower and slipped his fingers through my folds. But still, he didn't give me what I needed.

I slammed my head back against the surface behind me. "Please," I demanded, ready to beg.

He rubbed his lips against mine. "Be patient," he said, voice taut.

"I don't want to be."

"That's unfortunate for you. But you'll be glad I don't take orders from bossy little brats like you," he said, something of a smile in his voice. He flicked his thumb against my clitoris as he said it, and any outrage I might have felt at his comment was obliterated under a storm of sensation.

I was shaking when he did it a second time and practically sobbing as he did it a third.

Then, finally, he circled the entrance to my body with one thick finger before slowly pushing inside.

I came. Just like that, with nothing more than a few strokes of my clit and his finger lodged inside me, I came. He swallowed down the mewling cries I made and continued to stroke me, stoking the fire inside me higher and higher.

When he had me clamoring and all but begging for him to make me come again, he stopped.

"You're a bastard," I said against his mouth.

"So I've been told." He took me up into his arms and carried me over to the bed. He lay me down and said calmly, "Wait here." He walked off, and when he came back to me, he caught the waistband of my jeans and dragged them down before stretching out between my thighs, pressing his mouth to my pubic bone. "I'm going to taste you," he said in a blunt voice. "I wanted to eat you up practically since the first minute I saw you."

I shivered at the words, remembering my dreams. "I'm not opposed..." The rest of the words dissolved into a harsh moan as he pressed his mouth to me and kissed my pussy in an open, lavish kiss.

He thrust his tongue inside me, licking at me like I was made of candy. I shoved my hands into his hair and cried out, unprepared for...this. I hadn't ever felt anything like this, anything like him. This was a raging storm and everything I had known before this was like a spring rain.

He screwed two fingers into my cunt and caught my clitoris

between his teeth, tugging on it. "Don't come yet," he said, voice ragged. "Don't."

He crawled up my body and rose up onto his knees. I grabbed the hem of his shirt and demanded, "Off."

I wanted to feel his naked chest pressed to mine. I wanted it more than I could remember ever wanting anything.

Well, maybe not *anything* – I wanted to feel his cock inside me pretty damn bad.

He hesitated a moment, then grabbed his shirt and pulled it off, tossing it aside. His chest was broad, skin stretched taut over muscled skin, and when he pressed against me, the heat of me flooded me with an overload of sensation. Shaking from the intensity of it, I caught his arms, my nails digging into his skin.

He went rigid for a brief moment, his hard body a rigid line against mine. His mouth slammed down over mine in a kiss that tasted of need and darker things.

But then, after only seconds, the kiss changed, softened.

There was still hunger, but there was a control that hadn't been there just seconds ago.

I didn't want him *controlled*.

Raking my fingernails up his arms, I arched against him. "Lukas, please..."

He splayed his hand wide over my throat, and I could feel my pulse rabbiting against his touch as the kiss continued. But I wanted *more*.

He pulled away, and I groaned.

"Greedy," he growled.

I would have reached for him, but he pulled something from his pocket – a condom. Okay. He could take care of that.

As he tore the foil open, I let myself study him, taking in the body I'd suspected lay below the flannel and denim – and under the Armani. Wide shoulders, a heavy chest that was corded with muscle. He shoved his jeans down just past his hips and my mouth parted as he freed his cock, casually stroking himself before pulling the condom from the packet.

Swallowing, I looked up to find him watching me as I stared at him.

I expected some arrogant remark...*Like what you see*?

But the look in his eyes was stark and naked, pure, heated desire – the kind I'd never had directed at me.

That look was as raw, as intimate as the kisses he'd given, as raw and intimate as the way he stroked his hands over me.

The hunger pulsed, throbbed in the air, dancing along my skin, and I wondered what I was going to do when he unleashed it all on me.

A moment later, I was bracing myself as he cupped my hips in my hands, drawing me closer.

I was all but shaking, so ready for him – so ready to feel the weight of that hunger – I hurt with it.

His mouth brushed mine just as he pushed his thigh between mine.

Reaching up, I caught his shoulders, my nails sinking into his flesh.

He wedged his hips between my thighs.

Shuddering, I arched up, so achingly ready, I hurt.

He brushed against me, once...twice...

"Quit teasing me," I begged.

He fisted a hand in my hair and held my head in place, staring down at me. With his free hand, he reached between us, and I gasped as the head of his cock rubbed against me.

The head rubbed over, around...and then he was inside me, stretching me and I cried out at the pleasure of it.

He slid deeper, then pulled out.

Slow, lazy thrusts.

Slow.

Lazy.

It was sweet and easy...

And *wrong*.

"More," I demanded, twining my thighs around his hips and grinding against him. That didn't do it, but I hadn't expected it to. I grabbed his biceps and sank my nails in deep – *that* made him stiffen, and he groaned, hips already tucked tightly against mine. He ground them in closer, head arched back and teeth clenched.

"More, Lukas," I said. "Give me more."

He grunted and pulled out, driving into me harder.

Pleasure lingered on the horizon, and I knew if it was just this, we'd both love it, welcome it…enjoy it.

But it still wasn't enough.

I reached up and caught the back of his neck, hauling his head down to meet mine. I pressed my mouth against his, and once he was kissing me, I bit his tongue. "I want…all of you," I rasped against his lips as he snarled.

He tensed, his body going still.

But a tremble racked him. From head to toe, I felt the aftereffects as his cock jerked inside me.

"All of you," I said again, tightening around him.

"Be careful," he whispered against my mouth, just before he bit my lower lip. "You just might get it."

Then he shoved back onto his haunches until he knelt over me. Cupping my ass in his hands, he brought me in closer. He grabbed my wrists next and pinned them over my head as he began to swivel his hips in the cradle of mine. He felt bigger now, his cock pulsing and throbbing so that I felt every last fraction of movement.

"So good…" I whimpered, tightening around him.

He thrust, deeper, harder, lifting my ass up so I could take him deeper.

The hand on my butt slid up my side, along my torso, then up more until he had my throat in his hand. He squeezed lightly, his blue-gray eyes locked on mine, searching for…something.

"Lukas." I whimpered, unable to hold all the need and desperation inside.

His response was to pull out and flip me over onto my knees. A second later, he was inside me again, and he felt thicker, bigger. "Open," he ordered when I instinctively tensed around him. "Take it, baby...that's it..."

I wailed as he withdrew and slammed deeper inside me.

My hands scrambled at the sheets, clung for purchase.

He slid one of his around and pressed his fingers to my clitoris, working it until I was rocking back and forth between him and his hand, uncertain which one I needed more – the heavy pillar of flesh that filled me or the clever fingers that threatened to drive me insane.

"Be still, Stella," he said just when I *almost* came.

I couldn't be still. Couldn't. It wasn't possible.

He spanked me, the flat of his hand coming down so hard and sudden that it shocked a yelp from me.

"I said be still."

He began to pound into me, filling me with hard, slow thrusts that left me shaking, thrusts that felt like he was filling me all the way up to my throat.

"Tell me you want to come," he ordered.

Tell...him? I was practically already there.

As if he sensed what I was thinking, he backed off. He didn't just back off, though. He gripped one cheek of my ass and pulled, opening the bud of my anus. The shock was enough that it threw me off and the climax that had lingered just *there* fell away.

"Tell me you want to come," he said again.

"You bastard," I said instead. I'd told him that before, I realized.

"Say it." The tip of his finger brushed against me, that tight, narrow spot nobody had ever touched. "Say it...or..."

Terror bloomed in me, and I didn't know if I wanted to know the *or* or not.

"I want to come," I said in a rush.

He fell back into his rhythm, hard and deep, all over again.

I wailed out his name.

As if he'd just been waiting for that, he gave me exactly what

I needed, and began to toy with my clitoris, sending me right over the edge.

I came. It was brutal. It was beautiful.

He came too.

Yet...something told me, later that night, as we lay twined together, that it hadn't been...everything for him.

14

I woke with a smile on my face and an ache in my body – the kind of good, deep physical ache that came from a good, hard workout...or other things.

Lying in luxuriously soft sheets, I stretched, wincing a bit as the muscles in my legs pulled. The fog of sleep slowly drifted away, my mind clearing bit by bit.

Then, abruptly, it was completely clear, and I jerked upright as if some unseen puppet master had given my strings a hard pull.

The bed was empty.

Swallowing, I looked around.

My eyes fell on the clock, and I groaned when I saw what time it was.

Almost eleven.

I had no idea where Lukas was, but just then, I wasn't ready to face him anyway.

Slipping out of the cabin was a bit more complicated than one might think. Since it was daylight, plenty of people would expect it to be complicated, as I sure as hell didn't want anybody to notice me.

I ended up going out the back and taking the steps, using

one of the side paths that connected just about every building on the property. I backtracked a little bit so if anybody saw me, they'd assume I'd just been out walking.

That's all.

Nope, I hadn't slept with the boss last night.

Nope, nope, nope...

My face was burning by the time I reached my room, and I could only hope Aaron wasn't in there. I lucked out. Maybe he was looking for me, or maybe he'd spent the night with Terri. I had no idea, and I wasn't about to waste precious time looking for him or even wondering about his absence.

I grabbed my things, tossing my toiletries and clothes into my carryon with a lack of care that would probably appall me later, but just then, I didn't give a righteous damn. I wanted to be *out* of there before he got back, and he would be back because his things were all packed and waiting by the door.

It took me ten minutes, and I slipped out, going the long way around to get to the lodge. Yes, I was playing the avoidance game when it came to Aaron. I hadn't even changed my clothes, and I could still smell Lukas on me, but I'd deal with that later.

The gym.

I could change there. There was no way he'd be at the gym. I'd asked him about what gym he was using when I finally got into Denver, and he'd waved it off. "Oh, I'm not using one right now." I didn't really see him breaking that fast here in the mountains.

The gym was quiet, the lights flicking on when I entered, and I rushed into the women's locker room, bracing my back against the door once I was inside, feeling like a thief in the night.

"You need to calm the hell down, Stella," I told myself. It was nothing less than the truth, too. In less than an hour, I needed to board the bus, and Aaron, my cheating *ex*-boyfriend, was going to be on that bus. So were a lot of other people.

I needed to get my game face on.

❄

"MIND IF I SIT HERE?" I gave Breanna a hopeful smile as I lingered in the aisle.

"Be my guest."

Somebody had taken the seats in front and back, and the row across the aisle was already occupied so Aaron wouldn't be sitting directly next to me in any way. That was all I wanted for right now.

He and I could have our spectacular break up fight in private.

Even as I brooded about that prospect, Aaron boarded, and his eyes zoomed in on me, then locked on Breanna. His mouth tightened. I'd been one of the first in line to get on the bus, ducking behind a few others when I saw him looking for me. Childish, perhaps, but I needed to figure out what I wanted to say – other than *you cheating son of a bitch* – and I personally didn't want to hash it out with people around.

Aaron was dramatic enough to try.

He drew closer to me, and I looked away.

That didn't stop him from lingering by me in the aisle, though.

I could feel the weight of his gaze, and finally, as a couple of people behind him began to get restless, I turned and looked up at him. "Did you want something?" I asked coolly.

"Where were you last night? I looked around for over an hour trying to find you."

"Awww..." I gave a mock pout. "Weren't you worried that Terri would get lonely?"

His mouth tightened. Somebody in the seat in front of us made a choking sound that resembled a laugh.

Aaron's eyes cut to him before he looked back at me. "We need to talk."

"Oh, we will," I promised. Then I deliberately turned my back on him and met Breanna's eyes. "You were saying something about the two of us talking to Mark. That's the head of marketing, right?"

It was a deliberate taunt because I knew where the idea for the logo on the presentation Terri had been carrying had come from, and now that I was done playing nice, I was going to make sure the HR head knew exactly who'd designed that logo.

I sensed Aaron moving, and Breanna flicked a look past me a second later.

"He's gone." She cocked her head a bit. "Almost in the back – with Terri, it looks. Yeah, he's sitting down next to her." She looked back at me and winced. "I had a funny feeling about those two, but I wasn't sure if I should say something, considering we're really just now getting to be friends. Mind if I ask what happened?"

"I interrupted them at the sauna." I met her gaze for a moment before shifting back around in the seat, facing forward. "I'm going to pack up as soon as I get home."

"Do you have any place to stay?" she asked gently.

"No." I shrugged. "I'm not worried about it. I can stay at a hotel for a while as I look."

"I've got a better idea. Stay with me." She reached over and took my hand, squeezing it. "I can come with you when we get back to the city, help you pack. That will keep asshole Aaron from picking a fight, and you can have your talk with him on *your* terms, not his. Then you can stay with me until you figure out what you want to do."

I thought about that for a moment, then nodded, grateful to her all the way down to my toes. "I like that idea. Thank you."

❄

AARON CALLED me at nearly ten that night.

Breanna had been good to her word, although I hadn't needed her to drive me to my place. I'd been the one to drive Aaron and me to the office where the bus picked us up, and I'd given him a sunny smile right before driving away, leaving him at the office with his bag.

Terri had been walking toward him, so I wasn't worried about him getting a ride. He could always call a Lyft anyway.

"Where the fuck is your stuff?" he demanded in lieu of a greeting.

"Exactly where it should be," I responded. "It's with me. I moved out. Didn't you see my note with the copy of the key you gave me?"

"Don't you think you're overreacting? We had a fight, and I made a stupid mistake. It won't happen again," Aaron said, his voice reasonable.

That made me want to punch him.

"You're a liar, and you know what? I think you've made that... mistake before. I knew there was something going on with you and Terri, you asshole. I *knew* it."

Movement from the corner of my eye caught my attention, and I looked up to see Breanna standing in the doorway with a bottle of wine and two glasses. She wagged it back and forth questioningly, and I mouthed, *Yes, please.*

A moment later, I had a glass of wine as Aaron said, "For fuck's sake, Stella! We've been living apart ever since I got this job. What did you think I was going to do, turn into a monk?"

Anger fired in me and any lingering guilt I might have felt for sleeping with Lukas before I'd ended things with Aaron burned a hot, quick death. "Wow, I wish I'd known we were having an open relationship, Aaron. I would have been having so much fun that last year of school. I might have done the whole damn football team," I said in a sugary sweet voice. Before he could respond, I finished up. "In case you haven't figured it out, we're over. I'm so, *so* done with you."

I ended the call, dropped the phone in my lap and guzzled half the wine in the glass.

"Wow. That felt...good." Looking over at Breanna, I said, "That felt *really* good."

She smiled, but it faded quickly. "Think you'll end up quitting the firm?"

"I..." Huffing out a breath, I took another, slower, small sip of the wine. It was sweet and fruity, nothing like the dry varieties that Aaron usually bought. I loved it. "I don't know yet. I think part of that might depend on how the next few days go...what Mark says when we talk to him."

"You were serious about that," Breanna mused, shaking her head. "I wasn't sure."

"Ohhhh...yes. I'm serious. I don't think it was really Terri who stole my design, you see. I think it was Aaron." Biting my lip, I deliberated a moment, then confessed, "And I think he's been doing it for a while."

❄

I DIDN'T KNOW what to do or say when I walked past Lukas Monday morning. He was standing near the doorway, greeting everybody by name, although when I walked past, he simply nodded at me.

Heat shivered along my spine, my body prickling in awareness at the nearness of him. *Down, girl*, I thought wearily.

I took the seat Breanna had been saving for me and leaned back, wishing I had about five more cups of coffee than I'd already had. Not that my nerves needed it. Just coming into the office today had taken the last of my courage, and now, sitting with Lukas so close but so far away was about to push me to the brink.

I'd slept with him.

I'd had sex...hot, torrid, *dirty* sex with him.

He'd made me come quicker than I thought was possible, like I was primed to take him.

And now he was standing in front of the entire employee body, looking at us with eyes that were somehow jaded, professional, cool...*bored*, I thought. *He's bored by all of this.*

He hid it well, but somehow, I knew.

"I've chosen the winner." He held a small device in his hand, and with an economic gesture, he swept his arm back and clicked a button, bringing to life the screen on the wall.

My team's project was there.

"Stella and Breanna's team wins the competition." He glanced at each member, giving us a nod. "You've shown a great deal of understanding in how giving back to the community strengthens the company as a whole. We'll continue with the campaign – Stella, Breanna, it's your baby, so you'll continue to head it. You can decide if you want to work it with the rest of the team or choose a few select people. It's your call. As your prize..." He reached into his suit pocket and withdrew a thin stack of envelopes. "Each of you have a week at the lodge, to be used at any time you choose, all expenses paid."

He walked around the room, passing them out as he spoke. When he reached me, I took it in numb fingers, not exactly overjoyed at the thought of spending a week in the mountains. I needed to get over that, and I knew it, but I decided I'd take a bit more time first.

Once the congrats died down, he started to speak again. "I plan on talking to everybody over the next week or so. I want to know more about your strengths, your weaknesses, what your plans are. This is already the best advertising firm in Denver. We're going to make it into one of the best in the country."

His eyes then slanted toward me. "Stella, if you'll come with me, we'll start with you."

My heart jumped into my throat. "Me?" The word came out as a squeak.

But he'd already turned to go.

Aw, hell.

❄

"You didn't win the competition because we fucked," Lukas said the moment I closed the door behind me.

I didn't even see him at first.

Stepping farther into the room, I found him standing in the corner where two panes of solid glass formed a 180-degree view of the city. It was an elegant office, but it was dated, clearly designed by somebody with a stuffier style than Lukas.

Still, he didn't look uncomfortable.

Even as he delivered those blunt words, he didn't look uncomfortable.

Me?

My face flamed a hot red and indignation burned inside. He'd delivered that comment so calmly, so bluntly, and he watched even now, waiting for a reaction, and I had no idea what sort of reaction he expected...but I was *pissed*. "I'd sure as hell hope not considering our team had the better project," I snapped at him.

"How would you know?" he asked, cocking his head. "How much of their work did you see?"

"I saw enough to know that Aaron and Terri swiped the logo I've been using for the non-profit we took on last week. That's *my* design," I said without thinking. Crossing my arms over my breasts, I met his gaze.

He lifted a brow. To my surprise, he shrugged. "I know. I've monitored the online whiteboard – I noticed it the day you finished it. It's good work. And that's another reason why they didn't win."

"I...you..." Huffing out a breath, I let my hands fall to my sides, only to cross them over my chest again because I felt oddly naked, vulnerable in front of him despite the fact that I was wearing a cardigan and blouse, along with a slim-fitting skirt that made the most of my ass. Yes, I'd dressed to the nines today – I'd wanted Aaron to see what he was no longer going to have. Besides, it had made me feel better.

And maybe I'd wanted to see if Lukas noticed.

If he had, I couldn't tell.

"Do you have anything else to say?" He still had that arrogant expression on his face, watching me with that cocked brow and this almost-smirk that made me want to punch him. Or bite him.

Sadly, the biting had more to do with sensual pursuits than punishing ones, and the prospect of biting him was a lot higher on the list than punching him too.

"Was there a particular *reason* you felt the need to call me in here about this?" I asked.

"I thought you'd want to know."

Gaping at him, I echoed those words. "You thought I'd want to *know*? Do you have any idea how insulting you sound? The thought that you'd chosen my team because we had sex never crossed my mind until you went and threw it out there, thank you very much. I'm good at my job." Sneering, I added, "And I don't have to steal somebody else's work to *be* good at it, either."

"You're fresh out of college and young. I assumed you'd be... less confident." His lashes dipped low over his eyes.

"You know what they say about *assuming*," I replied sweetly.

Irritation flashed across his face. "You're being difficult. How in the hell did I insult you anyway?" he asked, cracks showing in that cool façade. "I just wanted you to know that you got the job based on the good work your team did. It had nothing to do with the fact that we fucked."

"You know what?" I said, pointing at him. "You need to work on your people skills. For the record, this isn't exactly how you talk to an employee – even somebody you *had a personal relationship* with."

"We don't *have* a personal relationship," he bit out.

I wanted to scream and was getting hard-pressed not to do it. "Again, you *really* need to work on your people skills," I said, pointing at him. "But then again, I could have told you that back at the cabin."

"That wasn't the impression you gave me Friday night," he said, his voice silky.

I gave him a deliberately insulting look. "I said *people* skills. Your bedroom skills are just fine. But unless you plan on sleeping with everybody in the firm, that's not exactly going to motivate people."

I don't know when it happened, but at some point, he had come around the desk, and we were now standing less than two feet apart. I felt the need to close the rest of the distance.

"Are you always this difficult?" he asked. "After the crash, I thought it was because you had a concussion. But I'm starting to suspect you really are just difficult."

"You think I'm being difficult?" I jabbed him in the chest with my index finger. Ouch. It felt like I'd just jabbed my finger into a wall of pure steel. "You're the one who's being difficult. All you had to do is say something like...*oh, hi, Stella, your team did good work. Just wanted you to know that. That* would have let me know that you appreciated the job. I didn't need to hear you point out it had nothing to do with what happened between us."

I went to poke him again.

He caught my wrist. I jerked back. He jerked me forward. I half-stumbled, my weight crashing into him. We stared at each other for a long, taut moment and then, despite my best intentions, my gaze flicked to his mouth. I tore my eyes away and tried to ignore the flicker of heat that had started in my belly.

But that flicker quickly fanned into an Inferno. How did one ignore an inferno?

"Let me go," I said.

Instead of doing that, he rubbed his thumb over the inside of my wrist. "Maybe you're right," he said agreeably. "Maybe I should have said, *Stella, your team did a great job*."

I swallowed hard. "Okay, thank you."

"I haven't said it...yet." And he didn't let me go.

"This isn't how you motivate people either." The words came out of my tight throat in a rough whisper.

"I'm not trying to motivate an employee."

And when I met his eyes, I saw a raging want there.

With a moan, I swayed toward him.

He leaned forward and met my mouth hungrily. Tongue sweeping in, he tasted me like it had been ages since he had touched a woman. I understood that need because my skin, my body, my mouth, all of me had been clamoring for just this ever since I had woken to an empty bed back at his cabin at the lodge.

He plunged one hand into my hair and twisted the strands around his fingers, cranking my head back. That hunger was enough to devastate me. How did one deal with that kind of hunger? I had no idea, and before I could figure it out, the kiss was over, and Lukas was on the far side of the room. "This is a bad idea," he said, voice hoarse. "You need to stay away from me. You don't want what will happen if we keep this up."

"Says who?" I asked, my voice shaking.

"You need to go." And he deliberately turned his back and stared out the window.

I had been dismissed, just like that.

15

My lips were still buzzing, and it had been hours since he'd kissed me.

It wasn't a surprise.

I'd felt like mini aftershocks had rocked my body for hours after I left his bed.

Maybe he'd meant to scare me away with that cryptic comment about how I wouldn't like where things would go, but I wasn't scared. More, I was starting to think I wouldn't just *like* it – I wanted it like I wanted my next breath.

Lukas had been rough with me, but not careless. I suspected he could get rougher, but he'd done something that Aaron had rarely bothered to do – he'd put me first, making sure I came each time.

And he'd *wanted* me.

Half the time with Aaron, I felt like I was just an available body.

And he definitely wanted one of those, I thought bitterly.

"Are you ready?" Breanna lingered at the entrance to my cubicle, and I glanced up, surprised to realize the day had slipped away.

I checked the progress of my work and discovered I'd gotten

more done than I'd expected. Most of the day had passed in a weird fog of want and frustration. I was *still* frustrated too.

That was what decided the matter for me.

"You go on," I told Breanna. "I want to wrap up what I'm doing. I'll grab an Uber or something. I might do some shopping on the way home too."

She hesitated. "Are you sure? You've been really quiet today. I thought we could go out for dinner, maybe get ice cream and bad mouth guys."

"No." I grinned at her. "Rain check?" Especially if the next few minutes didn't go as planned.

"Sure." She waggled her fingers at me and left. It wasn't long before I was the only one left downstairs, and I eased back from the desk, eyeing the steps that led to the upper level with more than a little trepidation.

Was I really going to do this?

I didn't know if it was panic or anticipation that had my belly fluttering, but I'd made up my mind, so I slid out from behind my desk, lingering just long enough to make sure my purse was locked up.

The stairs looked like they went on for a mile, and I found myself breathing hard after just a few of them, although it was all from nerves, not exertion.

Most of the lights upstairs were off although I saw a door open at the far end of the hall, the opposite direction from Lukas's office. I resisted the urge to plunge back down the stairs and hurry after Breanna.

Screw that.

The door to Lukas's office was closed.

But I knew he was in there.

Knocking, I held my breath as I waited for an answer.

It didn't take long.

"Yes?" The word came through the door muffled but curt.

I turned the knob and slid inside, shutting the door at my back. For good measure, I turned the lock.

Lukas stood beside his desk, and he had his tie in one hand.

The top button of his shirt was undone, and I could see the skin bared there. Recalling him in the heavy flannels he'd worn on the mountain, then the bare skin that had rubbed against mine back at the lodge, I realized I hadn't really had the chance to appreciate that wide, muscled tattooed chest without anything barring my view.

He'd taken his shirt off when we had sex, but I'd been...distracted.

I wanted to strip him bare and study him, from the top of his head straight on down.

And he just might laugh if I said it.

So, instead, I asked, "What exactly would happen if we kept it up, Lukas? What is it that I wouldn't want?"

His lids flickered. A muscle pulsed in his jaw. But he looked away instead of responding. "I'm not in the mood to play games with curious girls, Stella. Just remember what I said."

"I'm not in the mood to play either." Inclining my chin, I challenged him. "What did you mean?"

I had a feeling I knew.

Sex with him had taken on an edge that was wild and erotic, almost dark, and it had thrilled me. I might not have thought much of it, but I remembered those few, brief seconds where I'd seen him in the shed back at his cabin on the mountain, and I had speculations now.

Did he mean what I *thought* he might mean?

"You need to be careful," he said, finally sliding his gaze back my way. "I'm not your safe little boyfriend, sweetheart."

"I thought I told you?" I asked mildly. "He's not my boyfriend anymore. Not after I interrupted him and Terri in the sauna. I moved out as soon as I got back to town yesterday."

His lids did that mad little flicker again like he wanted desperately to shield his gaze from me, but at the same time, he didn't want to *not* look at me.

"So...what is this thing I won't like, Lukas?" I pushed away from the door, pacing closer.

He met me halfway. "There are some things that once you start them, there's no going back. You should leave...now. Go on home, have a glass of wine and come back in to work tomorrow. We'll forget all about today."

"I don't want to."

Seconds ticked by.

Ice flashed in his gaze.

I didn't look away.

Abruptly, he moved, hauling me to him. His brow pressed to mine, but he didn't kiss me. "You really want to know, sweetheart?"

"Yes." It came out on a ragged sigh.

One big hard hand came up, cupped my ass, and I braced myself, but he held still, rigidly so. "You dressed up so fucking sexy today. Was it all for me?" His eyes bore into mine. "Or was it because of the dickhead?"

I flushed. "What does that matter?"

"Answer the question or leave."

It was such an arrogant demand, I almost *did* leave. I didn't know what compelled me to stay, but something did, and I found myself opening my mouth to speak before I'd even made a conscious decision to do so. "Both." Inclining my chin, I met his gaze levelly. "If Aaron would rather have that bitch, then fine. But I'm not above rubbing his face in what he missed out on. And...yes, some part of me wondered if you'd notice."

"I noticed." The hand on my ass tightened. "But you wasted your time on the dick. He doesn't even know what he's throwing away." He traced one finger along the line of my panties as he murmured, "But I noticed. Every time I saw you bent over your desk...and you bent over it a lot...I noticed. You've got one last chance to walk out of here, Stella."

Heat flooded me, staining my cheeks red at his confession. "I don't want to walk."

"You may well change your mind." He spun me around, and in an instant, I found myself bent over his desk, and the rasping sound of my zipper sounded in the room. Was it always that loud? My heart thudded in my ears, in my throat as he dragged the skirt down. It pooled around my ankles. I could feel the fabric. I was almost painfully aware of everything in that moment.

"Know what I wanted to do every time I saw you bent over that desk?" he murmured, leaning forward and bracing one hand near my head.

"No."

"This."

I expected him to pull my panties down.

He didn't.

The hard, stinging blow from his hand was a shock I couldn't prepare for. Yelping, I jerked upright, but he had braced one hand on the small of my back, holding me steady.

"Now are you ready to walk?" he asked, voice still calm.

"I..." My head was spinning. My ass felt stung where he'd struck me, but while there was a minor pain, I didn't really *hurt*. Gulping for air, I answered in a raspy voice, "I don't know."

"You better decide." He spanked me a second time.

A rush of wetness between my thighs caught me off-guard, the punch of arousal so visceral, I didn't know how to process it.

The hand on the small of my back slid up to tangle in my hair as he held me in place and spanked me a third, then a fourth time. After that, he slid his fingers down between my thighs and tested me. "You're wet. But that doesn't mean you want this. Are you ready to walk?"

I knew the answer.

"No."

He spanked me again, and I shuddered, realized I'd lifted up for that blow. After a seventh then eighth swat, a fine sweat broke out over my body. He stopped at the tenth and pulled me up, staring down into my face. "Kneel."

The word came out clipped and tight, and it never occurred to me not to do it.

"Unzip me. I want that mouth on me. You're going to swallow my cock."

I moaned, and my hands shook as I obeyed his orders. He was bigger, thicker than Aaron, and I had to stretch my mouth wide to take him. He didn't immediately grab my head and try to ram himself straight down my throat. He let me learn him, and in turn, he learned me, one hand fisted in my hair, guiding me until he found my natural rhythm, then he fell into it, fucking my mouth as surely as he'd fucked my body the last time.

"Play with yourself," he ordered, the command coming as if from a distance.

But again, the thought of not obeying just didn't occur to me.

I slipped my fingers inside my panties to find liquid wetness, my flesh swollen and slick. Just the feel of myself so aroused was another turn-on, and I had to stop for a second, pulling away from him and resting my head on his thigh.

He didn't say anything, waiting for me to come back to him, and there was no question – I was going back.

The head of his cock was thick and round, angled off to the side just the slightest. I'd had that penis inside me. He'd made me come harder than I'd ever come before.

I raked my teeth across him.

He shuddered.

Sliding one finger inside my pussy, I gasped around his cock at the intense sensation. It hadn't ever felt this good while masturbating.

"Keep it up...make me come. Make yourself come, Stella," Lukas said. He gripped both sides of my head now, rocking to meet me, shuttling his cock back and forth past my lips.

I swallowed the head just the slightest, and another faint shake rocked him.

The first liquid drops of precum seeped free, and I licked them away before moving faster on him. I would have begged for more, desperate for the climax now, but I was in control. Or so I thought. I caught his balls, squeezed.

He reached down, covering my hand with his and adding pressure, more and more until my grasp was so tight, it had to hurt.

A growl escaped him.

He thrust deeper and held still, the head of his cock at the very back of my throat. My eyes watered. Under the ministrations of my thumb, my clit was stiff, pulsing.

I rocked against my hand one last time, and it was all over.

I came apart just as he started to come, flooding my mouth with his release. I would have pulled away, desperate for air, but the fist in my hair held me steady, forced me to take more, and more.

The need for air, the need to moan out the rhythm of my climax rose inside me and then I was free, still kneeling in front of him, my head pressed to his thigh as the aftershocks of my climax pulsed.

Wow, I mouthed to myself.

But I didn't say anything out loud.

I was a little afraid to.

❄

LUKAS HAD SLID down to sit in front of his desk next to me.

Without conscious thought, I slumped over and rested my head on his thigh.

He tensed, but after a moment, he reached up and combed his fingers through my hair. "You still glad you stayed?" he asked after what felt like an eternity.

"Yes." Rolling my head around so I could look up at him, I said softly, "I'm glad I stayed…and I want more. More of this, and I'm not just talking about us having another go against the desk once my knees are working again."

A faint smile quirked his lips up, but he didn't answer right away.

His gaze slid away, and he stared out at nothing for what felt like an eternity. "I'm not sure that's a good idea, Stella."

"Why not?" I cocked a brow at him as I met his gaze.

"I just..." He stopped and shook his head, still not looking at me. Finally, after a moment, he said, "I'd have to think about it."

And something told me he meant that in the very real sense of the word.

16

He must have been doing some serious thinking, and he was doing all of it away from me.

I barely saw him during the days that followed.

And I *looked*. Well, I looked when I had time, and that wasn't as often as I would have liked.

We were slammed. It turned out that the 'project' he'd had us working on over the retreat wasn't just a speculative thing. No, he'd actually used the retreat to get us to come up with some ideas he could pitch to a local non-profit, and now, I was in charge.

In charge. I wasn't just helping Breanna or working with a team, I was in charge. I was due to have lunch with the head of the small, local non-profit later this week, and Breanna had beamed at me as she turned over a company credit card. "Use this power wisely, young one," she'd intoned, and we'd both laughed,

Logically, I shouldn't have had a chance to even think about Lukas at work.

But I did.

Too much.

By the time Friday rolled around, I was wondering if he'd

even meant it when he said he needed to think about it and whether he'd bother telling me if he'd decided he wasn't interested in pursuing anything else. I wasn't even sure myself just what *anything else* might entail, but I definitely wasn't done.

My phone rang almost before I had a chance to put my things down as I entered my cubicle, and I hesitated to pick it up. Both the head of marketing and a couple of others had been treating me with more than a little cool distance, and I'd seen them talking furtively with Terri from time to time. My meeting with Tony, the head of marketing, about the two team 'projects' had been strained at best. I told him that I'd been at work on the logo that had been so similar to Terri's for well over a week. I even shown him the timestamps on my work.

He'd brushed it all off and started on a heated monologue, detailing just what I should and shouldn't do with the company expense card and what was going to be expected of me as I headed up such a large project.

I'd felt about two feet tall when I left.

He'd called me into his office two more times since then, and each time, I'd left with similar results.

If this was him...

Another chime from my phone, and I picked it up. "Stella Best speaking."

"It's Lukas. Come to my office, please."

My heart lurched up into my throat.

"Yes, sir. Of course."

As I put the phone down, I saw that my hand was shaking.

❄

LUKAS SAT BEHIND HIS DESK.

He looked cool and in control as I shut the door, a sharp contrast to me and my trembling fingers.

"You wanted to see me?"

He gestured to the door. "Lock that, will you?"

I did so and hazarded a few more steps deeper into the room, but I didn't take one of the seats. It was easier to clasp my hands behind my back – and hiding their tremors – if I remained on my feet.

"Have you changed your mind about the request you made?" he asked softly.

"No."

Something flickered in his eyes. I couldn't tell if it was relief or what. It didn't make the nerves dancing in my belly go away. Licking my lips, I thought calming, soothing thoughts and when that didn't work, I thought about how wild and crazed I'd felt with him. That boosted my confidence some. I'd felt...*wanted.* Not just sexually, which was always nice, but there had been something about the way he touched me that made it clear he was touching *me* – it wasn't just a sexual release he was after, but he'd wanted *me.*

That helped, and I met his eyes with more self-assurance.

"Have you decided?" I asked calmly.

"I have." He gestured to one of the seats. "Why don't you sit?"

Emotions unfurled inside me, and they were both terror and relief – because I already knew what he'd decided. If he'd decided against the two of us pursuing...whatever this was, he'd just say no and send me along on my way. There would be no reason for anything else.

"This isn't going to be a relationship," he said bluntly. "You need to understand that right off the bat. I'm not looking for romance, and I'm not going to offer any. If you want that, you should get up and leave now. I won't blame you one bit."

Mouth dry, it took me a second to form the words to respond. "There wasn't a lot of romance happening the other day. I still want more." My nipples were already tight and throbbing, sensitive to the point of pain, I wanted so much more.

"No." Lukas stroked a finger down his jaw, his eyes lingering on my mouth. "There wasn't. But that barely scratched the surface. You may have already guessed that I have...issues about control. As in, I want all of it. This won't be a give and take thing."

"Does that mean you get all the orgasms?"

To my surprise, a heated smile curled his lips. "Well, perhaps there will be some give and take. I'll give you pleasure, the likes of which you can't imagine. I'll take pleasure too. But it's my rules, Stella. Can you handle that?"

"I got an indication of just how you liked to play the other day." I tried for a casual shrug, and I think I somewhat managed well enough. "I can't say I've got much experience with it, but I've never had any desire to..." I hesitated, trying to sound much more sophisticated about the matter than I really was. "Take the lead, so to speak."

"You didn't have any problem back at the lodge."

Pursing my lips, I pondered the way I'd kissed him, then I shrugged. "True. Are you telling me that if I get it in my head to kiss you, you don't want me to?"

Lukas cocked his head, and I could actually *see* the way he thought that over, and to my surprise – and his, I think – he said, "Actually, I don't think I'd mind you kissing me. But you won't be the one in charge here. I will. Again, if that unsettles you and worries you, it's best you leave now."

"If I was unsettled or worried, I never would have told you that I wanted more." I still ached, still burned for more.

"When I tell you to do something, I expect obedience."

"What if it's something I don't want to do?" I countered.

"If you're really against it, then tell me. But I will push your limits, Stella. Be prepared for that."

"You've been doing that since I first met you. I wouldn't expect you to stop now."

That familiar, wolfish smile settled on his face, and he nodded. "I think we understand each other then. Just remember...what you and I will share will be purely physical – sex, nothing more. It isn't going to end up in a happy ever after with a white picket fence. That sort of future isn't for me."

It made me sad for him, and I thought about what I'd seen him doing in the shed, but I held my tongue. He'd already made it clear this wouldn't venture into emotional ground. I doubted he wanted to hear that I'd seen him at a time when he'd been stripped so bare, so vulnerable.

"Is there anything else?"

He crooked a finger at me, and I got up and circled around the desk. He pulled me between his legs and rested his hands on my hips, studying me lazily. I felt as if that slate-blue gaze could see straight through me, and by the time he reached my eyes, I felt more naked than I'd ever felt in my life.

"Kiss me," he said.

Slowly, I bent down and pressed my mouth to his.

"Do better than that, Stella."

I traced my tongue along his lips, tasting him again and knowing, just *knowing*, I'd never in my life find another man who made my knees weak the way he did.

Then you better enjoy it while you can, I thought. I twined my arms around his neck and leaned into him, letting him take my weight as I deepened the kiss. He let me, remaining passive as I slid my tongue into his mouth. The kiss was slow, decadent and deep...and completely one-sided.

Breaking away from him, I fought to control my breathing. "Is something wrong?"

"No. I was just checking something." He reached up and touched one finger to my mouth, but he didn't elaborate beyond that. "Come back here."

This time, *he* kissed *me*, and if I'd been breathless before, it was nothing compared to how much I struggled for air when he broke away this time.

"Go," he said curtly, pushing me away so unexpectedly, I stumbled back a few steps. "We both have work. I'll text you later."

❄

"LUNCH?" Breanna stood at the entrance of my cubicle with a hopeful look on her face.

I grinned at her gratefully. "Lunch, absolutely."

I'd been hoping she'd want to go out. I felt like I was coming out of my skin, sitting around waiting for a call or text that might not come until later tonight. Tomorrow, for all I knew.

But we were almost out of our work area when my phone chimed, signaling an incoming text. I pulled my phone out and almost died when I read the message.

It was from Lukas. It was short and simple, although I could in no way call it sweet.

I WANT you to go to the restroom and take off your panties before you leave.

SWALLOWING, I shot a furtive glance backward, but I didn't seem him. How he knew I was leaving, I had no idea.

NOW, Stella.

"BREANNA," I said, hoping my voice didn't betray the nerves I felt. "I'm going to run to the restroom before we head over there. The one at the restaurant is always so crowded."

She glanced back at me as she went to pull her coat from the series of hooks near the employee entrance. "That's a good idea."

I nearly died a second time when she followed me, and once we were inside, I went straight to the stall on the far side of the wall, moving with an almost deliberate casualness in hopes she wouldn't notice anything weird. If she did, she said nothing.

Once I was in there, I sat down and pulled out my phone to re-read the message.

Yes.

He wanted my panties off.

Blushing despite the fact that there was no way he could see me, I slowly stood up and lifted my skirt.

I couldn't believe I was doing this.

❄

After you're done for the day, come to my office.

It was almost four by the time I got another text from him.

I'd known one would come.

He wouldn't have made me take my panties off and then...*nothing*.

I was acutely aware of the fact that I was bare under the skirt, and I was so glad I'd worn a longer, pencil-style skirt today, one covered in tiny little pin-stripes. The thin red silk blouse I wore had long sleeves and buttoned at the nape of my neck, but did little to help with the odd chills that racked me off and on.

I knew what it was – arousal. A long, drawn-out session of terminal horniness brought about by my own anticipation of wondering what he was up to. And he was up to something.

Now, as I read his message, I swallowed hard and debated. Finally, I replied.

I'm wrapping up the Big City, Big Love campaign. Should have it done in 1hr. Do you need me before then?

Seconds ticked by, me sitting there hyper-aware that somebody might see me staring at my phone, mesmerized. Nobody did, and it was nothing unusual for one of us to be eying our phones. We texted clients, surfed the web looking for inspiration or stats. The world had become a technological one, and the advertising industry was definitely one that relied heavily on it.

But I was paranoid somebody would look at me and just *know – you're flirting with the boss*!

Nothing happened, and after a few seconds, his response popped up.

You can finish the job. The client wants it first thing Monday, and you won't be working any this weekend.

I huffed out an annoyed breath. No, I wouldn't. Of course, I also had plans on Sunday that involved me and Breanna, not him. Maybe I needed to go over limits of my own. I had to stay *me*. I had a terrifying feeling he could consume me.

But that was something that could wait until later.

Turning my eyes back to the monitor, I told myself to focus.

Normally that was something that came easily to me, but ever since Lukas had come into the equation, focus had become harder and harder to come by.

❄

"What is that?" I asked weakly, staring at the garments carefully laid out – *displayed* – on the desk in front of me. My jaw dropped as one piece in particular jumped out at me. "Is that... that's a corset. Please tell me that's not for me."

"It would look funny on me," Lukas said, deadpan.

I shot him a look and realized he'd just told a joke. A small one, but a joke nonetheless.

"I'll look like a cow in that getup," I said. "And what's the point?"

"We're going out," he said. "And no, you'll be beautiful." He took a step toward me, eyes on mine. "Did you forget our deal?"

He was testing me, I realized.

"Or is this something that makes you too...uncomfortable?"

Swallowing, I shook my head, then held still as he reached up and freed the button at the nape of my neck. He stripped the blouse away and studied my bra. "That won't work. But that's alright – I prepared for that." I held my breath as he stripped my bra away, and in seconds, I stood in front of him wearing just my skirt and heels – *just* those two items. He'd had me take my panties off hours ago.

And he was thinking about that, too, I realized as he reached for the tab of the zipper on my skirt and dragged it down.

"I thought about you naked under this skirt all day. Were you thinking about it too?"

"It was hard not to," I admitted.

His eyes held mine as he reached between my thighs and cupped me. A fire flared in his irises as he found me wet. "You apparently enjoy the games I play," he said, referencing the comment I'd made earlier.

I swayed a little as he circled my entrance, but that was all he did before withdrawing his hand and lifting his finger to his lips and licking the wetness away.

I swallowed the whimper and locked my knees as he stepped to the side. "Get dressed."

17

He had to direct me a couple of times.

There weren't any panties, per se, but it came with a shaper skirt with a pair built-in. Still, I felt terribly bare because the crotch on the shaper skirt opened and the dress he directed me to pull on over it only went down an inch or two past the lacy band. From mid-thigh down, I was bare.

That was right up until he gestured to the white garments at the very end of the desk – stockings. The kind that needed garters to stay up, and the garters were attached to the skirt.

I was starting to worry I'd look like a tramp, but gamely, I kept on. He'd also had a white bra which, unsurprisingly, fit me perfectly. Somehow, I didn't see Lukas Grayson picking up anything that was less than perfect. The dress looked like some sort of abbreviated version of an Edwardian nightgown, with full, bell-like sleeves that fluttered around me every time I moved.

Once I was done pulling it into place, he picked up the corset. 'I take it you haven't worn one of these," he said as he fitted it into place.

"No." I looked down, watching his agile, beautiful hands. "But I'm pretty sure you're putting it on backward."

"Give me some credit...it's part of the look." He began to pull and tug on the laces.

I braced myself, expecting to feel all the air get squeezed out of my lungs, but to my surprise, he stopped shy of that, and when he was done, the corset provided surprising support.

"Go look." He bent his head to murmur in my ear, lifting up to turn and nudge me in the opposite direction. That was when I noticed the door there. A bathroom, I discovered, complete with a full shower and a full-length mirror.

When I saw myself, my jaw dropped.

I looked...sexy. Actually, I looked beautiful *and* sexy. I'd expected to look like a tramp, but that wasn't the effect at all. I looked like a seductress. A beautiful one.

Movement from the corner of my eye had me turning.

Lukas stood there, staring at me. "I'm going to fuck you later, while you're wearing everything you have on now."

"I..." My mouth dried as I realized just what that open crotch in the shaper skirt meant.

"But we need to go now. Otherwise, we won't make it to the party."

"What kind of party is it?" I asked.

He reached into his pocket and withdrew a lace mask dotted with specks of jewels. "A masquerade."

❄

WHAT LUKAS HADN'T MENTIONED WAS that the party was at a BDSM club.

My skin was flushed from excess stimulus almost the minute we stepped inside, and it wasn't just because Lukas had his hand at the small of my back.

There was a show of sorts going on – a woman on stage being tied in a way that was almost erotically beautiful. Two others were already bound next to her, and when Lukas saw where I was looking, he said, "Shibari. You look...intrigued."

I wasn't sure that *intrigued* was enough to describe it, but instead of answering, I swiveled my head around, looking at everything else going on. There were two other small, raised platforms.

Lukas caught my chin and guided my head back to his.

Before I could say anything, he kissed me. "We've got all night. You'll see plenty."

He led me to the dance floor, and I saw right away that he was right. The show wasn't just taking place on the stages or those platforms. People were...well, I wouldn't call it making out – this seemed more intimate, deeper, the acts I was watching.

And while it was erotic as hell to watch a tall, powerfully built man spin his partner around and pull her back against him before palming her breast in one hand while sliding the other inside her skin-tight leather skirt, I knew that was one thing I couldn't do.

"Please tell me you don't expect to do that with me on this dance floor," I said, my voice shaking as Lukas pulled me up close to him.

"No. I don't share." He turned me so that I faced the couple. "But you like looking...don't you?"

Oh, hell.

He kept me facing them, and against my ass, I could feel his erection. "Don't you?"

"No. It doesn't matter to me." He nudged my butt with his cock. "This is because you've been naked and wet under your skirt half the day – and now you're practically naked. I could be inside you in five seconds. Are you still wet, Stella?"

"Yes," I said, my voice shaking.

How he heard me above the music, I don't know.

"Do you want me to fuck you?"

I nodded.

"Say it. Tell me."

"I want you to fuck me."

"Now...ask me nicely." He guided me back around to face him, bringing my arms up to around his shoulders.

I stared at him, feeling conflicted, but I knew, after a few seconds, what he was doing. This was another test – or part of the same one. All of this was a test.

"Lukas, will you fuck me, please?"

❄

"ARE we allowed to have sex here?" I couldn't stop the nervous question from breaking free as Lukas locked the door behind us.

There was a bed, a couch, TV...it looked for all the world like a rather lush, opulent hotel. Through the door to the right, I glimpsed a small, neat bathroom.

"It's sort of a...*don't ask, don't tell* sort of thing. The club is privately owned and while nobody can be coerced, forced, bought...if two or more parties decide to engage..." He shrugged. As he talked, he drew closer to me, and now he reached out, tracing a finger along the top edge of the corset. It wasn't a full one – he'd called it an underbust corset when I asked about it. As he stroked the edge of it, I could feel his touch along the underside of my breast. My nipples pebbled in anticipation.

His pupils flared, and he reached up to drag the elastic shoulders of the dress down. Dress...hell, it was more like a slip or nightshirt, barely covering my ass, but it was so elegantly made, it somehow managed to look classy even as it all but screamed sex.

He didn't completely remove it – the corset would have made that impossible, nor did he strip it off my arms. "Be still," he said, reaching behind me to remove my bra.

I swallowed as he took care of that task, taking the garment and tossing it aside. Once he was done, he tugged the dress even lower, tucking the elastic under my breasts so the weight of them held the material down. He turned me then, and I caught sight of the mirror that ran along the far wall – the *entire* wall.

"These tits drove me crazy all week," he said casually, reaching up to cup them from behind me. "The way you dressed...were you trying to get a reaction out of me, Stella?"

I didn't know if I wanted to answer that.

So maybe I had worn some of my most flattering clothes, items designed to highlight curves and disguise any flaws.

"Answer me," he said and tweaked one of my nipples, stopping just shy of pain.

"Yes." A rush of heat dampened the folds between my thighs, and I had to swallow the whimper that rose to my throat.

"You'll be punished for that." He let go of my breasts and reached down with one hand to cup my ass, making it clear what he intended to do.

My breathing hitched.

I had to be crazy.

I was getting off simply at the idea of him spanking me – and I didn't give a damn.

"You sound like you like the idea. Do you?"

"Yes."

"Say yes, Sir."

But I balked at that. "No."

His eyes flashed. "What?"

"You wanted to know what lines made me feel too uncomfortable – that does." I didn't know why, but addressing him as *sir,* or maybe even *master,* should he expect that, was too much. It didn't make sense because, at the office, I *would* address him as sir – or maybe that was the entire point. At the office, he *was* my superior.

Here, he wasn't. I elected to give him control and the idea of calling him *sir* chafed.

Lukas eyed me for a moment, then dipped his head to my ear. "Then say, *yes, Lukas*...and apologize."

That was easier.

"Yes, Lukas. I'm sorry."

"Good girl." He fisted a hand in my hair and cupped my

breast once more, staring at me over my shoulder. "I'm going to fuck you hard tonight, Stella. We should probably establish better rules."

"What rules?"

"You need a safe word." He dipped his head and raked his teeth down my neck. "I plan on pushing you to your very limit, and you might find it too much. If that happens, you need a way to make me stop."

"Why not just...*stop*?"

"Because sometimes, with these sort of games, pleasure and pain get blurred. You may think *stop* one minute, then beg for more the next. When you really want it to end, you need another word. Pick one. Something that isn't *no, stop* or anything like that."

Meeting his slate blue eyes in the mirror, I nodded. I had the perfect word. "Wolf."

Something that might have been curiosity flickered in those eyes, but he didn't ask.

I was glad.

As he turned me around, I tried to brace myself.

But that just wasn't possible.

He told me he planned on fucking me wearing the costume he'd picked out for me. Apparently, he hadn't been lying.

Unless he planned on untying me, there wasn't any way those clothes were coming off. Well, he could always cut them off, but I hoped he didn't choose *that* option.

If I had to choose the right word to describe the position I was in, it would be *hogtied*, or close to it. My ass was in the air, the skintight shaper skirt still in place, as well as the stockings. The slip-dress had fallen down around my waist, but the corset prevented it from falling any farther.

My breasts were still bare.

He produced a pair of restraints from somewhere, and they went on my ankles before he guided my wrists down and fastened them in place as well. The last thing he did was put a blindfold in place.

"You ready to cry wolf?" he asked, stroking a hand down along my exposed ass.

"No." My voice shook, and it was equal parts fear and arousal.

"Good." The words came out hoarse and raw, then his hand left my body.

A moment later, it came down in a hard stroke that set a match to the inferno waiting to light inside me.

I bucked, a scream trapping in my throat.

He did it a second time, and the scream broke free.

The third one was followed by the savage thrust of two fingers into my pussy, proving that yes, he very well could take me while I was still wearing the sexy little shaper skirt with its open crotch.

I clamped down around him, the beginning of a climax already rushing up to grip me in its tight, merciless fist.

He paused. "Don't you come until I say. Tell me you understand."

"I understand, Lukas." I barely managed to whimper the words out, and I wasn't even sure I *did* understand, but I knew what he wanted.

He scissored his fingers inside me, then spanked me again.

I moaned.

"Know what I want to do, Stella?"

I couldn't answer.

He spanked me, harder than he had before, and I yelped in response.

"When I ask you a question, you answer. Now...do you know what I want to do to you?"

"No, Lukas. What do you want to do to me?" I said, my face burning. Part of me was so ready to come, and fighting it off was sheer hell. I felt like I was going to fly apart at any second.

"I want to put my dick...here." As he said it, he withdrew his fingers from my pussy and grasped the cheeks of my ass in his hands, spreading me. Then he traced his thumb along the crevice in between, pressed against the tender spot he'd exposed. "Ever thought about having your ass fucked, Stella? Did Aaron do that to you?"

"No..." I breathed out.

Aaron had never shown interest.

But I'd wondered.

"It's time we start opening you then. Because you'll take my cock there before this is over."

I braced myself, but he didn't do anything except move away from the bed.

I remained where I was. How could I do anything else?

Unable to move, or even easily wiggle around, I fought to control my breathing. My nipples pulsed and ached, my clitoris did the same. And my core felt hugely empty. I needed him inside me.

Something pressed against me – *both* entrances.

"You want to get fucked, baby?" Lukas asked.

I sucked in my breath in anticipation – and forgot to answer.

The blow to my ass sent an avalanche of sensation through me, and I keened out his name. Still panting, I whispered, "Yes, Lukas. I want to be fucked. Please fuck me."

"Oh, I will...with this, but this time, since you're being so bad, I'm not going to let you come yet."

I didn't have any time to sulk at the unfairness of that because my senses were swamped at the next moment.

Something fat penetrated my pussy – fatter even than Lukas.

And something else tickled my anus.

I tensed.

"Don't do that," Lukas said, reaching up to cup my neck.

"You'll make it hurt. Relax…or push down. Make yourself take it."

"It hurts," I whimpered.

"It's a rod as thin as my little finger. You're going to learn to take it," he said impassively.

The pressure eased, and then as I gathered my breath, it started all over again.

I couldn't relax, so I did the other thing he'd told me to do – I pushed down. Pain flared, and the promise of more lingered just over the edge, but before it got to be too much, he eased off on the pressure. Then he did something, and the toy he was using began to vibrate. I cried out, the pulsing of it stroking against my already strained senses, an intimate caress that was almost too much.

"Oh…you like that, don't you?" It was almost a purr.

"Yes…" I pushed back as he started to withdraw, and he actually let me take the toy back inside.

"You're taking it all now. Want it harder?"

I nodded.

That's what he gave me.

I rocked back on the toy, the thin rod that penetrated my ass and the fatter dildo impaling my cunt, over and over again.

I pushed myself right to the brink of orgasm…

And he stopped.

The toy disappeared, and I was free of the restraints so fast I couldn't even understand what had happened until I was sitting on the side of the bed and Lukas had my face cupped in his hands. "You were almost a very bad girl, Stella. You were about ready to come, weren't you?"

"Yes. I'm sorry." The apology came easy, and I met his eyes levelly.

"Take my cock out. You're going to suck me off, and if you do a good enough job, I might let you come."

Instinctively, I clenched my legs together, remembering the first time in the office.

Hands shaking, I freed him. Feeling his eyes on me, I leaned forward to take him in my mouth. I went to wrap one hand around the base, but he stopped me.

"Don't touch me. I'm going to be the one doing it all – you're just going to take my fucking cock. Understand?" He pressed the head to my lips, but even though I opened for him, he didn't push inside. He simply waited for my response.

Staring into his eyes, I nodded.

His gaze held a steely sort of distance, I realized in that moment.

I was all but devastated by this.

And he was holding himself at a distance.

How could he do that?

I had no time to think it through though, because he thrust his cock inside my mouth, quick and deep, forcing me to all but swallow him, the head nudging the back of my throat with next to no warning.

He found my limit quickly and pushed me, over and over.

He hit his climax fast, and I swallowed his cum down, my lungs aching for air by the time he let me pull away.

"Stand up," he said, voice tight.

I did so, and he took my hand, guiding me to a pole in the center of the room. There, he turned me away from him and guided my hands overhead. I understood only a split second later as I was once more restrained. He kicked my feet apart, and before I could blink, he was inside me, stretching me, filling me, almost breaking me.

"Lukas!"

He stilled. "Ready to cry wolf?"

I didn't hesitate. "No."

He pulled out and thrust in, even deeper. "Brace your fore-arms on the pole," he ordered.

I did, and his weight was suddenly bearing into mine as he began to ride me, his hips slamming into my ass, his dick filling me.

"Are you ready to come?" he demanded.

"Yes...please...yes."

"Then do it."

I came. Hard and brutal.

But he didn't stop until he made me come a second, then a third time.

When he freed me from the restraints, I sagged against him.

He picked me up and carried me to the bed.

I turned toward him...but he didn't lie down. He simply adjusted his clothes and turned away.

I told myself not to take it personally. All we had was sex – the best sex I'd ever had, everything that had been missing with Aaron, for sure.

At least for me.

But Lukas...he was still holding back.

I could feel it.

18

A whirlwind week later, I found myself tied spread eagle to a four-poster bed.

It wasn't even the most erotic thing he'd done to me this week.

There was a tie for that. It was either the time he'd grabbed me and pulled me into the employee bathroom for a quickie, or the day he'd had me strip off my panties – again – then pushed a vibrating egg into my pussy before processing to set it to buzzing at various intervals through the day via a remote control he'd kept in his pocket.

By contrast, being in a hotel with relative privacy almost seemed tame.

Except he came toward me now carrying what he'd told me was a velvet whip.

"Ready to cry wolf?" he said for what seemed to be the tenth time this week.

"No."

He nodded and flicked his wrist.

It sent the silken lashes of the whip flicking over me.

One curled around my right nipple, and I gasped.

The sensation was caught right between pain and pleasure,

and I shuddered. If I could have withdrawn into the mattress at that point, I would have as my mind struggled to take in the mix of delight and torment.

But he didn't give me even a few seconds to process what he was doing before he did it again, then again.

He lashed me across the breasts, the belly, the upper thighs.

Then his gaze locked on the core of me. "Lukas, no–"

The very tip smacked against my clitoris.

It was a good thing he hadn't told me not to come, because I wouldn't have been able to stop it.

A shriek peeled out of me and I thrashed on the bed, jerking at the restraints and begging.

I had no idea what I was begging for.

Lukas had a better idea, and I felt another velvet lick between my thighs, the ends of the whip coming in contact with the folds of my pussy. Exposed, bare, swollen, the sensitive parts of me felt like they'd been set on fire as he stropped me lightly.

I was whimpering, desperate when he finally threw the whip aside and came to mount me. His hands went to my hips, and he knelt between my thighs. "You're sensitive now. I bet you can't tell if it feels good or not."

I shuddered. "I think it feels good. But it's too much, Lukas."

"Then what do you say?" He bent over me, his blue eyes catching mine, holding them in challenge.

A question popped into my mind.

Why are you so determined to scare me away?

If I could have reached up then, I would have caught him in my arms and held him.

"I'm not saying anything," I told him, determined.

Something flared in his eyes, but whether it was shock or satisfaction, I had no idea.

He drove into me, hard and deep, knocking the building scream right out of me with the force of the impact.

As I struggled to catch my breath, he fucked me hard and deep, his blue gaze relentless, his passion merciless.

And yet...

Yet there was still a wall.

I jerked against the restraints. "Let me go," I demanded.

"No."

"Yes!"

It became a challenge of wills, his head bending to mine. "If you want me to let you go...cry wolf."

I bit him instead, turning my head and sinking my teeth into his neck.

His body stiffened, and his cock swelled to near massive proportions. A growl rumbled out of him, and he battered me with his thrusts. The orgasm welled up, a leviathan that had slept inside me now rising to take me under. I cried out as it broke over me.

And still, he drove into me.

Teeth clenched, eyes locked on something I couldn't fathom, Lukas took me.

I came a second time, then a third before he finally found release.

I was breathless and shaking, my limbs sore and aching.

And still, I knew he was holding back.

❄

HE CARRIED me into the shower nearly a half hour later.

The tenderness of his hands on me was what undid me. I'd swear it to my dying day. I knew he wanted nothing more than sex, but some part of me was starting to believe he lied – to himself and me.

When he stroked that rag over me, handling me like I was made of spun glass, I couldn't help but wonder if he lied.

That was what weakened the stone wall I'd built inside me.

Nothing else would have done it.

A hundred times, I bit the words back, but after he carried

me back out to the bed and started to dry my hair, I couldn't do it anymore.

"I saw you in the shed," I blurted out.

He tensed, and the towel slid from my head.

Lifting my gaze to his, I swallowed.

His eyes had gone cold.

For the past hour, they'd been lambent, almost warm. I thought I'd glimpsed emotion in that slate blue gaze.

But maybe I'd been wrong.

Now, swallowing, I struggled to find my footing.

"I...um..."

He fell back a step, his hand tightening on the towel.

"I'm sorry," I whispered. "I was looking for you, the day we left the mountain. I heard noise coming from the shed. And I...I saw you. You were hurting yourself."

Lukas turned away from me.

The sight of his back, broad, beautiful and scarred, was like a fist in my gut. I rose from the bed, clutching the towel he'd wrapped around me.

"We're over, Stella," he said quietly.

But there was a controlled rage in his voice.

The words hit me like a full body slap – the sting came with confusion. "What?" I whispered.

He slanted a look at me, and I caught the coldness in his gaze then. "You heard me. We're over."

He walked away then, and I stared at his back as he proceeded to dress, quick, economical motions that made short work of the everyday task.

"Lukas, wait," I said, gripping the towel in my fist. "I...look, I wasn't asking for answers or anything–"

"Shut up, Stella," he said icily.

It was so brutally delivered, I felt like I had no choice but to do just that.

I shut up.

Numb shock gripped me for almost an hour after he left.

I sat there, wrapped in the same towel I had grabbed when he stormed out, watching the door in the hopes that he'd come back.

But it didn't happen, and I knew it wouldn't.

That didn't keep me from freezing my ass off, unable to move. Finally, my hair tangled and dried in twisted ropes down my back, I dragged myself upright and looked around. He'd left his stuff here. His watch, his jacket. Hell, even his wallet...

His wallet.

Seizing on that opportunity, I lunged for it, the towel dislodged by my sudden movement. It fell to the floor, but I didn't bother to pick it up. I grabbed the wallet and opened it.

His driver's license was in the neat front compartment, and I stared at the address, feeling like I'd been given a second chance.

I could go after him, find him. Apologize. Hell, I'd camp out on his front step for the duration if I had to. Even if he still wanted to end things, I at least needed to tell him I was sorry.

I *never* should have said anything.

He had made it clear he didn't want things going into emotional or personal territory, and I'd *known* what I'd seen in the shed was something deeply personal.

I dressed hurriedly and went into the bathroom, intending to make only a cursory attempt at straightening my hair but changed my mind. I knew the importance of making an impression, and the last thing I wanted Lukas to think was that I was so desperate that I'd come running after him.

Even if it was close to the truth.

I took my time straightening my hair, even dampening it and using my round brush and the hotel blow dryer to smooth out the tangles. It took longer than I liked, almost fifteen minutes, but I used that time to smooth out the tangles inside me as well.

It wasn't good that I felt so deeply enmeshed in this – in him.

Maybe it was a good thing this had happened, I told myself. It was fortuitous, perhaps, a way of keeping me from getting in over my head.

That had been coming for quite some time, if I was honest.

It had started the moment I let him talk me into taking off my panties in the office.

If he asked me to go braless under a silk top, I just might consider it.

And that was insane.

He was like poison, like candy, like a drug, all wrapped up into one, and I was addicted already.

Maybe it was good that he'd ended things.

But I didn't want them ending like this.

❄

THE AREA where he lived was clearly set aside for the well-to-do.

Even if I hadn't come from money, I'd know what I was looking at – the insanely, ridiculously rich. Just like my parents.

But from everything I'd read about Lukas, he'd earned his money the old-fashioned way.

He'd worked for it, making big business gambles that any sane investor would have ran away from – possibly screaming. He'd taken those risks and come out on the other side, smelling like a rose.

Maybe it was because it all bored him.

I could see it in his eyes during the group meetings he held with the company.

Maybe the risk was the rush, the reason he did it.

"Maybe you're stalling," I muttered.

Maybe I was. No. There was no maybe about it. I'd been sitting at the foot of the drive for nearly ten minutes, and that was after breaking nearly every traffic law known to man – or at least to me – to get here.

Heaving out a sigh, I threw the car into drive and started forward.

The drive wound through the grounds, treating the visitor to a view of the house that was nothing short of mind-boggling. It was done in a way that made me think the designer of both house and land had wanted to disturb the lush natural beauty as little as possible. It wasn't about showing off. I couldn't describe it, but the five-minute drive to get to the house made me appreciate the beauty of the land all that much more.

And the house – wow.

Tumbled timbers, panes of glass, natural stone. My heart ached a little seeing it.

It ached even more when I saw the car parked in front – a familiar car.

Lukas's.

He was here.

Drawing in a rough breath, I parked close to him, although it was just as close to the door as it was to him. That was what I told myself.

As I climbed out, I grew aware of how sweaty my palms were, how quickly my heart beat. I couldn't do much about my heart. I had never learned to meditate. It was something I might need to pick up if I expected to keep working around Lukas.

But I swiped my palms down the sides of the narrow-fitting skirt I wore. That took care of the damp palms, and I felt a little more prepared to face him.

"You'll probably get a butler with a stiff upper lip," I said, thinking of Eustace – George Eustace, to be precise – back home. He had been the family butler since I was five, and he'd taken over from *his* father. Also George Eustace. Our Eustace was the fifth in the line. The Eustaces had been with our family since the third Eustace.

While my family wasn't the kind to do so, there were those who'd refer to Lukas as *new money*, so he wasn't likely to have a Eustace V, and somehow, I couldn't see the man who'd served my family for so long being with a man like Lukas.

There would be somebody though. Maybe not a butler, I didn't know.

But Lukas would have people who tended to this house.

As I started up the walk, I found myself hoping it was a daytime staff. I didn't want to have to deal with a stern butler – or an even more stern housekeeper.

Grimacing, I looked down at myself, checked to make sure there weren't wrinkles in my dress. Some sins, after all, were unforgivable. According to my mother, at least.

Deciding it was better to hope for the best, I started for the door. My hopes were dashed when a gorgeous woman answered, dressed in severe black, her sharp eyes homing in on me. "Yes?"

"I...um..." My mind blanked out on me. I didn't know what to say, and the words that blurted out of me would have horrified my mother – and Eustace. "I'm looking for Lukas. Who are you?"

She cocked her head at me. "I'm Gracie. His wife."

19

His wife.

"Excuse me?" I said, the words coming out of me weak and thin.

"I'm Gracie." She smiled a friendly, polite smile. "Lukas is my husband." She hesitated a moment, then asked, "Are you a friend of his? Should I get him?"

My mouth dropped open at her words.

Here I was, dressed in a red silk blouse, a narrow skirt and a pair of *fuck me* heels, and she was offering to get her husband.

Suddenly, I understood what an *oh, honey* moment was.

I wanted to start sobbing out an apology, but when I spoke, the words that came flying out were *anything* but an apology.

After all, *I* wasn't the one who'd made vows.

That was her fucking husband.

"Your husband is a lying, cheating bastard, Gracie." That said, I turned on the heel of one of the *fuck me* heels I'd bought with Lukas in mind and stormed back to my car.

She called out behind me, but I ignored her.

I had to get out of here before I started to scream.

She'd asked if I was a *friend* of his.

And what pissed me off was the fact that I couldn't even say *yes*.

❄

THERE WAS something to be said about long, monotonous drives in cool, clear mountain air.

They proved to be very eye-opening.

I'd had some reservations about moving to Denver from the beginning. After the plane crash, they'd gotten stronger, but I'd never been one to quit just because things seemed hard. Then there was the mess between Aaron and Terri. Well, at that point, it would have felt like quitting, but maybe I should have just been okay with quitting.

Mom and Dad had told me they wanted me to get experience elsewhere before I went into the family business, and I understood the sense behind that, although I sometimes thought it was more that they'd rather I had my first major fuck-ups elsewhere than with the family non-profit.

But I'd actually had job offers while I was still in school. Maybe it was time to look into one of those. I didn't need Aaron or my family name to get me a job. I could do it – had done it – on my own.

And one thing was clear...I was *done* with Denver.

I should have left after the plane crash, and if not then, after finding Aaron and Terri practically in the act.

But I was a glutton for punishment.

By the time I pulled up in front of the small condo complex where Breanna lived, I'd made my decision.

I was quitting the firm. I'd wrapped up the project for the non-profit. What few odds and ends needed to be dealt with, Breanna could handle. She had more experience than I did anyway. I'd write up my resignation and send it off...fuck two weeks notice.

Something of what I was feeling must have shown on my

face because Breanna took one look at me and the spoon full of chocolate chip cookie dough ice cream froze halfway between the carton and her mouth. "What is it?" she asked warily.

"Men," I said, my voice full of venom. "They *suck*."

Without bothering to elaborate, I continued onto my bedroom and sat down on the bed with my laptop.

I wasn't surprised when Breanna appeared in the doorway. She lazily ate another spoon of ice cream as she watched me, swallowing before she asked, "Is this about Aaron?"

"No." I shot her a look and debated less than fifteen seconds before I answered, "Lukas."

Her brows shot up into her hairline, and once more, the spoon froze. It was empty this time, and to my surprise, she ended up putting it into the carton and leaving it there as she came closer. "You and *Lukas*?" she whispered. She pumped a fist in the air. "I *knew* there was something going on between you two! I could *smell* it. The chemistry...the pheromones..." She fanned a hand in front of her face, then went back to her ice cream. "So. What did he do?"

I bared my teeth at her. "He forgot to mention he was *married*?"

This time, the spoon didn't freeze. She did, and her hands must have gone numb, because the ice cream and spoon slid right out of her hands and hit the floor.

She didn't even notice. After a few seconds, she blinked and rubbed her eyes. "What did you say?"

Instead of answering, I pointed to the floor. "You're wasting good calories."

She scowled and scooped up the pint carton and spoon, turning around and hurrying into the kitchen.

While she was gone, I launched the word processing program on my computer and started typing up my resignation letter. She was back before I finished and done with cleaning up the small mess the ice cream had made. As she sat down next to me, I tried to ignore the press of guilt. I didn't really want to leave one of the few friends I'd made.

But those few friends weren't worth the misery that had come along with this job.

The plane wreck.

Finding out my boyfriend was cheating on me.

Then finding out I'd been made into the *other woman.*

"You're leaving," Breanna said softly, resting her head on my shoulder.

I knew she had to be reading the scathing resignation, but I didn't do anything to stop her.

Instead, I answered her question. "Other than you and a couple of other friends, I really haven't found much reason to stay. Now this thing with Lukas..." I shook my head. "It's too much, Bree. It's just too much."

She was silent as I finished typing up the letter.

Skimming it once, I decided it was good enough. I saved it before opening my email. Without giving myself time to think, I drafted a quick note to Lukas and the head of human resources, then attached the letter. I huffed out a breath as I hit send, then closed my laptop.

"Feel better?" Breanna asked quietly.

"No." Looking around my room, I took in the bedroom suite I'd just bought, the few furnishings I'd allowed myself to get as I tried to make this strange place into a home. I hadn't even had a chance. "But I will sooner or later. You want to keep the bedroom suite? Maybe use this as a guest bedroom?"

She gaped at me.

I shrugged. "It's not a big deal, but I can arrange to have it transported back home if you don't."

Which was smarter since I'd need it for when I found myself an apartment because I wouldn't stay with my parents any longer than necessary, that was certain.

"Um...I'll think about it," she said slowly. Then she grinned. "Maybe I'll donate mine and take yours."

I laughed. It almost felt good.

Rising, I went to lug my suitcase out of the closet, one of the nice things about the condo where Breanna lived. It was spacious and open, the kind of place I'd probably have to pay three times as much for to get in New York. Which meant I wouldn't get anything like this right away. My parents would float me the money, but until I got the bulk of my trust fund at twenty-five, I had to be careful.

"Anything I can help with?" Breanna asked, her voice husky.

I glanced up and saw that her eyes were wet. I went to her and hugged her. "I'll miss you."

She hugged me back. "Let's get this done before I try to talk you out of it," she said, pulling back almost immediately.

We worked in silence for almost twenty minutes and would have likely kept that up until we were done if it wasn't for the ringing of the doorbell.

Breanna sniffed and looked at me, grimacing. "Do you mind? I don't do goodbyes well, and I looked awful now."

I nodded and paused to hug her again before slipping out of the bedroom.

Shooting a quick glance at the clock, I saw that it was almost nine. I didn't think Breanna was expecting anybody, and I knew I wasn't so I had no idea who it was because I knew it wouldn't be Lukas.

I sure wouldn't have minded a pizza delivery guy right then though.

My belly rumbled demandingly, almost on cue, as I opened the door. Face flushed with embarrassment, I went to greet my visitor.

But the words froze on my tongue.

It was Gracie.

Lukas's wife.

20

We stared at each other for the longest time, the silence growing taut and heavy, moving well past the awkward stage and into the downright *weird*. But I didn't know what to say or do, and it seemed like Gracie felt the same.

Did she go by Mrs. Grayson? Had she hyphenated? Kept her last name? Should I ask?

The longer she watched me, the more uncomfortable I became, and I opened my mouth, desperate to shatter this quiet. Then I spoke – and I wanted to yank the words *back*.

"I didn't know he was married," I blurted out.

I braced myself for derision, for anger, for speculation.

What I got was a laugh. "I know that," Gracie said, her voice gentle. "Our relationship isn't publicized, and he told me that he hadn't told you."

"He...you..." Shaking my head, I asked, "He told you about us?"

"Oh, I've known for a couple of weeks. Lukas and I don't really have any secrets." She glanced past me, then said, "I'd like to come in, if I could. I know this must be awkward."

Awkward?

Yeah. We could start with that.

I was pretty sure that calling this awkward was like referring to the Titanic as a bit of disaster, but what the hell. "Sure." I stepped back, crossing my arms over my belly as she came inside.

She didn't bother with any pleasantries, just went straight to the couch and sat down, clearly waiting for me to follow suit. Since I wanted this over, I did just that, sitting in the armchair across from her and crossing my legs. Gracie met my gaze.

"So Lukas told you about us."

"Yes."

"Might have been nice if I was informed," I said breezily, trying not to let the feelings of betrayal and hurt overtake me. We'd had a sexual relationship, nothing else. No reason to feel hurt over it.

"Lukas has...trust issues," Gracie allowed. Then she shrugged, sighing. "But yes, he should have told you. I'm here to try and...explain."

"What exactly is there to *explain*?" I demanded. "Do you two have some sort of...open marriage? If so, hey...fine. But that's not my speed, and the bastard should have told me."

She cocked a brow. "Agreed. And I wouldn't call ours...open, per se. It's more a marriage of convenience. You see...." She paused, licking her lips and drawing in a deep breath. "Lukas and I both get certain things out of our marriage. He gets a partner for dinner parties or the various cooperate functions he has to attend, minimizing the chance that he'll have to deal with flirtatious overtures that make him...uncomfortable. And I... well..." She paused and brushed her hair back. "Stella, I'm gay. My family is very conservative, and they have no idea. Before Lukas and I made this arrangement, I constantly had to deal with them trying to hook me up with this bachelor or that, various blind dates. It was awful. Now, they leave me alone."

I said nothing, staring at her as I processed her words.

A marriage of convenience.

"Why didn't he tell me?" I asked finally.

"I don't know." Gracie shook her head, lifting one slim hand in a gesture of confusion. "What I do know...he's...different since you came along. Lukas carries a lot of things inside him, and sometimes, he keeps too much of himself trapped inside. But he smiles more lately. I think it's because of you. I hope you'll give him another chance."

"Ha." I got up and paced over to the window, staring outside at the busy street, still crowded despite the growing lateness. "I think you're wasting your breath, Gracie. Lukas told me earlier that we were done. I made a personal comment and...whoa, was that a mistake."

"No, it wasn't," Gracie said, and there was stubborn determination in her voice.

Slowly, I turned and met her eyes. "Did he tell you what I said?"

"I know you've cracked his exterior. Whatever is doing that is something he needed to have done. He *needs* to start feeling. He never allows himself that bit of humanness, but I think you draw it out of him."

She rose from her seat, gazing at me. "You've been good for him, Stella. Nobody knows him like I do – and I've never seen him open up as much as he has the past few weeks. You're the reason for it. But I can't make you believe that. You have to choose to do so for yourself. Lukas has a great deal to give, but you would have to be patient with him. He would be worth it, I think."

She turned away.

"I saw him beating himself." I don't know what drove me to say it. "I mentioned it to him tonight. That's what set him off."

Gracie turned back to me, her mouth a perfect *O* of surprise.

"Wow," she breathed out. "That's...wow. Yes, I can see why he'd try to pull back on you."

"Why does he do it?"

"I can't tell you that," she said, shaking her head. "That's his story. It's one of the sadder parts of him. But...if you would be patient, he may well share it with you."

21

"Here." Gracie offered me a key. We sat in the car, the engine idling, parked in front of the big house. "I've got a date. Besides, I think this is something that belongs between the two of you anyway."

I blushed but accepted the key.

Folding my hand around it, I squeezed it hard enough that the edges bit into my hand.

Eying the front door with trepidation, I said, "What am I supposed to do if he doesn't want to talk to me? It's a far way for Uber to come for a pick up."

"He wants to talk to you." She gave me an encouraging smile. "I know him better than he knows himself."

I was taking an awful lot on faith here, but just gave her a nod and climbed out. The house towered over me, making me feel incredibly small as I made my way closer. My hand shook as I fit the key to the lock and slid it. The sound of the tumblers clicking into place seemed louder than necessary, and I didn't know if it was me or just the heightened awareness that made it seem so.

Slipping inside, I closed the door and braced my back against it, letting my eyes adjust as I took in my surroundings.

Gracie had told me she lived in the east wing of the house, while Lukas lived in the north. *Just take the stairs and keep going straight. His bedroom is at the very far end of the hall.*

Seemed simple enough.

My knees shook with each step.

Halfway up, I realized I'd left the key in the lock, and I hurried back down to retrieve it, tucking it into the pocket of my blue jeans. I'd changed before leaving the condo with Gracie, and I was glad I had. It had gotten colder, the temperature hovering in the forties. It didn't seem much warmer in the hall as I made my way closer toward Lukas's room, despite the jeans and turtleneck sweater I wore.

Was it the chill that made my hands continue to shake? Nerves?

I didn't know.

Coming to a stop outside the door, I took a deep breath and knocked.

"Go away, Gracie!" Lukas said, his voice low and intent.

Instead of correcting him, I slipped inside.

The chill here was worse, and it wasn't hard to see why.

He stood in the open doors of what looked like a balcony and wind blasted in.

He spoke without looking at me. "Damn it, Gracie–"

"It's cold," I said, interrupting him. "Can you shut those doors, please?"

He spun around so fast, it was almost comical.

Our gazes locked across the room and I inclined my chin, refusing to look away.

"You..." He stopped for a second before continuing on. "What are you doing here?"

"Gracie brought me here."

His lids flickered. Bit by bit, his expression closed until it was like staring at a closed book – his features gave nothing. Save for that slight flicker of his lids, I might as well have been staring at a statue.

"Why?" he asked quietly.

"Well, I haven't decided," I said softly. "I could be here to kick your ass for not telling me about her. I could be here to apologize for intruding on your personal business…I just haven't decided."

His mouth tightened, some of the icy façade fracturing. A split second later, it smoothed over, gone as if the fracture never existed.

Fine. He wasn't going to take the first step. I'd do it.

"I shouldn't have intruded on your personal business. I'm sorry," I said.

His head bowed, big shoulders shuddering on a heavy sigh. When he looked back at me, I thought maybe he was going to say something…explain, even. When he looked away without saying anything, I wanted to scream. But I did nothing. I wasn't going to push again. I knew better now.

"I should have told you about Gracie," he said, each word slow and halting, like they had to be dragged from him with rusty, iron hooks. "What we have…we're friends. The marriage is a convenience. There's nothing else between us."

"She told me." I wasn't sure if I entirely believed her, because I didn't see Lukas giving so much of himself to just a friend. But that could be just because I was jealous she had so much. And I wasn't going to push. Not for anything.

Another gust of wind blasted through the open doors, and I shivered, wrapping my arms around myself. Lukas jerked as if coming out of a fugue. He turned back to the doors and pulled them closed, then gestured to me. "Come over here," he said gruffly, beckoning toward a fireplace that took up most of one wall. He hit a switch and gas logs flared to glowing life.

I let him pull me closer to the fire, and a sigh escaped me as warmth penetrated the chill that had gripped me for what felt like the past several hours. Lukas stood behind me, rubbing his hands up and down my arms, adding to the warmth.

Something brushed the back of my head.

I thought it might be his lips.

Another shiver raced through me, and he said, "Still cold?"

"It's getting better," I told him, the words husky. Slowly, I turned in his arms and tipped my head back to meet his eyes. "You told me it was over. Is it?"

He caught a fat curl in his fingers and stroked it. "You sent a resignation. Should I accept it?"

Instead of either of us answering the other, the two of us swayed closer.

His mouth met mine. It was hard to say who kissed the other first.

His tongue swept into my mouth, a hungry, deep kiss that I felt from the tips of my toes all the way up. My breasts heated, the nipples tightening. He slid one hand under the hem of my sweater, and I gasped at the shocking heat of his hand on my naked skin.

Clothes fell away.

I'd glimpsed a massive bed tucked up on a platform on the far side of the room, under a triangular frame of windows, but it seemed so far away now. When he swept me up into his arms, I moaned, because I didn't want him to stop kissing me or touching me long enough to carry me to the bed. I didn't even want him to stop touching me long enough to get me naked.

To my delight, all he did was carry me over to the couch that faced the fireplace and laid me down, stripping my jeans away without once pausing in the kisses he pressed to my mouth, my neck. Once he had me naked, he came down over me.

I fought with the buckle of his jeans, hurriedly freed him and wrapped one hand around his cock. Skin stretched smooth and tight over his erection and his heavy length pulsed in my hand as I stroked down, then up. He caught my hand and dragged my wrist up over my head, pinning them in place as he wedged his hips between my thighs.

He watched me as he pressed up against me, the moment almost painfully intimate.

The moment he slipped inside me, we both groaned and I arched up, deepening the connection.

Lukas grunted as I clenched down around him, withdrawing and driving back inside, hard, fast. I felt his balls slap against me, felt him swelling. "Lukas," I breathed out.

His mouth took mine, swallowing down the sound.

Our breath mingled, the ragged moans becoming one.

His heart slammed against mine, and the hand gripping my wrist slid up to twine with my fingers, palm to palm.

Panting, moaning, desperate, I scrabbled underneath him, needing to be even closer. One big hand cupped my ass and tilted me up, deepening the contact. I cried out as each thrust now had him scraping over my clitoris, the head of his cock bumping against me just right.

"Lukas!"

He bit my lower lip.

I climaxed with a whimper.

He didn't stop.

Neither did my orgasm. Not until it slid into another, then another.

When he finally reached his, I was a melted puddle of flesh, so weak and boneless I could barely move. He shuddered against me, arching into the cradle of my hips one last time.

Then, a harsh groan slipped from him, and he climaxed so hard I felt the jerking rhythm of his cock. His mouth was buried in my hair, and his voice was muffled. But he whispered my name just before sinking down to lie on me for just a moment.

I heard him.

He murmured, "*Stella...*"

22

"My father was abusive."

The words, spoken in the quiet stillness of an early morning, caught me off-guard.

Lukas and I had lain awake together for nearly twenty minutes without speaking, facing each other, just enjoying the silence and warmth of the other.

So when he spoke, and the words were what they were, it came as something of a shock.

I steeled my jaw against trembling, refusing to let myself tear up the way I wanted to. I also had to fight against the anger that burned inside.

"He used to beat me...whenever. If I didn't do good in school, or if he thought I was being a show-off, bringing home good grades. If it rained and I had to stay inside, or if it was sunny and I asked to go outside. It got to where I didn't ask for anything – I just got by. If I was hungry, I stole whatever food I could find because if I asked, he'd belt me. If my clothes were getting too small, I'd steal them, too, or find them at shelters, whatever it took."

"Lukas–"

"He was a mean bastard. He liked to hurt people, and I was

an easy target, Stella." His eyes flicked to mine. "And I'm his son."

He paused then, and I tried to puzzle through whatever it was he was telling me.

I wasn't having much luck.

He must have seen the confusion on my face because he stroked my hair back, then pulled me in and placed a kiss on my forehead. "I'm his son. Sometimes, anger burns inside me so bright, the need to strike out...I can't explain it. But I worry that if I don't do something to blunt that edge, I might strike out and start hurting people...like he hurt me. That was why you saw..."

It clicked then, and I understood what he was telling me.

He was explaining about the shed.

"Lukas, you can't tell me you were in that shed because you felt some deep urge to hurt me," I said, reaching up to touch his cheek.

"It wasn't *hurt* on my mind," he admitted gruffly. "But I don't trust myself. Besides..." As I watched, his cheeks went a dull, ruddy red. He was embarrassed, I realized. I waited for him to pull back, to hide away from me again, but he continued and said, "All the things he would say to me...I still hear them. In here." He tapped his temple. "I've been away from him for a long time, but I hear him all the same. It's like he's on repeat in my head sometimes and when I..."

As his words trailed off, understanding filled me.

"You're punishing yourself. What he used to do, you're taking over."

"In a way." I could tell he didn't want to look at me now, but he did it anyway.

I hurt for him. I wanted to draw him into me and stroke away all those pains, all those fears. I also wanted to hunt down his father and beat him stupid, but that wasn't going to help anything, was it? But maybe I could help with this.

"You're not the only person who's hurt himself for a reason like this," I told him, brushing his hair back. "Others have done it – others do it all the time. What you have to do is figure out a healthier way to deal with this...edge you described."

"Healthy." He snorted and sat up. "There's nothing *healthy* about the shit I've got going up here." He tapped the side of his head again.

While I agreed he had some unhealthy ways of dealing with some rough shit, I suspected there was just as much broken in his soul as in his mind. But I wasn't going to go there. Not right now, maybe not ever.

But...

Clearing my throat, I said, "Can I ask you something?"

His face took on that familiar shuttered expression, but he said softly, "I can't guarantee I'll answer."

"That's fair." I smiled at him. Then, taking a deep, shaky breath, I dove in head first. "Maybe I'm wrong, but I get the feeling when we're...intimate, there are things you're holding back from me. Am I right?"

The shuttered expression didn't disappear, but I caught a flicker in his eyes. It might have been surprise. "What makes you think that?"

"Instinct?" I shrugged, smiling weakly. "I don't know. I just... it's hard to explain. I get more from what we have together than I've ever gotten from any man, but something tells me you're not giving me everything. I don't mean *personal* everything. It's just... you're holding back on me, aren't you?"

"You won't even call me *sir*, Stella. I'm not sure you're ready for anything more intense than what we're already doing."

"I don't call you *sir* because it puts me in the mind that I'm not your equal, and I am," I said tartly. "I've lived most of my life with people making me feel like I'm less than them. Maybe they don't even do it intentionally, but the reason we're even involved is because I made the choice to cede control to you. That means *I* have some level of power in this relationship. Calling you *sir* when I've already ceded control is just...it's not me."

He latched onto one thing in all of that.

"Whoever it was that has made you feel less...they are wrong," he said, cupping my cheek in his hand. "That is all there is to it."

My heart threatened to flip. I held it in check through will alone.

"Smooth," I said, keeping my voice light. "But I'm still not calling you *sir*."

He laughed, the sound rusty. "Fair enough."

"Will you tell me what you're holding back?" I asked, not expecting an answer.

"It's not any one specific thing, Stella. There's no formula for this. You say you don't want to have sex in front of others and I'm too greedy to share, but if I tell you I wanted to strip the blouse from you in the middle of the dance floor and show the other men that I had something they wanted...what would you do? If I'd touched you..." He cupped one breast in his hand. His lids drooped as he found the nipple puckered and tight. "Would you be as aroused as I think you are now? Or would you pull away?"

"I don't know," I said, voice raspy. "But I'm willing to try it."

"And when I tell you that I plan on fucking your ass and listening to you beg me to stop, then beg me not to...does that scare you or turn you on?" he demanded, his hand moving from my breast to tangle in my hair.

"Both."

"It will hurt." He caught my hip now, fingers spread wide to curve over my ass. "I already know that, and I don't even care because that means I'll be the first one to sink my cock into that hot little hole. What does that make you feel?"

"Hot." The word was almost more of a squeak than anything else. Wiggling in closer, I pressed my lips to his chin. "Almost everything we do scares me a little. But that's one of the things I love about it. It's what's been missing from my life, Lukas. Stop holding back."

23

I gasped as Lukas finished screwing the butt plug into place.

I was already a quivering mess of sensation, thanks to the minutes he'd spent putting nipple jewelry into place, drawing it out under the guise of *adjusting the fit* – and then doing the same when it came to a pretty little piece that he'd told me was a clit clamp.

It sounded painful.

It felt...unreal.

My clit was engorged and already swollen, and now, as he spread the cheeks of my ass, clearly looking down at the plug he'd just put in place, I thought if I had to so much as *move*, I'd come.

Then he moved me, straightening me away from the desk and turning me to face him.

"You'll keep all of it in place all day," he told me, brushing the back of his fingers down my cheek.

"Yes, Lukas." I nodded, but I was so caught up in the sensations, I barely knew what I was saying. He could have told me that he wanted me to walk naked down to my cubicle, and I might have agreed.

Or...maybe not.

A minute later, as my head slowly cleared, I held out my hand for my panties, and he hesitated.

"I need my panties, Lukas," I said, almost desperate. I had a conference call in less than ten minutes, and I had to get down to the bathroom.

He lifted the lacy silk scrap to his mouth. "But I like them."

Throwing a look at the clock, I gave him a pained look.

"But I *need* them."

"You do know what to say, right?" He was pushing me, I realized.

"I'm insanely wet," I said, pushed to the edge. "If this...thing falls off me..." I gestured to my front. "Or if I started..." I hesitated, not certain how to explain. "What if I sit down and end up standing with a wet spot on the back of my skirt?"

Lips pulled to the side, he considered me, then slowly, held out the panties.

I grabbed them and all but ran from the room.

In the bathroom, I hurriedly cleaned up, terrified I'd dislodged the clamp. I wasn't worried about the plug, but... whoa...the way it felt inside me. Sitting down was going to be interesting.

Once I'd wiped off as best as I could, I pulled my panties back on and wondered if maybe I should start wearing pants to work.

It had been two weeks since that weekend when we'd opened up a little bit to each other – I'd spoken to HR the weekend I came back, asking if I could please withdraw my resignation. Naturally, it was just for form. Lukas already knew I'd changed my mind and had contacted HR as well. But still, it was the courteous thing to do.

During those two weeks, Lukas had done exactly as he'd said he'd do. I'd asked him to stop holding back.

He'd promised to try, and *wow*, was he holding up that promise.

One morning, I'd come in with a voice so hoarse, people had thought I was coming down with something.

No, but I hadn't been about to tell them that Lukas had made me scream myself senseless and my voice was trashed because of it.

Another day, he'd confiscated not just my panties, but my bra. Fortunately, I'd worn a pantsuit with a double-breasted blazer that day, which had probably given him the idea.

But nothing he'd done compared to what he was doing now. Each step was torture, an exercise in exquisite sensation and maddening patience as both the nipple and clit jewelry teased those areas into points of surreal pleasure, while the plug seemed to be a locus of heat that pulsed from within.

I was already wet again by the time I reached my desk.

Just in time for the phone call too.

❄

I WAS all but quivering by the time Lukas led me into his room.

He took the overnight bag he'd asked me to pack and dropped it on the floor, then turned to me.

He held out a hand, and I stepped closer, putting mine in his.

Just that light contact had me shivering, and he dipped his head to murmur in my ear, "You look like you're about ready to come, just standing there."

I managed a jerky nod.

"It makes me want to toy with you even more. Should I?"

"Please don't, Lukas," I said, the words hardly more than a moan.

"Would you cry wolf?" He fisted a hand in my hair and dragged my head back, staring into my eyes with a gaze that burned.

I didn't answer.

"I've watched you all day, knowing that your nipples must be aching, that your clitoris must feel the same. I've watched you all day, wishing that it was my dick in your ass and you can't even give me that?" There was something almost...teasing in his voice.

I opened my mouth, almost ready to say it.

But he kissed me before I could make myself.

"We'll find another way to bring you to your knees, Stella." His tongue licked into my mouth, and I curled my arms around him as he pulled me closer, but the press of his chest against my over-sensitized nipples was too much, and I tore my mouth away, shuddering.

"Lukas...please. It almost hurts," I said.

He reached for the buttons on my blouse, that gaze of his still burning hot. "I want to see you."

He stripped me bare, and when he had peeled every last stitch of clothing from my body, he circled me, pausing to tug on the chain that connected the two nipple charms. I cried out, feeling an answering pang in my cunt. He slid his finger to my shoulder and continued on his slow journey around my body. When he reached the front of me again, he startled me by going to his knees and staring at the apex of my thighs, an avid gleam in his eyes. "You're so wet, I can smell it on you." He leaned in and stabbed at my clitoris with his tongue.

I came.

The touch of him was like liquid lightning, and I'd been primed for him all day long. With a broken gasp, I caught his shoulders and squeezed, struggling to stay upright.

He caught me by the back of the thighs, supporting me with his strength, but the moment the orgasm ended, he was on his feet, his face rigid as he glared down at me. "You came without me giving you permission, Stella. Say you're sorry."

"I'm sorry, Lukas."

"Kneel," he ordered.

I did so, my mouth watering at what I thought was coming.

"You like sucking cock so much, I should find a better punishment," he muttered. He threaded one hand through my hair and reached for the slim, silver buckle on his belt with the other. "The problem is, your mouth is one of the best damn things I've ever felt. I don't want to give that up."

When his cock sprang free, I leaned in, taking him in my mouth, but Lukas wouldn't let me take the lead. He grabbed my head between his hands and fucked my mouth, slow, lazy motions that denied the frustrated hunger building inside me.

When I would have reached between my thighs to stroke it away, he said, "Don't you play with yourself. You're my toy right now. You touch when I say you can."

I moaned, but his words made me burn.

His toy.

His.

Even if only for this.

He came inside my mouth after only a few more strokes, each one rougher than the last, making me think the game we'd been playing affected him as much as it did me.

He pulled back almost immediately afterward, his cock still half-erect, and he made a bemused noise in the back of his throat. "I should be ready to sit and have a glass of scotch after that, and all I can think about is taking a look at your ass to see that plug. Stand up, Stella."

Once I did, he had me turn around and put my hands on the bed. I was far enough away that I had to lean forward to do so, and I bit my lip at the open, vulnerable position he left me in. The charms still dangled from my nipples although the clit clamp had fallen out of place, probably when he'd kissed me.

And the butt plug...

He pressed his thumbs to the cheeks of my ass, spreading me open.

I could feel him watching me.

"I'm not ready to fuck you here yet. I won't be gentle, and you need to be more prepared first."

"I don't care if you're gentle," I said desperately. I had a huge, yawning void inside me and I just wanted him to fill it.

"You will. But for now..." He thrust two fingers into my pussy. "Feel how tight this is, Stella?"

I barely heard him. The feel of his fingers invading me while the plug narrowed down my passage was too much, and I swayed forward, almost collapsing. It was only his hand, gripping my hip firmly that kept me upright.

"Move closer to the bed," he said.

I couldn't.

I couldn't move, could hardly breathe.

Breath shuddering out of me, I tried to follow his fingers as he withdrew – then plunged them back inside.

"Fuck, you're already about to come again...not without me," he said brusquely. He withdrew his fingers and slapped my ass abruptly. "Don't come without me, Stella. You hear me?"

"Yes, Lukas."

A moment later, I felt the head of his cock probing me, then he was inside – but he didn't thrust. I didn't know if he *could* – he was wedged in tight, thanks to the plug, and the feeling was indescribable. Whimpering, I bounced up on my toes trying to lessen the pressure – or take more, I had no idea.

He withdrew and began the slow process all over again. Each thrust took him a little deeper, and I was shaking, shuddering, begging, pleading.

"I can't hold it back, Lukas, I can't!"

"You will." He spread both hands across the base of my spine and rocked against me. "You won't come yet...not yet."

I cried out. "Bastard!"

"I know. But...bad girl, calling me names. You just enjoy being punished, don't you?"

Something slapped the cheeks of my ass, and I jumped.

The sting was sharper than it had been with either the velvet whip or with his hand, and I gasped. He did it again, and I arched upward, squirming. I couldn't decide if I wanted more or not. Then he did it again – and the twist my body made in reaction seated his thick, heavy cock completely inside me.

Oh...yeah. I liked.

"Little witch," Lukas breathed out. He threw something down. I saw it from the corner of my eye, and when my gaze focused on it, I realized it was his belt.

At that point, I didn't care.

He could paddle me with a switch, and I'd light up for him no matter what.

"Lukas...please...please...please..."

He grunted and withdrew, his hips swiveled forward as he slammed into me, driving deep despite the tightness caused by the plug. I shrieked out his name. "I have to...please... come...please..."

"Come for me, baby girl," he said roughly. "Come for me."

I came apart, and it was...amazing.

Just like everything about him was amazing.

Shuddering, I twisted on the thick shaft impaling me, riding the climax to the very end. If it was possible to die from pleasure, then I'd choose this as the way to go.

❄

Breanna, Gracie, Lukas, and I shared a table at a brewery just down the street from work.

Gracie had mentioned it to me, and I'd asked her if she'd like to join Breanna and me.

Breanna had given me a look like I was some alien life-form when I'd told her, still confused about the marriage business, but finally, she'd said, "If you're cool with it, I'm cool with it."

That had been a week ago – right before Gracie and I met for pizza...and to talk.

Gracie had issued the invite then.

Now, after issuing the invite to both Gracie and Breanna *and* Lukas, I tried to figure out just how I'd describe this time in my life if I ever had to do so. *Well, I hung out with my...sexual compan-*

ion, his wife, and my new best friend. And we somehow managed to get along great.

And we did.

There wasn't any tension, but part of me thought it was because Lukas, Gracie, and I all knew there was nothing expected between any of us.

Lukas and I were in this for the sex, right?

Lukas and Gracie were in it for something else.

As Breanna and Gracie laughed about a TV show they both loved, Lukas nudged my knee with his under the table. "Somebody is giving you a dirty look. Should I go mess up his face a little?"

I didn't have to ask who he meant. I'd seen Aaron come into the pub about five minutes after we'd been seated, and I could feel the hard weight of his glare arrowing into my back.

"Nah." Lifting one shoulder in a shrug, I said, "He isn't worth it." And I meant it. "He and Terri are welcome to each other."

"He still doesn't need to be giving you dirty looks." Lukas looked like he was debating, but finally, he hitched up a shoulder. "If it doesn't bother you, then I won't worry about it."

❄

"Mr. Grayson?"

The graying, grizzled older man didn't look up at first, so I spoke louder. I'd been directed to the outdoor patio by one of the employees here at the assisted living center. After looking for him for the past week and a half, I'd finally tracked down Lukas's father – and the man who'd raised his hands to the boy Lukas had once been.

Just before I would have said his name a third time, the older man stirred in his chair and lifted his head, blinking at me with bleary, sleep hazed eyes. He might have been resting, I had no idea.

As his gaze focused on me, I lifted a hand. "Hello, Mr. Grayson. My name is Stella. We spoke on the phone."

In response, he reached up and scratched his chest. He blinked and looked around, clearly searching for somebody, but finally, he focused on me and gave a short nod. "You called asking about that brat, Lukas."

"Yes." He hadn't had kind things to say about him on the phone, so I wasn't surprised by the vitriol now either. Irritated, yes, but not surprised. "Have you seen him since he left home?"

"Seen him?" Gilbert spat on the ground. "Shit, no. Why would that no-good piece of trash have any time for me? Not like I raised him, took care of him, put food in his mouth, did I?" The sarcasm was so thick it could have been cut with a knife. He curled his lip, glaring at me with rheumy eyes. "Then he goes and makes himself some money, and what does he do? Forgets the people who helped put him where he was."

I wanted to ask what Gilbert had done to put him where he was, but that wouldn't help, I didn't think.

No, if anything, it would make it worse.

"Would you mind if I asked what he was like as a kid?" Part of me yearned to know as much as I could about him, but I was asking for other reasons. I didn't know what I was looking for – some rationalization in this man's mind for why he'd done what he'd done. Honestly, I was starting to think I'd wasted my time tracking him down, wasted my time calling him, wasted my time coming here, but now that I was here, I felt like I needed to get something.

"He was a brat, got even worse after his mother died." Gilbert scowled, looking off into nothing. "Did he think it was easy for me, taking care of him with his mama gone? It's not like he was my kid, anyway."

I jerked in response to those words.

"What?"

His eyes went sly then. "What...you can't tell?" He held out his hands. "Look at me. Then go look at him. Ain't no way that boy is mine. His mama went and cheated on me. I always knew it. No kid of mine would have been so disrespectful, so mouthy. I had to backhand the boy just to get him to do his fucking chores. His mama spoiled him, then she left me to raise him."

He snorted and reached for the plastic cup on the little table next to where he sat. "All the shit I put up from him, looking at him and seeing his bastard father's eyes glaring back at me... then he goes and makes it big and forgets all about me."

Dazed, I slumped back into the chair and gaped at him, struggling to process the information he'd given me.

"So you're positive he isn't your son?" I finally managed to ask.

"Ain't you been listening?"

"Yes, sir." Swallowing to try and find the spit to moisten my dry mouth, I looked away. "You know who the father is, then."

"Yeah. There was this scrawny bastard...Holden Richmond. He used to chase after Penny like she was a bitch in heat." He paused, then laughed. "Guess she was. They fucked at least once, I know it as sure as I'm sitting here."

He continued to rant on, talking about how it was Penny's fault he'd had to be so rough on Lukas. If she hadn't given him a bastard, he wouldn't have to cuff the boy just to get his attention, that maybe he would have listened like any decent kid would do.

As he spoke, his face reddened, his anger clearly growing. Abruptly, I couldn't take anymore. Rising, I pasted a patently false smile on my face. "I'm sorry, Mr. Grayson, but I need to go. Thanks for all your help."

I hurried out of there in the midst of him demanding to know what the hurry was. It was rude, but I didn't care.

Out in my car, I sat there, gripping the steering wheel in my hands convulsively as Gilbert's words tumbled through my mind over and over.

Hardly any of it made sense, but one thing *did* connect. Clear as day.

Gilbert wasn't Lukas's father.

24

Ask him, I thought.

No, another part of me argued.

It was a foolish thought.

Foolish, maybe, but with Thanksgiving bearing down on us in less than a week and my flight only two days away, if I was *going* to ask him, I needed to do it now.

In the back of my mind, I was spinning some fairy tale about how I'd be able to reunite him with his father. I'd managed to locate Holden Richmond. He lived in New York, not that far from the home where I'd grown up with my parents.

If I could talk to Holden, then get Lukas to talk to him...

But first I had to get Lukas to come to New York.

Sure, I had Aaron's ticket, which he wasn't going to be using, and sure, I could contact the airline about switching it over to Lukas. I could work something out.

However, if I waited much longer to *ask* him, it wouldn't matter.

It wasn't like the two of us had gone and become a couple or anything. We were...almost friends, I thought.

But friends sometimes spent holidays together and why wouldn't he want to spend it with me? And it would certainly make things easier on me. The thought of traveling back home without some sort of buffer between me and my parents was enough to drive me crazy. Especially now that Aaron and I had broken up.

It was going to be worse this first time.

Not that Aaron was the only reason I wanted Lukas to come with me.

I knew I'd *miss* him.

That, right there, was the best reason *not* to invite him. We weren't supposed to get attached. We weren't supposed to get emotional.

But emotional and attached were apparently part of my make-up because I'd already been attached before the first time he touched me, and I knew it.

The knock at the door caught me off guard. Throwing a look at the clock, I realized it was time for Lukas to pick me up. It was our last chance to see each other before I flew out – unless I invited him along and he accepted – and I was wasting time with my head in the clouds.

Not that we were doing...well, much.

There was a movie out that I'd mentioned wanting to see the last time we'd all grabbed dinner, and he said he was interested in it too. I'd offhandedly mentioned going to see it together, and a few days ago, he'd asked if we were still going.

So...here we were.

But it wasn't a date.

I'd offered to meet him at the movie theater, and he said it was easier to just take one car. I didn't bother to tell him that I would have taken the bus, mostly because I wanted to spend the time alone with him.

I was a glutton for punishment.

Moving through the empty apartment to go answer, ignoring my open suitcase on the bed that reminded me I still had to pack, I hurried to the door. Breanna had left yesterday to go visit her family in Boulder. She would be spending the week with them. She'd invited me to come with her but I had told her I was expected back in New York.

She had cocked an eyebrow at me and drawled, "Expected, huh? That sounds so fun."

Yeah, I wasn't expecting Thanksgiving to be fun.

Things with my family rarely were. At least not for me.

Opening the door, I found Lukas on the other side and his eyes took a slow, leisurely tour down my body. I hesitated there, one hand resting on the door itself. "Do you want to come in?"

"Yes." His lids drooped. Then he shook his head. "But I'm not going to. We'll be late for the movie if we don't leave now."

❄

AFTER THE MOVIE was over he declined the invitation to go grab some food and escorted me back to the house.

"When do you leave for New York?" he asked as we headed up the sidewalk.

"Two days," I said, forcing a smile. *Ask him.*

"It's just as well." His expression was distant, almost remote. "There is a lot of work I have to handle over the next week. We wouldn't see each other much."

Well, hell.

I glanced over at him. Lightly, I said, "And here I was debating about asking you if you wanted to come with me."

"To New York?" He slanted a look at me.

"Yes." I shrugged, feeling self-conscious now and wishing I'd kept my mouth shut. "I'm going back to visit my parents and sisters for the holiday. It's expected."

The smile that came and went was almost identical to the one that Breanna had given me

"That sounds like fun," he said in an eerie echo of her words.

"That's why I was hoping I could have some company." I made a face at him. "You workaholic."

"Sorry." He shook his head. "I've got too much going on here. I was barely able to carve out the time for the movie."

Something about the way he said it made me feel like I should apologize, but I didn't let myself. He was the one who said he wanted to see it. And I was *tired* of apologizing for things that weren't my fault. I'd spent most of my life doing that, first with my parents, and then, although I had only started to realize it, with Aaron.

So instead of offering a fake apology, I gave a fake smile and said, "Okay."

I unlocked the door and went to step inside, but before I could, he brushed his fingers across my shoulder. "Enjoy your trip, Stella," he said, something almost sad in his voice.

I looked back at him, wondering what was wrong, wishing I had the right to ask, but I'd learned there were some lines I couldn't cross in our relationship and I worried this was one of them. Even if we were almost friends now. "Is there anything about the job you're working on that I can help with?" I offered. It was the closest I could let myself come to asking what I really wanted to ask. "I could take some work with me." Grinning, I added, "Or better yet, it could be something super urgent and I could tell them my very important boss absolutely needs me to stay and work through the holiday."

He gave a shake of his head, and whatever I thought I had heard in his voice didn't show in his face. "No. This isn't related to a client. It's a company matter." Eyes locked raptly on my face, he watched me as he spoke.

"Ah, I see." I didn't, not really, but I had no idea what it was like to run a company – and he ran any number of them. "I imagine you've got your hands full with all the businesses and companies you run."

He shrugged like he didn't do anything more than organize a couple of fundraising dinners. And that was enough to make me feel like I wanted to hurl. "Well, I guess I need to get inside. I've got packing to do," I said. Lamely, I added, "Especially since you won't save me and make me work over the holiday."

"You don't want to face them alone, do you?"

"Whatever makes you think that?" I pasted a bright smile on my face as I stepped inside, facing him over the threshold now.

"I'm sorry. Things are just too...complicated now." That sad note came into his voice again and it made me think he was apologizing for more than just not being able to come with me. "Ask Breanna. I've heard she breathes fire. She might scare them into behaving."

I laughed. "I would, except she's got family stuff planned." Gripping the door knob, oddly reluctant to let the moment end, I searched for something more to say. A thought popped into my head just as I realized I needed to say goodbye. "Hey! Do you think Gracie might come? Or did you two have plans?"

"No. We don't have plans." Head cocked, he considered the idea, then nodded slowly. "You should ask her."

He leaned in then, closing the distance between us in a movement that startled me. "Try to enjoy your time off, Stella." He kissed the corner of my mouth, then turned.

Mouth tingling from the contact, I sagged against the doorway and blinked to clear my suddenly hazed thoughts. Such a light, casual kiss...and it melted me.

I'd better be careful or he was going to look at me one day and see just what it was he did to me.

25

"So, Gracie...just was it that you do?"

I groaned and shot Gracie an apologetic look, but she just smiled. She'd told me something about her family on the flight to New York, and the two of us had decided we had a great deal more in common than just affection for Lukas, even if hers was more fraternal than mine.

Our families were almost carbon copies.

The question from my father didn't even seem to faze her.

Edward Best sat at his seat at the head of the table, politely waiting for a response as Gracie lowered her wine glass to the table.

"I'm a photographer. I mostly work for a modeling agency in Denver, but I freelance some." She smiled at my father, a slight incline to her head. "A few of my images of the Grand Canyon were included in an exhibit in D.C. – a tribute to the National Parks."

"How lovely," my mother said.

I think she actually meant it. My mother was a huge supporter of both the arts and the nation's parks.

"It was one of the proudest moments of my life," Gracie said honestly. She slanted a look at me. "I imagine it was about how you felt when you scored that job for the philanthropy group at the firm."

Blinking in surprise, I fumbled with the glass of wine I'd just picked up, saved it – barely – and realized I was now the center of attention. All of my sisters were looking at me, as well as my parents.

"What job?" Farah asked.

My oldest sister, she was...perfect. She'd done everything right her entire life, from getting the right grades to marrying the guy and joining the family business. She was *sweet* too. Genuinely, honestly sweet. The kind of person who just *cared* about people, and things too.

So when she looked at me and asked, *what job*, I knew she really wanted to know.

Squirming uncomfortably, I took a sip of wine and wet my throat before answering. "There's a philanthropy group in Denver that's doing a big push on public awareness – how helping others helps us all. There were a couple of teams who put ideas together on how to tackle the job and mine was selected."

"That's wonderful!" Farah clapped her hands, her big blue eyes sparkling. "You've always wanted to focus more on helping than doing something with advertising. This sounds right up your alley."

"You've only been there a few months," Annette pointed out, her lips pursed. "Why would you have been selected to head up a team?"

"He liked my ideas on other projects I'd done," I replied, not surprised at all by Annette's question.

I also wasn't surprised when she redirected the room's attention to her husband's upcoming campaign fundraiser. I was almost even glad for it. Shooting Gracie a look, I mouthed, *I'm going to get you for that.*

She grinned back.

❄

GRACIE HAD DECIDED she was in the mood to go shopping, so after she climbed into a cab, I called for one myself.

We'd promised to meet for lunch – she'd been to New York and was familiar with Times Square so we were meeting close to there.

For now, I had my own plans.

I hoped I wasn't going to make a mess of things, but I had Holden Richmond's address, thanks to the online background check I'd run on him, and I was going to talk to him.

Hopefully, he wasn't the ass that Gilbert Grayson had been.

Hopefully, he's home, I thought ruefully as I climbed out of the cab some forty minutes later, looking up at the sleek skyscraper where Holden owned a penthouse.

Sunlight glinted off the glass in a dazzling, blinding display, and I blinked away the momentary blindness as I walked toward the entrance. A doorman waited, and I prepared my best *I belong here* smile. I wouldn't get to the penthouse if Holden didn't want to see me, but at least I could get inside...if I was lucky.

I was lucky. He smiled back and opened the doors for me, allowing a rush of heated air to come out and kiss my skin, chasing away the chill of the November morning.

Inside, a prim woman manned a desk, and I approached, ignoring the nervous knocking of my heart against my ribs. *You're doing this for Lukas,* I reminded myself.

"May I help you?"

"I'd like to speak to Holden Richmond if he's in," I said, offering another smile.

"Is he expecting you?" The woman reached for something out of my sight – a phone, likely.

"No." I hesitated, then added, "Tell him it's related to Penny Alpert."

Although I was like 99.99% certain that I had the right guy, at least this way I'd knock that question right out before I wasted any more time. The man's address had been listed in New York for years, but he *had* lived in Denver for the first part of his life – and during that time, the records indicated he'd lived on the same street as Penny.

Online records searches were amazing things.

I fiddled with the strap of my purse as the woman made the call, and to my relief, she gestured to the elevators. "He'll meet you at the elevators. It's the seventy-fifth floor."

I nodded my thanks and turned to the elevator, praying I could get through the next few minutes without rambling or stuttering or tripping and falling on my face.

Holden Richmond was indeed waiting for me as the elevators opened on the seventy-fifth floor. A handsome, distinguished looking man, he looked at me with blue eyes – and I knew instantly.

Still...

Swallowing, I summoned up a smile as I stepped out of the elevator and offered my hand. "Thank you for agreeing to see me, Mr. Richmond."

❄

"YOU REALLY THINK Lukas is *my* son," he said.

I held my coffee cup in my hands and remained quiet. He wasn't asking for confirmation, I didn't think. After all, he'd said those very same words twice already.

He was just...shocked.

I'd told him my suspicions, then asked, as politely as I could, if Lukas's birthday lined up with the time he and Penny were together. We'd both blushed.

I found it charming that a man old enough to be my father could still blush.

Of course, that was silly, because I hated the fact that *I* blushed – considering the things I'd done with this man's son... and that just made my blush deepen so much more.

"The timing is right," he mused. It was clearly directed at himself, softly spoken and pensive.

He faced one of the expansive floor to ceiling windows that let all the sun's light shine in. His penthouse was clearly meant to be a home, not a showcase, and I found myself oddly comfortable there, more comfortable really than I sometimes was at my own home, a strange thing considering I had never stepped foot inside this place before today.

After what felt like an endless silence, Holden looked back at me. "It's possible," he said slowly. "He could be my son."

"He looks like you." Offering a hesitant smile, I added, "Some. The shape of your face...your eyes."

Something that looked a bit like amazement brightened the man's face and he looked ten years younger. "Wow. Isn't that something?"

"Would..." I bit my lip, because here was the tricky part. "Would you maybe want to take a paternity test and find out?"

Head cocked, he considered the idea. The expression on his face and the way he looked in that moment was so like Lukas, it was eerie. He nodded slowly and said, "I'd consider it, but only if he wants to proceed. I can't force myself into his life at this late date." Sadness darkened his features and he looked away. "I wish I'd known earlier. When Penny died..." The words trailed away and he shook his head.

"I think he'll want to know," I said. "I can't swear to it, but I think he'll want to know."

Anything would be better in his mind that having Gilbert as a father.

And after meeting him, I couldn't say I blamed Lukas for feeling that way.

26

Nervously, I smoothed out the card Holden had given me as I approached the stairs. This was probably coming perilously close to the line I shouldn't cross. But knowing how miserable Gilbert had made Lukas as a child, and the fear he carried inside him that he was like the man he believed was his father, staying silent didn't seem to be the right option.

The morning had dawned cold and dreary, the iron-gray skies bearing the promise of snow. I hadn't even made it to work before that promise proved to be true and there was already an inch of the fluffy white stuff on the ground. It would have dampened my mood but I was too excited, too nervous.

If Lukas took the paternity test and it proved that Holden was his father, what would that mean for him?

I didn't know.

But it had to be *good* – something good.

My hand trembled a little as I knocked. Not wanting to risk him sending me away before I could say who it was, I called out, "Mr. Grayson?"

So far, unless he was on a call, he'd never once told me to come back at a different time.

He didn't this time either.

I slipped inside at his gruff, "Come in," but upon seeing the room full of suits and lawyers, I immediately tensed.

"This is a bad time," I said softly. I summoned up a smile, disappointed but determined to hide it. "I'll come back."

"No, please." Lukas inclined his head. "Stay." He gestured to the others, and as they started for the door, I stepped aside.

"If this is important–"

"It is, but I needed to speak with you regardless." He waited until the last suit left the room and I recognized her – she was from legal, I thought. She'd joined Breanna and me for lunch a week or two ago. She'd seemed friendly enough then, but now she wouldn't look at me as she closed the door.

A strange tension settled over the room as I turned to meet Lukas's eyes, and I had the weird feeling it had nothing to do with the excitement that had been vibrating inside me. I'd wanted to call Lukas and tell him what I'd discovered over the weekend, but each time I called, he'd been too busy to talk or the call had just gone to voicemail.

Now, I wished I'd left the news on voicemail so at least he had some idea and wasn't staring at me with distant eyes.

"Somebody's been skimming from the company," he said, his voice toneless.

Taken aback, I gaped at him. "I...what? You're sure?"

"I've spent the past week going over records, checking everything over. I brought in accounting and even had a friend who works in forensics accounting look things over. Yes. I'm sure." He paused a beat. "You look surprised."

"Well..." I laughed weakly. "I am. You're the last person I'd think anybody would steal from."

"Really." He moved behind his desk and sat down, that distant expression still on his face. Leaning back, he steepled his fingers in front of his face. "I don't suppose there's anything you want to tell me, is there?"

"I..." I frowned at him, then realized, dimly, what he was

implying. The card I'd been holding fell from numb fingers. "You think I did it."

He remained silent, but his eyes had iced over, back to the frozen expression he'd so often watched me with initially.

"I haven't stolen *anything*," I said vehemently. "My family is *rich*, Lukas. What reason would I have to steal?"

"It's been my experience that people take things for many reasons – a need for money isn't always the reason," he responded, lifting one shoulder. The cool disdain in his eyes was enough to make me want to shudder, but I managed to hold still.

"How much?" I asked, my mouth so stiff it was hard to form the words.

"What?"

"How much money do you think I've supposedly *stolen*?" I demanded.

"Nearly twenty thousand has been...removed from petty cash or...misspent," he said.

That cold look in his eyes was killing me. "What does *misspent* mean?"

"Can't you guess? All the lunches you take?"

I barked out a laugh and went to shove a hand into my purse to pull out receipts, only to remember it was downstairs. "I go across the street with Breanna and I pay with my debit card, you ass. Again, I *didn't do anything wrong*."

"The facts don't lie, Stella." He shrugged. "You're fired. I'm not reporting this because I'd rather our...personal interactions not come to light, but you're not to come onto these grounds or speak to any of the clients who have business with this firm. The non-compete clause is good for two years. But...if I were you? I'd stay away from them for much longer."

The threat in his voice was clear.

"Don't worry," I said woodenly as the impact of what he was saying hit home. "I won't be anywhere near this place *or* your clients."

On wooden legs, I walked down the steps and back to my

cubicle. Two security guards were already waiting there, one of them with two filing boxes, the collapsible kind, in his hands. I stared at them dumbly as he held them out, not understanding. "You have to take your personal belongings. We will, of course, monitor what you're taking. No company files, thumbdrives, SD cards or anything will be allowed. I'll watch everything." He delivered those words in a cool, remote voice then nodded at the woman at his side. "Meredith will check your computer for any company files. You need to unlock it."

"My computer?"

"You declined having the company purchase one for you, said you had one of your own. You accepted that search when you signed on with the firm," he said.

Of course.

I went to the desk and sat down – for the last time, I thought. As I was logging onto my laptop, Breanna came rushing in, neither of the guards quick enough to stop her.

"What's going on?" she demanded.

"I've been fired," I said flatly. Looking from one security guard to the other, I finally looked at Breanna. "Lukas thinks I've been skimming money from the firm."

Her mouth dropped open. "He *what*?"

Dimly, I noticed the shocked expressions that danced across both of the guards' faces before they smoothed back into implacability but I didn't care enough to wonder why they might be surprised.

"You heard me."

"Oh, I'm going to go tell him a thing or two," she said, spinning on her heel. It made me think about what Lukas had said – she breathed fire.

Reaching out, I caught her hand. "Don't," I said gently. "It won't matter. I couldn't stay here now anyway. Not after..." I dropped her hand and turned back to the computer. "Not after this. I should have gone back home after I found Aaron cheating on me. I just..." I laughed bitterly. "I thought I could make something of my own. Thought I could have *something* on my own. Without my family."

What a joke that had turned out to be.

I unlocked the laptop and picked it up, turning it over to the stern-faced Meredith. She sat in the only other chair and put the laptop on her legs, fingers flying across the keyboard.

Turning back to my desk, I accepted the boxes from the other guard. I hadn't caught his name – couldn't even remember if he'd offered it. Nor did I care.

He watched me with cool eyes as I carefully took down pictures of my nieces and nephews, of me and my sisters. I went to remove one of the cards from the ad set I'd done for the philanthropy group, but he said, "That's company property."

My heart sank a little. I'd put my heart and soul into the project, and I couldn't even have that simple card to remember it by.

"For fuck's sake, it's a *postcard*," Breanna said.

"It's company property," he repeated.

She turned on her heel and strode away. In the cubicle next to mine, I could hear her muttering, swearing – inventively.

It almost made me smile.

Almost.

27

"Stella!"

The sound of Breanna's voice had me stilling at the bottom of the snowy steps. The snow was coming down quicker than the groundskeeper could clear it, fat, fluffy flakes that had already covered the grassy areas completely.

Numb, I turned back to face Breanna as she rushed down the steps.

My teeth were chattering by the time she reached me and she scowled. "You need to put your coat on," she said, reaching for the heavy garment I'd thrown over top of the two boxes I carried.

"I'm fine." I barely felt the cold. It was shock and disbelief hitting me more than anything else. I'd been *fired*. I couldn't believe it. I'd been *fired*. "He thinks I stole twenty thousand dollars from the firm."

Dazed, I turned around and started for my car.

Breanna followed along next to me, her arms crossed over her midsection. "I'm going to go back in there and kick his ass. He can't do this!"

"He can," I said weakly. "He did. I guess I should be glad he didn't call the cops." A weird, hiccupping noise that sounded like a mix between a laugh and a sob escaped me. "He said he wasn't calling the police because he was worried our sexual relationship would come to light. Lucky me, huh?"

Breanna looked like she wanted to hug me.

The boxes were in the way and I was glad of that. I felt like my bones had turn to brittle glass and the slightest touch would shatter me. "Let me get the door for you," she said, stepping closer and slipping a hand into my purse. "Are you sure you don't want me to kick his ass over this, honey? You know I will."

"I know. But you need to keep your job."

The two of us wrestled the boxes into the small hatchback and when Breanna grabbed my coat and turned it over, I obediently pulled it on. She leaned into me and I hugged her close.

"Here," she said, pushing something into my hand.

I looked down and saw one of the postcards from the campaign.

Tears blurred my eyes but I blinked them back. "Thank you."

She brushed my hair back. "What are you going to do?"

"Pack." Bleakly, I stared at the falling snow, clutching the postcard like it was a lifeline. "I'm going to pack and go back home."

Her face fell and I squeezed her gently.

"There's nothing for me here, Bree. I should have just listened to my gut from the get-go."

She didn't argue with me this time, and after a moment, she hugged me tight and murmured, "I'll miss you."

We drew apart and she gave me a wobbly smile.

"Take care of yourself."

❄

My eyes were dry by the time I got home.

Tears had threatened for the first fifteen minutes of the drive, but I hadn't given into the urge to cry and I wasn't going to. Not yet.

I had to pack.

I had to call home.

I had to figure out if I was going to drive or fly back and arrange for the car to be transported. Hell, maybe I should just sell the damn thing. But I discarded that idea almost immediately, because I *liked* my little sports car. It wasn't as practical as it could be for driving on snowy Denver streets but I was tired of always being practical.

Granted, that lack of practicality was going to prove to be a pain in the ass if I decided to drive this tiny little car back home.

Home.

My heart panged inside my chest as I glanced west toward the mountains. I couldn't see them, and although I didn't exactly want to travel up into them, I'd gotten used to the view. Denver had been becoming home.

But I hadn't lied when I told Breanna there wasn't anything for me here.

I'd come here for all the wrong reasons.

At least I'd leave for the right ones.

❄

Listlessly, I went about doing the one simple thing that could be accomplished as I struggled to make decisions.

Packing.

Packing had to be done no matter what.

But even an hour into the task, I still had no idea what I wanted to do or how I wanted to do anything.

In the few short months I'd been here, I'd accumulated a *lot* of stuff, and the thought of moving everything across country was a nightmare I didn't want to think about. The thought of booking a flight and worrying about my stuff being on one side of the country while I was in New York was another nightmare I didn't want to consider.

It was that thought that decided me.

I'd arrange for a moving service to come get all the stuff that wouldn't fit in my car. Maybe I'd be lucky and they wouldn't be too busy this time of year.

The boxes I'd used in the move were tucked in the back of the closet, one small miracle in a very dim, gray day and I found the packing tape I'd used stash in the bottom of my junk box. Some of my stuff still wasn't unpacked at all, stashed away in the storage unit that came with Breanna's apartment.

All in all, I'd have to pack up about half my life. A quarter of it was still in boxes and the rest was furniture...like the new bedroom suite I'd bought, an arm chair, some pictures.

I picked up a framed one that sat by my bed and stared at the blue-eyed man in the frame. He hadn't noticed I'd taken the picture. I'd printed it out at one of the kiosks at a local pharmacy and used one of my favorite frames so I could have a picture of him close.

Now, with careful, precise movements, I undid the hinges on the back that held the image secure. Flipping it open, I took the picture out and studied it up close.

Then, in an unexpected fit of fury, I tore it down the middle.

A knock at the door kept me from tearing it completely to shreds. My heart leaped up into my throat. Lukas?

But immediately, I quashed the thought.

I didn't want it to be Lukas. I was better off without him and I didn't even have to convince myself of that.

After today, what I needed to convince myself of was that I would *eventually* be able to trust myself when it came to men again. I had no idea when, but it had to happen.

Dropping the torn halves of the picture onto the floor, I walked through the apartment, ignoring the hammering of my heart. I knew it wasn't him, but some stupid part of me was still hoping. I wanted to *throttle* that piece of myself. I settled for mental chastisement as I reached up to put a hand on the door, bracing myself before leaning in to peek through the Judas hole.

Gracie stood out there.

I opened the door and steadied the smile even as it threatened to wobble then fall right off my face. "Hi."

"I heard." She came inside and hugged me tightly before drawing back, studying me. "At least, I heard some of it. I'm confused though. Please tell me that Breanna got it wrong – tell me Lukas didn't fire you because he thinks you were embezzling from the company."

"I can tell you that," I said weakly. "But I'd be lying."

Her face crumpled and she dropped her head onto my shoulder. After a few seconds, she pulled back and muttered, "That *dumbass*."

"I've had similar thoughts a few times today." Lifting a shoulder, I admitted, "And that's the most complimentary."

With a scathing laugh, she replied, "It's the most complimentary thing going through my head right now too. When I see him, I swear, I'm going to tell him a thing or two."

"No." I stepped back and waved her in. "Come on inside. I'm in the middle of packing."

"You're going back to New York, aren't you?" she asked as she trailed after me into my bedroom.

With a grim smile, I faced her over the bed. "There's no reason to stay, Gracie. This job was the only reason I came out here. So far, I've made two real friends and that's not enough to keep me here after everything that's gone wrong." I laughed, but the sound was strained even to my own ears. "To be honest, very little has gone *right*. I'll do better in New York. At least I've got family and friends there."

"But your family sometimes sucks," she reminded me.

I flinched at the gentle reminder.

"Yeah. There is that." Dejected, I turned and leaned against the bed. "I just can't stay here, Gracie."

She came around the bed and leaned against it next to me, slipping an arm around my shoulders. "I'll miss you."

Resting my head on her shoulder, I said, "I'll miss you, too. If things hadn't gone so badly, I'd stay. You and Breanna would be worth it. But nothing...hell, I think Denver just hates me. That or the mountain air and me just don't click."

28

"I've seen happier faces when I'm talking budgeting for the upcoming year to the members of the board."

That was my father's attempt at a joke and I managed a vague smile for him as we sat down to breakfast.

Mom didn't even attempt to use humor to try to break the ice, but I guess I should have been expecting it. It had been a week since I'd moved back home, and if I looked as glum as I felt, then it was a wonder people didn't break out into sobs when they saw me.

"Are you ever going to tell us what has you so moody? Or why you left Denver?" Mom asked as she cut into the grapefruit she always ate for breakfast.

I went to brush the question off – as I'd done every day since moving back here – but then I stopped. I had to face the music sooner or later, and avoiding it wasn't helping. Taking a deep breath, I met my mother's gaze, then glanced over at Dad. "I broke things off with Aaron. That's..." I almost lied outright and said that was why I'd left Denver, but in the end, I just hedged a little. "I caught him cheating on me and I ended things. After that...well, I tried to make everything work, but it wasn't happening. I thought I'd be happier working closer to home."

Mom's lips pursed and she sighed. "Darling, what happened?"

"He cheated," I said, holding up my hands and shrugging. "I told you."

"That's not what I meant." She glanced at my father, her cheeks coloring a bit before she met my eyes once ore. "Men don't stray unless they have reason. Did you...give him reason?"

My jaw dropped open. "Did I...*what*?" I demanded.

"Sweetheart, any number of young women make similar mistakes," she said, speaking in a comforting voice now.

But that came far too late. I didn't want to be *comforted* because they thought they could advise me about how to avoid making some *mistake* I'd made with Aaron.

"The only mistake I made with Aaron was not seeing that he was such a douche earlier on," I said cuttingly. Laying down the spoon I'd been using to stir my oatmeal, I added, "He *cheated* – not because of anything I *did* – unless you count not being there while I was in college, in maybe not asking *how high* when he said jump."

I got up then, too mad to see straight.

"Stella," Dad said, his voice firm.

I stilled, recognizing that tone.

"You won't speak to your mother that way."

I jutted my chin up. "What way? Implying that maybe I deserved *respect* from my boyfriend, and when I didn't get it, I ended things?" It was the sharpest I'd ever spoken to either of them – and probably the closest I'd ever come to *being* disrespectful – but I was tired of pretending that their jabs at me didn't hurt. "I'm not perfect, but I don't deserve to be treated like trash by my boyfriend."

Turning on my heel, I strode out of the room, refusing to linger.

If I had, Dad would wear me down, and I *would* apologize. I knew it.

And I couldn't do it this time.

I wasn't wrong and they'd been unfair.

❄

For the past few days, I'd driven around, dropping off my resume at various firms and advertising agencies, but nobody was looking to hire this close to Christmas. There were only a few weeks left in the year, and it was entirely likely I wouldn't be able to find a new job until the beginning of the year. Longer, perhaps. They'd call my old job, and once they talked to HR, they'd get the impression that I wasn't rehireable.

Breanna had offered to be a reference, and she'd told me that at least two others there had promised the same, which was better than nothing. But still, if my former employer – my *only* significant employer – didn't consider me to be *rehireable*, that said quite a bit to a prospective employer.

After the debacle with my parents, I wasn't up to dealing with the harsh realities of life – or any of the polite but firm, *we're not really looking at hiring at this time* responses I'd been getting.

But I wasn't staying in the house either.

So I left to go see my sister Camilla. I would have loved to have spent a few days with Aunt Millie, but for the past few years, she tended to head south as soon as the temperature dropped below fifty degrees.

I wasn't certain I'd find much sympathy with Camilla, but visiting Annette was out of the question. She was almost *always* in campaign mode. And Farah would be at work. She wouldn't mind a visit, and if her bubbly personality wouldn't make me feel worse, I could go see her, but I didn't want to risk running into my parents while I was there.

She'd been working with them almost since she graduated,

and my mom and dad rarely let a day go by that they weren't singing her praises. It was exactly what I didn't need.

When I arrived at Camilla's, it was to find the place tastefully decorated like a house out of a Martha Stewart magazine.

If it lacked a little bit of imagination, well...so did Camilla.

She liked the status quo. Change and adventure scared her.

But she was also dependable and honest and wasn't out to prove how much better her life was than somebody else's. In short, I could count on her, and I desperately needed a shoulder just then.

She ushered me in out of the cold, and in no time flat, we were sitting down with tea and scones she'd made the day before.

Tea and scones.

It was so Camilla.

If I came over in another week – in the afternoon, of course – it would be hot chocolate and Christmas cookies.

"I take it Mom and Dad are already driving you crazy," she said as she picked up the scone she'd selected for herself. "You would have waited until the weekend to visit otherwise."

"What makes you say that?" I sipped at my tea, still cold from the trip from the car to the house.

"Because that's just you. Why did you leave Colorado? What happened between you and Aaron?" She lifted her own tea cup and took a small drink, sighing in pleasure. As she lowered it, she kept it cradled in her hands.

"I..." Licking my lips, I floundered for an answer. *Just tell her what you told Mom and Dad*, I thought. "I...well...Aaron cheated on me."

There. That wasn't hard.

Then...

"I had an affair with my boss. Well, it wasn't an affair, really. We made arrangements and decided that it was just sex, but I started having feelings for him...then he *fired* me. He accused me of embezzling money from the company."

Camilla blinked at me over the rim of her cup. Slowly, she lowered it down, eyes resting on the delicate china.

She was quiet for so long, I didn't know if she'd answer.

"Camilla?"

"Wow. When you do something big, you do something big, don't you?" She laughed a little, like she'd told a funny joke, but whatever it was that had amused her, I couldn't tell. She took another sip of her tea, then put the cup down. "Exactly *why* would he accuse you of embezzling? I mean, you wouldn't do that. It's not like any of us *need* the money."

"Exactly!" I flung up my hands, then let them fall to my lap. Exhaustion battered me, and part of me wished I'd just stayed in bed. It was nice, though, to at least hear my sister's conviction that I wasn't a thief. Nibbling on my lip, I shot a look around, then leaned forward. "Can I trust you to keep this to yourself?"

She blinked at me. "Keep what?"

"Camilla!"

"Fine, fine." She waved a hand at me.

The story came pouring out of me, and it was all I could do to edit some of the details that she would find more shocking. I said nothing about the ways Lukas liked to have sex, nor did I mention that he sometimes beat himself – anything that was personal to him, I kept quiet. But I did tell her we'd struck up a *mutually beneficial sexual* relationship. Her cheeks had colored when I said it, but she nodded and asked why I'd done it.

I told her the simple truth.

I needed something for me...and I wanted him.

Her response had been, *But didn't you want Aaron*?

I hadn't been able to answer that though.

At the time, I *thought* I'd wanted Aaron, but since then, whatever emotions I'd felt for him had taken on a lackluster shine, a tarnish of sorts, and I didn't think it was all entirely due to the fact that I'd found him cheating.

Now, as I finished up telling her about how Lukas had claimed that money was missing and everything seemed to point to me, I had to fight to keep my voice steady. There was this massive ache in my chest and the pain of it was breath-stealing. It hurt *so* much – too much, in fact. This hurt more than it had when I'd found Aaron with Terri. I didn't even understand how that was possible. I'd been with Aaron for *years*. What Lukas and I'd had, it had started just weeks ago.

It wasn't supposed to be anything more than sex either.

I was the one who'd been foolish enough to let emotions enter the equation.

"And so...I moved back home." I shrugged, feeling drained now, like I'd run a marathon or something. I had no idea how long I'd been talking. I knew that Camilla had refilled my tea at least once, and my bladder had become a pressing issue, but as my sister studied me, I couldn't force myself to move yet. "I came home. I didn't know what else to do. But I *miss* him. It hurts being away from him. It hurts to *think* about him."

"I guess it does. It sounds like you fell for him rather hard," she said. She leaned back in her chair, a sympathetic smile on her face. "I could have told you something like this would happen. You always have such big dreams, Stella. You always do everything so...big." She sighed and looked away. "Maybe it's time to start focusing on reality."

29

Paying for the cashmere sweater, I stepped to the side so the next in line could move up. The clerk next to the one manning the cash register adeptly boxed the sweater, then, with a snip of the scissors and a few quick folds of shiny paper, she had it gaily wrapped for Christmas. I accepted the card and quickly wrote *To Mom, From Stella* on it.

She bagged it for me, and I mentally checked another gift off my list.

I hated shopping for my family.

All of them had everything, so anything I bought was just... stuff. None of it really mattered. At least, it seemed that way.

Leaving the department store, I headed out into the shopping center, still brooding over what Camilla had told me the day before.

Did I really try to do everything...*big*?

Was that what happened with Lukas?

It didn't take more than a few seconds of consideration to acknowledge that it could be a possibility. I was a romantic. I'd grown up with my head in the clouds, and all of my sisters had had their feet firmly planted on the ground. My mother and father loved each other, but their true passion was their non-profit.

It wasn't ever us – their kids – it never had been.

It wasn't that they didn't love us.

I knew they did.

But they gave...*more* to the work they did for charity than they did to us. They always had.

Each of my sisters had somehow managed to find their perfect match, but not a one of them had any sort of deep, staggering match-made-in-heaven sort of love.

The one who came the closest was Camilla, with her marriage to her high school sweetheart, but the two of them weren't exactly what I'd called star-crossed lovers. More like a well-worn, comfortable pair of old shoes, even though they were both just in their twenties.

I'd been the one who daydreamed about having secret admirers or going off to Europe to travel after college, where I'd meet some cute guy and he'd turn out to secretly be the prince of some small, perfect kingdom and we'd fall in love and he'd ask me to be his bride.

I'd had those daydreams even after I'd hooked up with Aaron.

Now the only daydreams I had were that things had worked out with Lukas.

Maybe I did dream too big, too much, too hard.

It was a depressing thought.

❄

"I'm sorry," I said softly as I passed the folded piece of paper across the desk to Holden Richmond.

He'd given me his contact information for both home and office, and I'd contacted him earlier to let him know I wouldn't be able to help him with Lukas. I hadn't reached him at home so

I'd called his work, planning to leave a message, but the receptionist had asked if I'd be willing to come by.

So I'd had to deliver the news in person.

It made looking into his crestfallen face a necessity, and I wished I could have pushed Lukas for an answer about this over the weekend.

Don't be silly. He was investigating you over the weekend. That's why he was being so stand-offish.

Silencing the mentally chastising voice, I went silent as Holden nodded and rose from behind his desk. "It sounds like this is a permanent thing for you."

"It is." I debated on how much to tell him and finally said, "I've moved back to New York."

He gave me a surprised look. "I'm...well, I'm surprised to hear that. I would have thought there was...well, I suppose I'm being out of line, but I had the feeling there was something between you."

"No. There was nothing." Blushing, I looked away. "The information to contact Lukas is on the paper. It's all public information. I'm sorry, I don't feel comfortable giving you his private information. You can try leaving a message and see how that goes."

"Of course." He nodded at me, eyes lingering on my face.

"I'm sorry."

"Don't be. You did something a lot of people wouldn't do. I appreciate it." He folded the page and tucked it under the edge of a crystal paperweight.

Recognizing my cue to leave, I stood. But I couldn't just walk out yet. "Are you going to contact him?" I asked nervously.

"I...I don't know," he said, voice quiet. "I want to. But I'm not certain if I should, if it's my place. I'm not even certain if he'd want to hear from me."

"He would." Hoping the desperation I felt inside didn't come through in my voice, I gave him a smile. I wanted it to convey confidence. But who knows. It could have looked like a clown's smile for all I knew. "Trust me. He'd want to know."

Holden didn't respond, and after a moment, I turned and left.

He said nothing as I walked out the door.

As I rode the elevator down, my phone rang, and I tugged it out of my purse.

Seeing Gracie's name on the screen had me tightening my hand around the case of my phone, but I didn't answer. I shoved the device back into my bag and slipped out of the elevator to the jangling little tune of it as it rang a third, then a fourth time before finally going silent.

I had no idea what to say to her.

She'd ask how things were – they sucked.

Knowing Gracie, she'd offer to talk to Lukas – I'd rather roast in hell before accepting the job back from him out of pity.

She'd want to know if I'd found another job – I was tired of even *looking*.

What was I supposed to say?

It was easier to just not answer right now. Maybe in a few weeks, when I had a job.

❄

"So how is the job hunt going?"

For all the reasons I'd dodged answering a call from Gracie, I should have also considered dodging a call from Breanna, I thought grimly. Laying on the bed, I stared up at the ceiling of the room I'd slept in as a little girl. With the phone on speaker and a glass of wine in hand, I was close to falling asleep. Even though I hadn't done much more than a bit of Christmas shopping and gone to see Holden, I was worn out.

"Stella?"

"I'm here," I said. "I'm just trying to figure out a way to answer that won't make me sound like a loser."

"You're not a loser." Breanna's voice was stern. "You're awesome." She lapsed into silence then for a brief moment. "No luck yet?"

"Nobody is interested in hiring right now with the holidays so close. Well, unless I want to work retail." I grimaced. "And... hell no on that front."

"I don't blame you," Breanna replied with a lusty sigh. "I've been there, done that. It's hell on two wheels."

"I did it for a year in college. Don't *ever* want to do it again."

"You worked retail?" Breanna laughed with glee. "Damn, rich girl. I would have thought you would have spent all your time hanging out with the sorority girls."

I made a face at the phone. "I didn't join a sorority, much to my mother's horror."

"Why didn't you join one?"

"To horrify my mother," I said with a grin. I took a sip of wine, then put the glass down, slumping lower in the bed. "So how are you doing?"

"Okay, I guess. I met a guy at the Asian place we liked – we're going out this Friday. His name is Jack. He's...wow, hot."

I could practically see her waggling her eyebrows. "And...?"

"And nothing, yet. We haven't gone out." She hesitated a moment, then said, "Work is...work. Things are kind of weird. Tense, like. And Grayson–"

"I don't want to hear about him," I said quickly, cutting in. "I'm sorry, but I just don't."

"Okay. I'm sorry." A moment of silence stretched out before she added, "I don't blame you. Anyway, things are weird. Not as much fun as they were when you were here. Terri has become almost *insufferable*, snapping at everybody over the smallest things."

"Maybe she's figured out that Aaron wasn't worth it," I said waspishly. "I sure as hell have."

"Nah. She's not that bright. It would take her a decade and

evidence of four or five affairs before she figured out that nugget of wisdom."

"Shit." I snorted. "It took me a couple of years and evidence of one."

"Proof that you are indeed smarter than her."

My phone clicked, and I turned it to glance at the screen. Guilt clutched at me as I saw Gracie's name, but I still wasn't ready to talk to her. She was one step closer to Lukas than I wanted to be just then. *Later,* I thought. *Later, when it doesn't hurt so much.*

Dropping the phone back, I focused on Breanna. "So...what are you doing for Christmas?"

❄

"YOU HAVE A VISITOR, MISS STELLA," Eustace said from the doorway.

I sat curled up in my favorite seat in the one room of the house I loved the most – the library. Putting down the book I was reading, I rose. "I do?"

"Indeed." Eustace slipped me a smile before turning to lead me from the room. "She's in the small salon. I believe she said she was a friend of yours from Colorado, Miss Stella."

"What?" Confused, I drew even with him, ignoring the old butler's very inbred sense of propriety. He took great pride in what he saw as his role in the house and that included *presenting* guests, etc.

He must have sensed what I was feeling because he brushed his fingertips down my arm. "She appears upset. I'll bring cocoa, if you wish to greet her alone."

"Yes, yes, please." I smiled my thanks and rushed forward, wondering what might have brought Breanna out here when I'd just talked to her yesterday.

Only it wasn't Breanna.

"Gracie!"

She rushed toward me, lifting her hands to grasp mine. "I'm sorry for dropping in like this, honey," she said, squeezing my fingers. "I just...frankly, I didn't see that I had much choice. I need you to come back to Colorado."

I jerked my hands back.

"No."

"Please," she said, her voice urgent. "Lukas is behaving..." She laughed wildly, sketching her hands abstractedly through the air. "I can't even describe it. But he's hurting himself more now than I think he ever has. He acted rashly when he fired you. You and I both know that, but *he* figured it out and now he feels guilty and he's taking it out on himself."

The knowledge was like a punch to the gut.

"What am I supposed to do? Go back so he can take it out on me?" I asked bleakly. "He thinks I'm capable of stealing twenty thousand dollars." Throwing my arms wide to encompass the salon, I demanded, "Do I look like I need twenty thousand dollars, Gracie?"

"It's not about the *money* with him – it's about taking what he sees as his." She sank down onto the edge of a chair. "He had to scrap for everything he ever had, and he guards it with a near mad possessiveness."

"And he blamed *me* for something I didn't do."

"I know that!" Gracie shouted. Her face crumpled then. "I know that," she repeated, sounding defeated. "But...Stella, please. I'm scared. I've never seen him like this. I'm afraid if something doesn't change soon, he'll do something..."

The words trailed off and she looked away.

The silence spoke more than her words could, and I dropped into the seat opposite hers.

"What good could it do for me to go back?"

Gracie canted her head to the side. Voice soft, she said, "You're the only thing that's mattered to him in years, Stella."

"Ha." Bitterness filled me. Rising, I started to pace. "If I *mattered*, he would have listened–"

"You're the reason he bought the company, Stella."

Those words brought me to a quick stop, and I spun to face her. "*What*?"

She inclined her head. "You heard me. You're the reason he bought the company. After he brought you into town, he found out where you were going to be working. For a man like him, it wasn't hard. He reached out to the owner – turns out he'd been interested in selling anyway. Lukas showed up at a good time and paid the asking price." She shrugged. "He didn't want to lose contact with you but it's not like he was going to just...show up and ask you on a date. He bought the company because of you. Don't say you don't matter."

Stunned, I staggered back and might have just kept on going until I hit the wall, but my hip bumped a table that held one of my mother's prized Tiffany lamps. Out of self-preservation, I managed to catch it before it fell, and I stood there, staring at the beautiful shade on it as my mind spun with everything Gracie had just told me.

"What are you going to do?" she asked softly.

Closing my eyes, I took a deep breath. Slowly, I turned and met her eyes. "Pack."

30

I was freezing.

I'd grabbed the first coat I saw, and the leather ankle-length garment was far from the warmest I owned. It was a lot colder in Denver that it had been when I left just over a week ago, and snow was coming down in fat, fluffy flakes as I made my way up the walkway to the house where Gracie and Lukas lived.

Gracie had given me her key and dropped me off, telling me she thought I'd do better if I was alone.

Lukas isn't opening up to me at all. If I'm there... She'd trailed off and just shaken her head.

I wasn't entirely comfortable being alone in the big sprawling house with Lukas considering how we'd parted, but I'd agreed.

Now, as I fumbled the locks open and stepped inside, using her fob to disarm the system, I wondered what I was going to say, what I was going to do.

Would he listen to me?

Would he try to send me away?

I didn't know what I was going to do if he did.

It wasn't like I could *walk*.

That thought, more than anything, settled me, because Lukas wouldn't let me walk, which meant I had time to get through to him.

I started up the steps, listening for the music I'd heard the one time I'd seen him hitting himself with the belt.

But I didn't hear music.

It was almost eerily silent, but once I reached the hall that led to his room, I heard a rhythmic noise. Something slapping flesh. Swallowing the bile that rose up in my throat, I hurried down the hall. Something sharp bit into my hand, and I looked down, realized I'd tightened my fist around the key until the teeth were cutting into my palm.

Swearing, I shoved the keys into my coat pocket as I came to a halt in front of the door.

I went to turn the handle, determined to get in there and make him stop whatever he was doing to himself.

But the door was locked.

Swearing, I hit my fist against the door. "Lukas!"

The noise coming from inside didn't so much as pause. I hit the door with my fist again, and called out louder.

Nothing.

Swearing, I drew back, studying the door – and the lock. Then I smiled, reaching up into the messy topknot I'd twisted my hair into. I'd been a brat of a child, so different from my perfect sisters. I used to sneak into Annette's room and read her diary – she was actually a little less perfect than she let on and *her* diary had been fascinating. Eye-opening, really. Once she realized I was sneaking into read it, she'd started locking her door and hiding it. So I'd learned how to pick the lock...and it had been a lock almost identical to the one on Lukas's door. About as simple to pick as one could hope for. Squatting down, I told myself to ignore the noise and focus. I was a kid again, just trying to go somewhere I didn't belong, and it was that much more fun for it.

The hair pin I'd pulled from my hair almost wasn't long

enough, but finally, there was a satisfying click and I turned the knob as I rose to my feet.

The view in front of me was enough to have me sucking in a horrified breath.

Lukas hadn't just been thrashing his back – he'd destroyed his room. Looking around, I took in the devastation, a little dazed.

Movement to the left had me turning, and I shouted, "*Stop*!" just as Lukas when to strap his back again. It was covered in angry, ugly red welts, and a few looked like they might actually be bleeding.

My heart broke a little.

Lukas flinched at the sound of my voice, but the strap landed anyway.

"I said *stop*!" I shouted at him, rushing over and grabbing his wrist as he went to lift his hand again.

He froze at my touch, his clouded eyes zooming in and locking on my face. He blinked, confusion in his gaze. The clouds slowly cleared, and he shook his head. "You're here."

"Who did you think was shouting at you?" I demanded, tugging on the belt.

He didn't let go.

"Give this to me," I said, pulling harder.

He yielded this time, letting the belt go and reaching up with his hand to touch my cheek. "Why are you here?"

"Because Gracie told me you were being a dumbass," I said, trying to smile, but it wobbled, then fell from my face before it even fully formed.

Lukas shook his head. "You should have stayed away after what I did. I was an asshole – I *am* an asshole. I didn't even give you a chance to defend yourself. I should have..." He stopped talking and turned away.

The sight of his back made my stomach hurt, and I closed my eyes. I went to rub at my face, but the leather of the belt touched my skin. I dropped it, repulsed. He'd done himself so much damage. Taking a long look around the room, I asked, "Are you doing this because of me?"

"I'm doing it because if I'm *not*, I'm hurting somebody else. You, Gracie. Even the people at the firm. None of them can stand to be around me and I don't give a flying *fuck* about them, but it's my company now and I need to make sure it's fit to run on its own before I turn it over to somebody else for the day to day operations."

He laughed bitterly. "Fantastic fucking job I'm doing." He spun to look at me, his eyes glittering. "Did you do it? Steal the money?"

"No." I lifted my chin. "My family is *loaded*. Why the hell would I need to steal?"

"Some people do it for the thrill. But that's not who you are. And I should have known that." A wild look entered his eyes, that self-directed rage leaking through once more. "I *should* have. But I'm too much of a self-absorbed asshole."

"You *are* an asshole..." I said softly. "Sometimes. But everybody can be that way." Taking a step toward him, then another, I hoped none of the heart-wrenching emotion I felt showed on my face. I knew he didn't want it. But it overwhelmed me. "Lukas, you're not a bad person."

"The hell I'm not. It's stamped on my DNA. My dad was like this – *I'm* like this. Maybe if my mother had lived, I might have had a chance, but I came from shit and shit is all I ever knew – so that's who I am."

"No." Throat tight, I shook my head. I had to tell him. "Our DNA doesn't make us who we are. Hell, if it did, I'd be as perfect as my parents are – as my sisters are. But I'm not. And you... Lukas, I don't think Gilbert Grayson is your father."

His head jerked up at the sound of that name. "How do you know who he is?"

"Because..." I took a deep breath. "Because I did an online background check and found out. I went to talk to him and he said..." Biting my lower lip, I hesitated a moment before blurting out the rest of it. "He said some pretty awful things about you and your mom, but he also said that he wasn't your dad. He told me your father's name was Holden Richmond. So I looked him up too. He lives in New York, and I went to see him. Lukas...you have his eyes."

He hadn't moved, hadn't blinked since I started talking.

Now, he staggered a little. One hand went out, grasping the nearest post of the magnificent bed and slowly, he sank down. The eyes – eyes just like his father's – stared blankly at nothing for what felt like an eternity. Finally, though, he shifted his gaze to me. "Are you serious?"

"Yes." I twined my fingers together, nerves biting at me. What was he thinking? How did he feel? Well, other than *shocked*. That much was obvious. "I know I shouldn't have gone meddling, but I was trying to understand how anybody could lay hands on their child. What I realized was that, even if you were his, Gilbert would have hurt you. He's just plain mean, but genetics aside, you're not his son, Lukas."

31

He stood staring out the window, as he had for the past ten minutes.

I'd almost think he'd forgotten I was there, but every couple of minutes, he'd glance over his shoulder at me, nod slowly to himself, then go back to staring out into the falling snow.

By the time he finally turned to look at me, my stomach was in knots.

"Are you angry with me?" I asked nervously.

"No." He looked dazed, but to my surprise, some of the brackets that had seemed permanently stamped on his face looked...less. "I'm not. I can't...hell, I always wanted to believe I was adopted or a foundling or something. I never actually thought there was any real chance that Gilbert would turn out to not *be* my father though. This is like an early Christmas present."

He flashed a smile that looked surprisingly young, almost vulnerable.

My heart flipped over in my chest at the sight of it.

I wanted to go to him and hug him, but everything between us still felt too raw.

"You've got to figure out a better way to handle things when you're on edge." Deciding to test the waters, I moved closer to him and lifted a hand, lightly tracing the red edge of one of the marks just barely visible on the upper curve of his shoulder. "You tore yourself up today. You can't keep doing this."

"I had to do something," he said gruffly. "There was too much..." His gaze slid away. "I've got ugly shit inside me. I'm angry with myself, Stella. I shouldn't have treated you like I did."

"No," I said, agreeing with him. "You shouldn't have. But you've got to find other ways to deal with it."

At some point, I'd stopped touching the mark on his shoulder and just let my hand rest on his chest. Now I was exquisitely, almost painfully aware of his heart as it beat against my palm. Tension, like electricity, buzzed between us.

"What do you suggest?"

Licking my lips, I said, "Well, I've got one thing in mind...for now."

He reached up, cupping my cheek. "That's a bad idea with me in the frame of mind I'm in."

"I'm not in the brightest frame of mind myself, Lukas." I tipped my head back. "I'm not afraid of you. I can take it."

His pupils flared. "Don't tempt me, Stella. I'm weak right now. And when it comes to you, I'm not all that strong anyway."

My nipples puckered and tightened. The heat of him seemed to reach out across the inches that separated us, but it wasn't enough. I needed more. Stepping closer, I lifted my other hand and reached up, sliding my fingers along his skin until I could link them behind his neck. "Come on, Lukas. See if you can make me cry wolf."

His mouth came crushing down on mine in the next moment.

I only briefly had time to wonder if maybe, just maybe I was asking for more than I could handle.

If so...well, I was going to enjoy every rough, wild minute of it.

He carried me to another bedroom.

"This one isn't fit for what I want to do to you," he told me.

He left me standing at the foot of the bed and said brusquely, "Be naked when I get back. Those clothes won't be in one piece if you're still wearing them when I walk through the door."

I was naked when he came back. Although I was a little chilly, I didn't climb into the bed.

The look in his eyes had warned me not to, and I was glad I'd listened to my instincts.

He was only gone a few minutes, and when he returned, I was standing where he'd left me, but my clothes were now folded neatly, waiting on the dresser.

It's a vulnerable position to be in, standing naked in front of somebody while the other person is completely clothed. Lukas made no attempt to disguise his perusal of me, and I was painfully aware of the flaws, the curve of my belly, thighs that would never be model slim.

But whatever it was that he saw pleased him – it was obvious in the way his pupils spiked, the black swallowing up the blue of his eyes. He came closer and tossed something on the bed behind me. I didn't turn to look. Yet another lesson he'd taught me. Whatever it was, I'd find out soon enough.

"Get on your knees. I want to fuck your mouth," he said, voice raw.

I knelt in front of him and reached up, unbuttoning his trousers and dragging down the zipper. I went to free him, which he allowed, but when I started to wrap my hand around the base of his cock, he shook his head. "Hands off." He shoved one hand into my hair and fisted the other around his cock, holding it steady as he pressed the tip to my lips. "Swallow me. Take me deep."

He didn't give me much choice either, thrusting in the moment I opened for him. He used his hand to mark my limit, then he did exactly as he'd said – he *fucked* my mouth. It was raw and primal, his need savage. I gripped his thighs to ground myself, feeling battered by the hunger I sensed inside him. My eyes teared up and a few drops broke free and rolled down my cheeks as he thrust past my lips, the head bumping against the back of my throat with each stroke.

Wet gathered between my thighs.

My nipples ached.

I wanted him to touch me.

I wanted to touch me.

But if I did it right now, without his okay, I knew he'd make me suffer for it.

He groaned and tore me off him. I whimpered and tried to follow, but he kept me in place with his hand tangled in my hair. "I'm going to come on you," he said starkly. "There's not going to be an inch of you that I don't taste, mark or fuck by the time the night is over, Stella. You understand me?"

As he spoke, he fisted his cock, stroking himself roughly, up and down, his fist swallowing up the head of his dick in quick, rapid pumps.

I whimpered at the sight of it.

"Say you understand."

"I understand," I told him, eyes still on the magnificent cock in front of me. I licked my lips.

He came.

I gasped as his semen splashed across my breasts and belly, and still, he stroked. A drop of the white fluid slid down between my thighs, and I groaned. My skin seemed to have shrank down on me, becoming two sizes too small, just not big enough for all the sensation swimming inside me now.

"Get up."

The second I stood, Lukas hauled me against him and slammed his mouth down on mine. He crowded me back up against the bed as he thrust his tongue in, then out, mimicking the motion his cock had used earlier. I bit down on him, then sucked, and he caught the cheek of my ass in his hand, squeezing tight.

I responded by arching against him and wiggling against his still-rigid penis.

He spanked me, then pulled back. His mouth was wet as he said, "Turn around."

Obediently, I did so and when I did, my gaze fell on what he'd tossed on the bed.

It was a bag. Several things had fallen out of the small duffel, and I shivered at the sight of the velvet whip. He reached past me and pulled something out. Seconds later, I discovered what it was – a cord to secure one of my wrists to the bed post. A second cord was withdrawn to tie my other wrist. Then he pulled out the whip. "Spread your legs, Stella."

I was almost afraid to do so, but, knees shaking, I did as he asked. He caught my hips and tugged me back a half-step. There was enough give in the wrist restraints to allow it, and I wondered at it – right up until he lashed me the first time.

The whip curled around my side, the very tip kissing the underside of my breast.

"Ahhhh..." I cried, curling in on myself as much as I could, uncertain as of yet whether it was ecstasy I felt or something else.

"Be still." Lukas's voice came out as cool, almost dispassionate.

I struggled to comply as he plied the whip again and again, up and down my back, my thighs. Then...I shrieked as I felt the kiss of it *between* my thighs, the tip of it flicking against my swollen, engorged clit.

Erupting, I jerked against the restraints and fell forward, shuddering in a climax.

A hard arm came around my waist, and he steadied me as the orgasm rocked me.

The tugs on my wrists gave way as he freed me and guided me facedown onto the mattress. Something soft and gentle brushed over my back, and I shivered, every part of me electrified, oversensitized.

I moaned, lifting my hips seekingly.

"Do you want to be fucked, Stella?" he asked.

"Yes...please...Lukas, please," I moaned.

Something prodded my entrance. It was uneven in some places, smooth in others. I wiggled, but he put a hand at the base of my spine, holding me in place.

"I told you there wouldn't be an inch of you that wasn't touched, tasted, or fucked," he said against my ear.

Then, whatever it was, he thrust it deep, deep, deep.

I wailed as it set off another mini-orgasm.

It was still shaking me when Lukas flipped me over onto my back and shoved my thighs wide, hooking them over his shoulders as he dove for my pussy. He thrust the object inside me in as he flicked my clit with his tongue. Withdrew. He blew a puff of air on me. Thrust. He bit me. Withdrew. He sucked on me. Thrust. Another slow suck.

I could feel myself climbing up, up, up again, and I gasped, not certain if I could take so much sensation at once.

But he stopped and rose up, staring down at me with his hands braced on either side of my hips. He licked his lips, shuddering a little before he looked up and met my eyes. "I love the taste of you," he said. Then he lowered his head back down.

It was slower this time, as if he wanted to make sure he did as he'd promised, tasted, touched, fucked me so thoroughly, no part of me went undiscovered by him. One hand roamed down my left thigh, gripping my ankle, then cupping my foot and tracing a pattern over my instep. He twisted the heavy, hard object he'd thrust up inside me, and bit my clitoris, then shifted his hand to my right knee, trailing it down, down, down, so he could toy with my right ankle, then my foot.

I was all but vibrating by the time he was done playing with me, so desperate and ready to come and he knew it. Each time I got close, he backed off. Frustrated and ready for him, I shoved my hands into his hair and arched up against his face. "Please!" I begged.

He tensed for a moment, then he caught my ass in his hands and hauled me to the very edge of the bed until I was half-dangling off. He flipped me and shoved me up onto my knees. "Get rid of this," he muttered, pulling the long, thick ridge from my cunt before pressing his face to me like he was just going to eat me up.

I cried out, my hands fisted in the covers.

He spanked me, and I came so hard, I *felt* the wetness as it flowed from me. He growled and licked at me like he was dying of thirst, and when finally, the tremors ended and I would have sagged onto the bed, he held me up. One steely hand gripped my hip. The other...

I gasped as he probed the entrance of my ass.

"I'm fucking this ass tonight," he said. His voice wasn't so calm and dispassionate now. It was low and raspy, full of possessiveness and need, and just the sound of it was enough to make me quake.

Still, wariness flooded me at his words.

At this point, I was no stranger to anal play, but it seemed the gloves were off now. There was a rawness to his hunger that he'd never let me see before. And he wanted to have anal sex for the first time?

I was about to voice my reservations when he pushed against me – his fingers, not his cock, slick and wet with lubricant.

I pushed down instinctively as he'd instructed me to do and he grunted in approval. "You're going to grab my cock just like that, baby. I can't wait. Here...take this now."

I gasped as he pulled his fingers from me, whimpered when something else pressed to my entrance – I thought it might have been whatever he'd fucked me with a few minutes ago. Something brushed my thigh, and I realized abruptly what it was. The whip – the whip's *handle*. The velvet lashes of it were rubbing against my calves as he rotated it.

"Ahhh...." I groaned, my spine arching as he slowly screwed the handle inside me, settling it deeper and more firmly in my ass than any of the toys he'd previously used.

He bent over me then, his lips almost touching my ear. "That's the whip handle. I'll have to buy a new one after this, but you needed to be fucked so badly. You got it soaking wet, Stella. You know that?"

He nudged it again as he spoke, sending a tremor of sensation through me.

"It's almost as long as my cock and you took the whole damn thing."

He straightened up, and I sensed him pulling away from the bed, circling around, and I looked up to see him standing at the side, staring down at me. The look in his eyes was molten.

He circled back, and I gasped when I felt the lashes of the whip flick against my clit, between the folds of my pussy. It was almost too much. He did it again and again, and I began to rock back, seeking the contact.

That was when he began to thrust the handle inside me, slowly at first, but then, harder, harder.

And he was no longer flicking my clit with the whip.

It was all about the thrust of the handle and me riding it.

"Stop," he said, gripping my hip and bringing my movements to a halt. He withdrew the handle with almost surgical precision, leaving me aching and empty. "The first time you come like this, it's going to be with you wrapped around my dick."

I whimpered at his words, but went still. Fine tremors shook me, and they became more pronounced when he fit the head of his cock to my ass. He soothed me, stroking one hand along the curve of my butt. "You know how to make all of this stop."

"I don't want it to stop," I rasped out.

And I didn't. I was almost scared of what he was about to do, but I didn't want it to stop.

"Good."

With his hand now gripping my hip, he held me steady and began to slowly, slowly invade me. Pain threatened as I stretched to take him, but he didn't relent. He did withdraw a bit, then began the process all over again. That was the way of it – he'd feed me more of his cock, then slowly withdraw just a little before rocking more of the way in. I barely had a chance to adjust to what I'd taken before he was giving me more, but before I realized it, I was rocking back to meet him, *seeking* more.

I groaned when I felt his hips press to my ass. "Good girl," he said, rubbing my hip. "I knew you could take it all."

He twisted his hips, pulling a whimper from me. He did it again, and I sagged, dropping my upper body flat to the mattress. He caught my wrists in one hand and secured them to the small of my back. Using that as his hold, he began to rock me back and forth on his cock. "I like watching you take me, Stella. You're stretched so tight around me. Does it hurt?"

"Yes...no...I don't know..." I moaned out my response, barely able to summon the breath to answer.

"Do I stop?"

"Please don't!" I felt stuffed so full, so completely possessed and owned by him.

He laughed and slid one hand around and under me. He speared his fingers through my curls and they slid wetly across my slick folds as he sought out my clitoris.

Just that one light touch was like liquid lightning on my skin.

I tensed.

He flicked me.

I froze.

He did it again – and rolled his hips.

"Lukas..."

He did it again...and again...and again...

I lost it, tightening around him and coming so hard, black dots danced in front of my eyes.

He let go of my wrists and grabbed my hips, shoving me down to the mattress where he began to ride me with hard, fast, deep digs of his hips, his cock dragging over sensitive tissues and eliciting more cries from me as I rode my orgasm to the very end.

He ended up collapsing against me moments later, his arms shaking.

Crushed under his weight, I struggled to breathe, but it only lasted a moment before he rolled to his side and pulled me into the hard curve of his body.

We were a mess, a sticky, sweaty mess, and I never, ever wanted to move from this spot.

Lukas's breath came out of him like a bellows, and I covered the hand resting on my belly with one of my own.

He surprised me by half turning his hand and twining our fingers.

"You can't tell me this isn't a better way to deal with all that... mess you carry inside you," I said softly, unable to stay quiet.

He kissed my shoulder.

"This is a better way to deal with just about anything," he agreed. Then he pulled me in even closer, a heavy sigh leaving him. "Stay with me?"

"Yes."

32

I had no idea what woke me up. It could have been the pang in my belly telling me that I needed to hit the bathroom ASAP, or it could have just been the unusual quiet of the room. I always slept with a fan going.

But something woke me, and for a moment, disorientation washed over me. I knew immediately that I wasn't in my room. The mattress was a little too soft, for one.

For another, there was an arm thrown over my waist, and a hard, firm body pressed against the back of mine.

That was another indicator.

Immediately, memory slammed into me, and I had to close my eyes for a minute just to take everything in. I wanted to roll over and look at Lukas in the dim light, but the pressure in my belly told me I really did need to go to the bathroom. I slid from the bed and stood there, shivering for a few seconds as I tried to get oriented.

I hated waking up in a strange room at night.

Spying a door across the room, I hurried over to it vaguely recalling the shower we'd taken in the middle of the night. I was almost positive this was the bathroom.

It was.

Longing panged inside me at the sight of the deep, sunken tub and my aching body whispered how nice it would be to run a bath and slide into it, but that wasn't going to happen right now.

After taking care of business, I washed my hands and hurried back out into the bedroom. I spied his shirt on the floor and grabbed it, slipping my arms into the sleeves quickly then buttoning it up before slipping back under the covers and snuggling up next to Lukas.

His arm immediately came back around me, and he mumbled a sleepy, "Good morning."

I stared at him in the dim morning light. Before I could stop it, a smile spread across my face.

"What is it?" He sounded grumpy and tired.

"Nothing," I said, but there was a note of wonder in my voice. The lines that perpetually grooved his cheeks were gone. The deep furrow that was almost always between his eyebrows was gone as well. He looked ten years younger. Lighter, somehow. It was as if a weight had fallen off his shoulders in the middle of the night.

Lifting a hand, I pressed it to his cheek. Stubble that had grown in the middle of the night rasped against my palm.

He covered my hand with his and turned his mouth toward my palm, pressing a kiss to it. "Thank you."

"For what?" I asked.

Instead of answering, he pulled me on top of him and rubbed his lips against mine.

"I need to brush my teeth," I said.

"I'm not complaining." He rolled on top of me and slid his thigh between mine. I opened for him and he sank inside me, sweet and easy.

It was a slow, easy coming together, unlike any we had ever had before.

His lips met mine in a kiss so lazy and sweet, my heart felt like it was going to explode in my chest, while pleasure built inside me with every breath.

When it was over, he pulled me on top of him and threaded a hand through my hair. I kissed one flat male nipple and murmured, "What was the thank you for?"

"For telling me. For caring enough to find out." He brushed my hair back, and I looked up to find him watching me, head propped up on his forearm. "Something tells me you were reluctant to say anything."

"I was." Heaving out a sigh, I admitted, "I knew I was digging around in your personal business, and I know how private you are, but I couldn't let it go. Once Gilbert said you weren't his son...well, I knew you'd want to have answers."

"You're right. If I'd had any idea myself, I would have done the digging myself ages ago." His mouth twisted. "Gilbert has a lot to answer for."

I bit my lip, a mental debate waging inside me. In the end, I spoke up. "He's a miserable, angry old man. There's nothing you can really do that would make him more miserable than he's made himself. He'll never have anybody who truly cares about him." Brushing my finger across Lukas's lower lip, I said quietly, "I think, in the end, he's done himself more damage than you can. Why don't you let it go? Don't let him draw you back in that ugly, angry world of his."

Mouth tight, Lukas met my eyes. "I don't know if I can."

"Will you try?"

"For you." He pulled me in close again and kissed my temple.

We lay in silence for a while. He stroked a hand down my spine and said, "I'm not going into the office today. There's something I want you to help me with. I don't have any right to ask but maybe a fresh set of eyes would make a difference."

Pushing up onto my elbow, I met his gaze. "What is it?"

"I've got the books, files, documents, receipts, a lot of stuff here that I want to go over. I've missed something, and I'm determined to figure out who has been stealing from the company." His eyes flashed hot. "And who set you up. With you gone, they'll either stop or come up with a better way to hide everything, so I have to get it figured out now. I want you to help me look at everything."

"I don't know how much good I'll be. Accounting is not exactly my forte."

He shrugged. "Numbers are my area and I'm missing it. Maybe it's not in the numbers but something else."

"If you want me to try, I'll look." Teasingly, I said, "Since you're the boss, do you have to call in?"

He grinned. "I'll let my assistant know I won't be in. Everybody else..." He shrugged. "Let them worry. Somebody there is guilty."

33

It made a sickening sort of sense. I had to admit. Nearly three hours later I was finally able to see the pattern that Lukas and the accounting team had picked up on. Withdrawals from petty cash would be made out to my name and receipts would be close to the amount withdrawn, but the money was spent at extravagant restaurants. Something told me that there was more money going into the thief's pocket, because the cash tips left were *beyond* generous.

And that happened on more than one occasion. It got to the point where it was almost blatant and there were extravagant meals where one client's name appeared several times over.

"Is there a client by the name of Tad Fikes?" I asked. "A big one."

Lukas sat across the floor from me with his back braced against the bed. The remains of breakfast lay littered among all the papers. We had a mess to clean up. Neither one of us had shown much interest in taking care of any of it at this point though. From time to time, I found myself nibbling on a leftover piece of toast or another slice of bacon.

"Not that I know of, but I don't know all the accounts," Lukas replied, his eyes still on the stack of papers in front of him. His gaze moved to mine after he flipped over another page. "I know the name though. I saw it too. According to everything I found, you're the only one who has had contact with them."

"Well, I need to take better notes then. It would at least be helpful to know what kind of business they're in, what we do for them that entitles them five hundred dollar meal tickets, along with wine that costs about two hundred bucks a bottle." I rolled my eyes and fought to keep my voice light, despite the fact that anger burned in me. Whoever was doing this, they sure as hell didn't give a flying fuck what it did to my name.

Lukas shot me a grin. It surprised me, but he had been doing that off and on all morning. It was almost like the depressing task before us didn't faze him at all. But maybe it was just depressing to me. He might have found it exciting for all I knew. Trying to track down whoever was stealing from him might appeal to him. I could see that. To me, all the numbers and names were running together. And something else was bothering me. I just couldn't quite put my finger on it.

I kept going back to one particular file and studying the receipts, the names, the clients, but whatever small detail was niggling at the back of my mind remained just out of reach.

The more I tried to reach out and grab it, the more insubstantial it became.

I scanned over a few more pages before dropping them back into the pile, frustrated.

"What about from before I came? This is just the past couple of months. I was the only one hired recently, but I can't believe this just started when I got there. It's too smooth. At least at first. The past month has gotten even more bold. These fat tips and the fancy dinners? There's got to be more."

He shot me a look but nodded. "I have spreadsheets going back the past couple of years. I was hoping to find something in the hard copies, but I guess it's time to start looking at those documents."

"I'm comfortable with spreadsheets. If you want to keep looking at all of these, I can start looking at them."

Lukas pointed to the briefcase that was by the door. Apparently, he had been working on this off and on ever since I had left. This bedroom had become a second office of sorts, with several boxes of hard copies already stacked on the desk or the nearby file cabinet.

After opening the laptop, I got his password and he told me where to find the folder as well. I got to work and lost myself in the data. I couldn't find the pattern this time. Whoever it was had been more careful when they started out. Plus, Lukas hadn't been there to point it out.

In the end, it wasn't a pattern at all that made me realize just how long this had been going on.

It was that name again – Tad Fikes. It had something to do it this. I knew it did. I just couldn't figure out why it was bugging me. Did I even know anybody by the name of Tad?

"Wow. You two look busy."

The sound of Gracie's voice dragged me out of my reverie, and both Lukas and I looked up to find her standing in the doorway. There was a look of both relief and curiosity on her face, but the expression in her eyes was strained.

"It looks like you two manage to work things out," she said. "I'm glad."

I smiled at her while Lukas pushed off the floor and went to her, holding her in his arms for a warm hug. The affection between them was clear. "You're home early," he said, his voice soft. "Are you nervous about tomorrow?"

Tomorrow? I wondered what tomorrow was. But I didn't ask.

She laughed weakly. "I'm torn between whether or not I should do it now."

"Why? This is what you wanted. Shit, you spent months talking me into it."

Now my curiosity was really piqued. Surreptitiously, I shot them both a look. Gracie noticed. She must have been looking at me, and her cheeks flushed as she glanced back at Lukas. "It just seems...awkward. Things between you and Stella are different now, aren't they? I knew they would be if she came back and you talked to her." She glanced at me and smiled. "I'm not trying to talk about you in the third person. I'm sorry."

Unable to contain my curiosity anymore, I asked, "What are you talking about? What's tomorrow?"

Gracie shook her head. "It's nothing."

"It is something." He looked over at me and went on, "Gracie's planning on getting artificial insemination tomorrow. She wants a baby."

"That's wonderful," I said, climbing to my feet, but she shot me a nervous look.

"You might not think so once you know who the donor is."

She glanced at Lukas, and I immediately understood. "Are you thinking that because Lukas and I..." *What are we*, I wondered. We hadn't even talked about it. It felt like things were different but that didn't mean they were. And even if they were, this was clearly something that had been in the works for a while. Who was I to mess up plans that Gracie had already made?

"You should do this." Shaking my head, I gestured between Lukas and me. "We're still trying to figure things out, I think." I looked at Lukas, and he nodded. "But regardless of what is going on between us, that doesn't change anything you two planned to do. I mean, it's artificial insemination. If you're getting a procedure tomorrow, then he's..." I was blushing now. How stupid was that? "I mean, he's done his part. Hasn't he? Isn't that how it works?"

Gracie laughed. "That's how it works, yes."

She came to me, her hands catching mine. "Are you sure about this?"

"Absolutely. Don't give this up on account of me." I squeezed her hands. "Don't even think about it."

34

"Is it going to bother you?" Lukas asked. It was hours later, but I knew exactly what he was talking about.

I leaned against him and roped my arms around his neck. "If it bothered me, I would tell you. I'm not some passive, meek thing, in case it's missed your notice."

A grin crooked his lips. He had smiled more today than I'd seen him smile since meeting him. It was amazing the transformation that had taken over in the past twenty-four hours. The shadow cast by Gilbert Grayson on his life had weighed on him more than I could have possibly realized.

"Here I was thinking I'd gone and found me a sweet, passive submissive. I don't know, Stella. Now I'm thinking this just might not work out." It was clear he was teasing by the way he kissed me as he finished talking. It was a kiss that curled my toes and made it clear just how well this could work out.

"You know," I said, breathing a little harder. "We still haven't exactly defined what this is. I know we talked initially that this is going to be about sex, but Lukas..." I hesitated now because I wasn't sure if I could handle having my heart handed back to me if I gave it to him.

He surprised me though. He wrapped his hand around my

hair, forming a loose tail, and tugging my head back with it. "It stopped being just sex for me a long time ago. Couldn't you tell?" He rubbed his mouth against mine. "I think that's why it was so easy for me to believe that you were the one behind the missing money. I needed to believe it. I needed a reason to push you away. I needed to *find* a reason to push you away so I wouldn't end up hurting you."

Cupping his face in my hands, I hauled his head down to meet mine and kissed him. It was a soothing sort of caress, benediction and forgiveness all in one. "You know," I murmured against his lips. "It's more than just sex for me too. I felt something for you even up on the mountain. Even as rough and grumpy as you were." I wiggled my eyebrows at him, trying to get him to smile again.

It worked. Lips curving, he brushed his hair back from my face as he said, "You were a sassy little brat. I was up there for peace and quiet, and I had to deal with Little Red Riding Hood trying to sweet talk a bunch of wolves."

I snickered but the laugh faded as he tucked me in closer, his lips brushing against my cheek, then up into my hairline. "Stella..." His mouth was right next to my ear now, the words low, spoken in a hushed voice. "Stella, I think I'm falling in love with you."

The impact of those words was stunning. Tears blurred my eyes, and I couldn't speak. A knot swelled up in my throat, and even though I coughed to clear it, I couldn't respond right away. The words were there, but I just couldn't force them out.

His cheek moved against mine, the stubble rasping over my skin. "I understand if you don't have anything to say to me. Just tell me you'll give me a chance."

"Aw, Lukas..." I finally managed to say.

But I couldn't force out anything else, and he started to speak again. "I didn't think anything like this would ever happen to me. I didn't think it could. But it feels good. It feels right."

"It does," I agreed. "You deserve love as much as anybody

else does, Lukas. One day, you're going to believe that." We ended up curled on the bed, talking about everything, and nothing.

And then we ended up talking about Gracie.

I asked him about the plans for the baby plus another question that had been on my mind. "I don't understand something," I told him. "You were so convinced that Gilbert passed on his assholishness like it was a disease." Easing back, I brushed my hand across his cheek, meeting his eyes. "If you're that certain it has to do with genetics and DNA, why would you risk passing it on to a baby?"

"I never believed it was all just genetics. I believed it was his DNA, combined with how I was raised and what he passed on to me," he confessed. He gave a diffident shrug as he continued, "I never knew anything but the hell he taught me. With that being all I knew, I'll admit that I had reservations. I still do. But Gracie talked me into it."

"Are you going to be part of the baby's life?" Curious, I kept my head back to study his face. This answer mattered to me because, at some point, I'd always seen myself having kids, and if he couldn't bring himself to be around babies, it was something I needed to prepare myself for.

"She wants me to be," he said softly. "I'm not going to be the dad, per se. She's the parent, but she wants me to be involved in the baby's life. I'll probably fuck it up, but she's pretty insistent."

And he cared too much for his friend to say no, I thought. My heart squeezed inside my chest. And he thought he wasn't a good man.

"Don't be silly." I smiled at him, unable to hold it back. "Whatever role you have, I think you'll be good at it. We choose who we are in this life, Lukas, you know. The past can shape us, but it doesn't make us."

He brushed my hair back from my face. "Are you sure you're okay with all of this? The baby? Her living here? That was the plan all along, but I don't want to do anything that causes you to be uncomfortable with it. You'll always be number one for me."

It was a startling revelation.

I could see in his eyes that he meant it. Had I ever been number one for anybody? I didn't know.

I wanted to think it over and revel in the wonder of it, but he was still watching me, waiting for an answer, so I smiled at him and laid my hand on his cheek. "It'll be fine." Then, the light hit me and I realized something. "That means I get to be part of the baby's life too." Delighted, I threw my arms around his neck. "I love babies. I've always wanted to have a couple of my own."

Nerves jangled inside as I settled back down on my feet to watch him, but he didn't panic the way I'd expected.

"I kind of suspected." A half-smile crooked his lips. "The look on your face when she told you her plans. I've been mentally preparing myself." He cleared his throat then added, "Assuming you want them with me."

I rose onto my toes and kissed him. "Lukas, it's early yet, but when it's time, I would love to have your babies. But we can worry about that later." Hugging him, I leaned into him, enjoying the closeness, the intimacy, the simple knowledge that I had the *right* to do this. That he *liked* it.

That we *fit*.

35

Discontent woke me.

At least that was what it felt like, although I couldn't put my finger on exactly what it was that woke from a deep, deep sleep. I lay next to Lukas, wide awake, for the second time in less than twenty-four hours and tried to figure out just what had pulled me back to the conscious world.

My eyes were gritty with fatigue and my body ached with it.

I *wanted* to sleep.

But my mind was racing.

Get up, it whispered. *You've got work to do.*

Work. What work did I have to do?

I didn't have a *job*.

I wasn't angry with Lukas anymore because I could understand why I'd looked guilty – and more, I could understand why he'd pushed me away. But I *was* angry. I was angry with whoever had set me up. That thought set my mind wandering down the path of all the figures, the falsified reports and receipts – and they had to be false, right?

Tad Fikes. What kind of name was that?

A fake one, I thought. It had to be.

It's faked.

I jolted, those words sending a memory trembling through me, but it stopped just shy of me grasping it.

Damn it.

Next to me, Lukas slept on, his breathing deep and steady. Hoping I wouldn't wake him up, I slid out of the bed and picked up the laptop I'd left lying on the dresser. The bedroom was shaped like an *L* with a small seating area around the bend of the room. I headed over there and sat down in the window-seat, dragging the blanket over my bare legs. I had pulled on one of his shirts again. Pajamas hadn't been high on the list of my priorities when I'd packed, Besides, I liked sleeping in his shirts anyway.

I could smell him on my skin now, and I loved it.

I flipped open the laptop and turned down the brightness, not wanting to disturb him if he got restless.

The bed shifted, wood creaking gently as he rolled over in bed and I looked up, wondering if he was going to wake up looking for me.

But a few moments later, his breathing settled back into a normal pattern, and I focused back on the computer.

Tad Fikes.

The name was all but echoing through my mind now, a sick sensation spreading through my gut.

That name. Tad. Where had I heard that before? Finally finding it on the spreadsheet, I read over the entry, eying the date – Valentine's Day – and the total amount of money spent. It was just this side of insane, although I knew my dad had spent more when he courted new donors.

Valentine's Day. I sneered absently, thinking of the plans I'd made for Aaron and me, plans I'd ended up canceling the day before after Aaron called me and told me he had a big project and the boss needed him to stay in town to wrap it up.

Aaron...

The bottom of my stomach opened up and dropped away as that final bit of memory settled into place.

Tad Fikes.

It's faked.

Another Valentine's Day, this time back in college. Aaron showing up at my apartment, a bottle of cheap wine in hand and even cheaper chocolate. But I'd been so delighted I hadn't cared. The wine had been awful. I'd ask him how he had managed to get it, and he'd laughed. He didn't turn twenty-one for another two months.

The memory played through my mind.

He flashed an ID in front of me.

"My good buddy Tad helped me out."

I had snatched the ID away, looking at Aaron's picture on what looked to be a very real ID. But the name..."Tad Fikes?" I asked, laughing. "If you're going to come up with a fake ID, can't you come up with a better name than Tad Fikes?"

He wrapped his arms around my waist and pulled me up against him. "Shows what you know. It's an anagram, darling," he said, kissing me quick and hard. "Switch the letters up and it says *it's faked*. I'm laughing at everybody carding me. None of them have caught on."

Amused, I had looked back at the ID I still held. It had been a fantastic job. I wondered who had done it. Not that I knew much about forging IDs, but it looked real to me. I studied the name, and in my head, I rearranged the letters. Sure enough, *it's faked* spelled out perfectly.

"You must be so proud of yourself," I said, laughing at him.

"From time to time," he admitted. Then he dropped his head and kissed me. "Do you like your Valentine's Day present?"

"I do." The thought meant a lot.

"How about you tell me how much?" Aaron murmured against my lips.

I jerked to startling awareness just before Aaron would have kissed me again.

Even so, I wiped the back of my hand over my lips, not wanting even the memory of his kiss on my mouth.

"Tad," I murmured against my hand as I remembered the name. And nausea welled inside me, my gut turning.

Understanding hit me hard and fast. It was Aaron. Aaron and probably Terri. That Terri had been involved in setting me up didn't surprise me. But Aaron getting involved...? That hurt.

It hurt a lot. Tears burned my eyes and for a moment, I sat there, fighting to compose myself.

I wasn't in love with him. If I ever had been, those feelings had faded a long time ago as the boy I'd loved had changed into the player he'd become since graduating.

But the echo of that boy...memories of him remained inside me and to know that he could do this?

It *hurt*.

Tears threatened, but I didn't let them fall. He didn't deserve the tears anyway.

Once I knew I could talk to Lukas without betraying how upset I was, I got up. Cradling the laptop against my chest, I padded back over to the sleeping area and rested a hip against the bed next to Lukas.

His eyes opened almost immediately, and he looked at me with startling clarity. "What's wrong?"

"Nothing," I lied. I faked the smile and I had a feeling he could see right through it. "It's just... Well, I figured something out."

My fingers drummed nervously on the laptop and his gaze slid to it.

"What did you figure out?" he asked softly.

"It's about that name...Tad Fikes."

Lukas nodded. "I've already emailed my assistant. I want more concrete info on this so-called client. There's very little hard data that she's been able to find but I'm going to have her keep digging."

"Go ahead, but you won't find much," I told him. Taking a deep breath, I said softly, "The man doesn't exist."

Lukas said, "I'm rather certain of that myself." He cocked his head. "But what clued you in?"

"Nothing *clued* me in." Uneasy, I smoothed my hand down one of the wrinkles in the shirt before confessing, "I know he's not real. *Tad Fikes* is the name that Aaron used on his fake ID back in college. I just now remembered it."

For a moment, he didn't even blink.

Finally, a thick, heavy fringe of lashes fell down, shielding his eyes, and he averted his gaze, staring off at nothing.

"Aaron," he repeated in a low voice. "Your ex set you up."

"Well...I think he had help. I think he was doing it with Terri." I hesitated a moment, then said softly, "I'm sorry."

He reached up and cupped my cheek. "Don't apologize to me. If anybody deserves apologies here, it's you."

He pulled me in close, but he didn't kiss me. His brow touching mine, he simply held me.

❄

NERVES DANCED inside me as I followed Lukas into the office the next morning. I was wearing nothing more than a blouse and jeans because I hadn't exactly packed for a day at the office.

Technically I wasn't an employee here anymore, and I suspected I could have worn a paper bag for a dress and Lukas wouldn't have cared, but clothing was armor. I would have felt more secure if I'd been in one of my designer suits, with a pair of Louboutin heels to go with it.

Instead, I was in jeans and a pretty top with a pair of boots that went up to my knees and I was just going to have to fake it.

People slid me sideways looks as I walked along with Lukas up the stairs to his own personal office, and I could only imagine what they were thinking.

I hadn't been quiet about why I had gotten fired, and I knew that Breanna had been *furious* so whether or not she had stayed quiet about what Lukas had done, I had no idea.

But that wasn't my concern right now.

"Are you sure I should be here?" I asked softly.

"We wouldn't have figured it out as quickly as we did without you," Lukas said simply. He opened the door to his office and stepped aside, gesturing for me to enter.

I did so but turned back to meet his gaze one more time. "I still feel kind of funny."

He cocked a grin at me. "As you've made it clear several times."

He indicated for me to take one of the seats by his desk, but I elected to take one in the seating area in the corner instead. "I don't want to be the first thing they see," I said, making a face at him when he gave me a questioning look. I already knew he planned on calling Terri and Aaron. "It just seems...weird."

Lukas let it go at that and moved around behind his desk, pushing the button on the intercom to bring his assistant on the phone. "Good morning," he greeted her in return. He asked that she page Terri and Aaron and send them to his office.

"I should have gotten some coffee," I muttered, crossing my legs.

He was waiting in the corner opposite me now, hands in his pockets.

"You've probably got a minute," he said.

"No. I'm fine." Glancing at the door, I looked back at him and met his eyes. "After this, I might need something stronger than coffee. Like a screwdriver or a Bloody Mary."

"We can go get brunch." He jingled the change in his pocket restlessly, but at the knock on the door, his head whipped in that direction.

Terri entered, followed closely by Aaron. She approached him, speaking in a brisk tone, and if she had any nervousness inside her, I couldn't tell.

"I'm glad you called us in here, Mr. Grayson. I've been wanting to talk to you about the account Stella was managing. I'd like to take them over."

Aaron said nothing. Neither of them had noticed me yet.

I crossed my legs.

Some small sound alerted him to my presence, and he glanced over his shoulder and saw me. His eyes widened and nerves jittered in his eyes. He reached out, his fingers trembling the slightest as he brushed them down Terri's arm.

She ignored him, her attention raptly locked on Lukas.

"There is one account associated with Stella that I'd like to speak with you about," he said with a tilt of his head, an expression on his face that might have made one think he was considering Terri's request. "I've got questions…we might need to consider calling Breanna up. With Stella being new, she was supposed to have a senior member go over all her accounts."

"I'm certain I would know the account," Terri said, rather quickly. "I made sure to stay abreast of anything she took on."

"Did you?" Grayson's eyes were cold. "It's odd then considering…well, that matter is being kept between accounting and me."

"What matter would that be?" Terri asked, once again brushing Aaron's hand off when he went to grab her elbow.

Lukas looked at Aaron instead of answering. "Aaron, did you also try to stay abreast of the accounts Stella worked on? Since you brought her in, one would think you felt a responsibility in this matter."

Aaron opened then closed his mouth. He shot me another look, his face a dull shade of red. He was caught and he knew it. It was stamped all over his face and instead of responding to Lukas's question, he just shrugged.

Terri shot him a quick look and that was when she noticed me.

"Stella," she said, shock in her voice. "What are you doing here?"

"It's that account Lukas had questions about." I smiled at her. "I've got to admit, I've got questions too. So…that's why I'm here."

I would have said more but this was Lukas's show.

Except he seemed to want to turn the ball over to me. His slate-blue gaze slid to me. "Why don't you tell us more about this account, Stella? What was the client's name again? Are you familiar with the client at all?"

"I'm familiar with the name," I allowed, flicking a look at Aaron. "I just don't think he's a client. He's certainly not one of mine. Beyond that...there's not much to tell. The client isn't mine. Anything that's come out of petty cash that has my name on it that's linked to this...client? Well, I don't know what to tell you. I didn't have *any* expenses associated with him. I didn't have any dinners with this client. As a matter of fact, there were nights when I supposedly had dinner with this client when I was actually in the office working with Breanna." I slid a look in Lukas's direction. Once we'd started breaking down the expense reports, we found two nights where I'd been here with Breanna when I'd supposedly been wooing and wining and dining a client.

As I talked, Aaron's face got red and redder.

Terri's, on the other hand, was getting whiter and whiter. Malice and anger burned in the depths of her green eyes, though, making her gaze snap.

She was *angry*? Screw that.

Her anger was like a match, setting fire to mine. I met her angry glare with one of my own.

"I will tell you this though," I said, holding Terri's gaze with mine. *Bite me, bitch.* "This...person isn't even a client."

"What in the hell is that supposed to mean?" Terri demanded.

Instead of answering, I looked over at Aaron. I could almost *hear* the ice dripping from my voice as I said, "It's faked."

He clenched one hand into a fist.

Terri didn't get it. Apparently, he hadn't let her in on the little joke.

"Are you saying the client isn't real, Stella?" She gasped, the outrage on her face perfect.

I had to admit she was good.

"That is outrageous. It's insane," Terri said, her voice shaking.

I didn't bother looking at her. I simply waited for Aaron to respond.

He didn't though. He seemed frozen where he stood. Rising to my feet, I rose and walked over, stopping a few feet away. I held his eyes. "Nothing to say...Tad Fikes?"

At that moment, Terry realized she was caught. Turning to glare at Aaron, she demanded, "What is she talking about?"

"I did mention I knew the name from somewhere," I reminded her, turning to look at her. "He's used the name since college. Funny, huh?"

Knowledge started to glimmer in her eyes. Terri shifted from one foot to the other.

"You messed up," I said softly. "You two used the same name back on Valentine's Day. That's just one we found...I don't know if there are more, but if there are...?" I shrugged. Glancing at Lukas, I cocked a brow.

"I've already hired an outside team, specialists in forensic accounting. The books will be gone over with a fine-toothed comb."

Terri's composure snapped. Whirling on Aaron, she flung out her hand, pointing at him. "You dumbass! This is *your* fault! You went and messed up everything, you stupid asshole!"

At that, Aaron snapped out of his daze. Turning on her, he demanded, "Me? You're the one who couldn't stop having expensive dinners. You're the one who couldn't stop using petty cash as her personal piggy bank!" He took a step toward her, his face going thunderous. "Your dad got on you about that so many times and you still found a way to keep doing it. Don't you go blaming this on me."

The door opened but neither of them noticed. That was until two uniformed officers approached.

Terri froze. "What in the hell is this?"

"They're called cops," I offered helpfully.

Terri ignored me, spinning around to stare at Lukas imploringly. "What's the meaning of this? You can't be serious."

He spoke for the first time in several minutes. Coming around the desk, he stopped in front of her. "You were going to ruin Stella's career before she even had a chance to really build it. If she'd gotten arrested, you would have just sat by. You did nothing when she was fired. And you want to know if I'm serious?"

"You didn't have her arrested," Aaron said, stepping forward. He gestured toward me. I could tell he was trying to sound calm, but he looked like he was about ready to cry. "Is that because you're fucking her?"

Lukas took one step forward.

Aaron backed up three. "Look, okay...okay. That was uncalled for. I get that. Look, we can pay the money back. And maybe..." His eyes flicked to Terri, then back to me. "Stella's gone and moved back to New York. I mean, she's here now, but... you know..." He glanced at Terri.

He said nothing else, but Terri seemed to read his mind as easily as I did.

She moved toward him. "We can make this right." She laid a hand on Lukas's shoulder.

I was moving toward them, murder on my brain.

Lukas caught her wrist in his hand and pulled it away, which saved me from committing murder.

Terri didn't get the point though. "You can't have us arrested. You can't be serious."

"I'm very serious." He leaned in, his face the cold mask I'd first seen on the mountain. "If you hadn't tried to paint Stella as the thief, maybe I would have just let you pay the money back.

But that's not what you went and did. So now you get to deal with the mess you made."

He nodded at the officers. They stepped up, and as Terri and Aaron continued to beseech him, he came to me. "Do you want your job back?"

I considered it for a moment and then I nodded. "I do. But only for a little while. I think I'm going to go back to school. I want to finish my degree."

And this time, I thought to myself, I was going to find a career that actually made me happy, not just something that would please my parents.

36

"I can't thank you enough for making this happen." Holden had a tear in his eye when he glanced past me toward where Lukas stood waiting.

We'd agreed to pick Lukas's father up at the airport – and he *was* Lukas's father.

The paternity test results had come in, proving without a shadow of a doubt that Holden was Lukas's biological father.

I hadn't needed the test. Just looking into Holden's eyes had been proof enough for me.

But Lukas wanted it.

Now that he had it, he was waiting to meet the man who wanted to be part of his life.

Lukas was nervous, though, and looking into Holden's eyes, I could tell that he was too. Holding out my hand, I said, "Come on. He's nervous too."

Holden laughed a little and took my hand. "That makes me feel a little better."

A few awkward moments later, we were all sitting in one of the bourbon bars in the restaurant.

Lukas and Holden talked stiltedly while I tried to figure out a way to break the ice.

And...I figured out the right way.

Leaning forward, elbows on the table, I fixed a smile on my face and cleared my head. "So, Holden...you want to hear how Lukas and I met?"

Both relief and curiosity flashed in his eyes. "Absolutely."

❄

LUKAS HELD both of my wrists in one of his hands, keeping my hands trapped on my head. With his other hand, he gripped his cock as he guided it to my mouth. I knelt in front of him, jerking against my wrists, not really in an attempt to break free, but every time I tugged, he tightened his grip just a little and the eroticism of it drove me nuts.

He rocked against me, thrusting his cock into my mouth, a lazy rhythm that set an echoing pulse up in my belly. It spread from my gut up to my nipples, down to my pussy.

There was no urgency to him tonight. The want was there and so was the need but the hard, driving need that so often took the lead wasn't there tonight.

I moaned as he withdrew, his cock almost leaving my mouth. I tightened my lips and followed, but his grip on my wrists held me in place. Groaning, I tangled my fingers in my hair and waited for him to feed me the inches of his cock again.

He rewarded my patience with another slow roll of his hips.

I took him deeper this time and half swallowed once he hit the back of my throat.

The sound of his grunt was like music, and it was followed by a sharper noise, then a few muttered words that made no sense.

"You're a little witch tonight," he said, as he let go of my wrists and gripped my head between his hands.

He knocked the breath from me as he began to move in earnest, pumping his hips back and forth and forcing me to take him deeper and deeper. I loved it. Even the way he bruised and stretched my mouth. But he stopped just shy of coming – I could practically *taste* it. He pulled me to my feet, hauling me up against him.

"On the bed," he said. He didn't give me a chance to do it though.

"Lukas," I said, aching for him.

He hoisted me up onto the mattress. He caught both knees, hooking them over his elbows as he knelt. "I want to see you," he said, voice rough, soft, slow. "Look at how pretty you are as you take my cock."

His words left me floundering. As he thrust inside, he stared down where we joined and I stared at him. Slowly, he slid his gaze up to meet mine and that familiar, wolfish smile spread over his lips. "I still haven't made you cry wolf."

"You're never going to," I said, a challenge in my tone, despite the fact that my voice was shaking. I shuddered around the cock impaling me. "I want everything you can give me and more."

"Good." He thrust his hips again.

I moaned as the head of his cock rubbed over my g-spot, need shaking through me. My cry bounced off the walls, echoing back to us. It was soon joined by another and another as he fucked me with tender, ruthless determination.

I was trembling, sweating and begging by the time he let me come the first time. I would have begged for more, too, begged him to make me come again, but he was already pulling out and flipping me over onto my belly and then urging me on to my knees. He moved his hands down my ass, gripped my hips before driving inside. "I'll never get enough of you, Stella," he told me.

I had no breath, no voice to echo the words back to him.

His cock swelled inside me, and I shivered around him, already so close to that edge again. His hand came down on my ass and that first, startling smack was all I needed to push me over again.

Lukas shuddered. He bent lower over me, driving into me

harder, faster. I started to come as he groaned my name, a rare loss of control for him. I closed my eyes as wave after wave crusted over me. As strength drained out of me, I dropped down onto the mattress.

His hands tightened on my hips, and he growled, grinding against my ass. His cock jerked inside me, and I shuddered as sensations went dancing through me all over again. Slowly, he sank down next to me. He pulled me into the curve of his body.

Long moments of blissful silence.

"I love you," he murmured against my neck.

I covered his hand with mine and smiled into the darkness. "I love you too."

37

Fall was coming to Colorado.

It was September, and I'd started school that month.

I'd finally decided what I wanted to do – I was going to get a degree in psychology and work with troubled kids. It was something that had always drawn me, but up until this past year, seeking parental approval had been the most important thing.

I loved my parents, but I had decided months ago that I couldn't live my life according to what they wanted.

Bent over the paper I was working on, I tuned out the sound of the phone ringing.

It was harder to tune out the sound of Lukas's voice and I didn't mind that so much. I'd been at it for hours and could use a distraction.

Standing up, I stretched my arms over my head, groaning as the kinks made themselves known. I turned to see Lukas as he came into the room. He saw me and smiled, mouthing, *It's Gracie.*

He turned over an envelope to me as he continued to talk to Gracie, asking her about her parents. They were in the air, if I had my times right, flying in so they could be there for the birth of the baby.

She'd reached out to them not long after finding out that the artificial insemination had worked – letting them know she was pregnant. She'd also come out, telling them what she'd hidden for so long. She'd half-expected them to reject her and the baby, but they hadn't.

They were still uncertain about what to think, but they'd made one thing clear.

They loved her.

They wanted to be part of her life – and the baby's.

Paper rattled and I glanced down, saw the envelope in Lukas's hand. It was a large, legal looking one. Taking it, I eyed the open slit, then glanced at it. He grinned at me and nodded at the envelope. So I reached inside and pulled out the papers.

The sight of what was inside caused a band around my heart to unloosen.

I hadn't even realized it was there.

"The divorce is final," I said, the words shaky.

He nodded and started to lower the phone, his gaze intent on me. But at the sound of a sharp sound coming from the speaker, both of us jerked our attention to the phone.

Gracie's startled cry had been clear enough that I heard her across the room.

"What is it?" Lukas demanded, worry entering his normally calm eyes.

I was already across the room so I heard her words clearly as she said, "My water just broke."

❄

It was twelve hours later.

Gracie and her mom were in the delivery room and according to what the nurses had told Gracie's dad, it shouldn't be much longer.

Lukas was nervous.

I don't know if it was on the level of new dad nervous – I don't think it was, but there were definitely some jitters. Hell, *I* had a case of the jitters, and I was just going to be the aunt. Gracie had started calling me that in her fifth month, taking my hand and putting it on the hard mound of her belly when the baby kicked. She'd say silly things like, *Say hello to your niece or nephew, Aunt Stella.*

And I'd done so, with a goofy smile on my face each time.

She'd done the same to Lukas, ignoring his obvious discomfort until he'd managed to overcome it, and eventually that discomfort was replaced by something that looked a little like awe. I remembered the first time I saw a smile of wonder spread across his handsome face, and it still made my heart flip over in my chest.

"How much longer can this take?"

"It takes as long as it takes," I told him, reaching over and taking his hand.

He glanced over at me, then tugged. "Come here."

I blushed but obeyed, rising from the seat and letting him pull me onto his lap. Nobody was paying us any attention. Gracie's dad was on his phone, talking to one of Gracie's cousins, giving an update about the lack of updates, it sounded like. Two more of Gracie's friends were there and they were talking quietly in another corner.

Looping an arm around Lukas's neck, I let him pull me into the curve of his body and relaxed into him.

He had something on his mind and I suspected it was more than Gracie.

I didn't press him though.

There wasn't much point.

He'd talk when he was ready.

It didn't take him long.

"You told me once that you wanted to have kids. Do you still feel that way?" he asked softly.

"More than ever," I told him honestly. Pressing my lips to his cheek, I murmured, "I'd love to have your baby, Lukas."

He turned his head so that our mouths touched and he whispered, "How much do you want it, Stella?"

My reply was cut short by his kiss.

"Enough for you to want to marry me?" he asked.

I blinked, caught off guard. Tensing in his arms, I lifted my head and stared at him, mouth falling open.

He crooked a grin at me, and now, he looked more nervous than ever. "I was going to wait until I had you someplace romantic...a candlelit dinner or something, but I don't want to wait anymore. I had to wait until the divorce went through and that was long enough."

"I..." Blinking at him, I swallowed around the knot in my throat, then suddenly giddy with happiness, I threw my arms around him and laughed. "Absolutely, I'll marry you."

He kissed the laughter right out of me and I moaned against his lips, having to remind myself where we were.

Heat, excitement, need, and want rushed through me, and as he broke the kiss, my heart hammered in my chest. Leaning in, I pressed my lips to the spot just below his ear and murmured, "You know, this baby thing Gracie is doing is taking *forever*... what do you say you and me go out to the car and have a practice run of our own?"

He laughed and caught me up in a crushing hug.

His response was cut short, though, by the opening of the doors. Instinctively, we both looked and found Gracie's mom standing there. She wore a beaming smile on her face as she looked around. "It's a girl!"

THE END

PREVIEW: SEX COACH

M. S. PARKER

1

MICHELLE

"Damn, I'm good."

Leaning back in my seat, I added my byline to the article – *Michelle Nestor.*

Too bad my article wasn't for something a little more elaborate than a little local magazine, detailing all the hot happening places in a suburbia.

It was okay, though. This piece on Phoenicia, NY was another notch on my freelance belt, and the more notches I had, the more I would get.

And now that this boring piece was done, I could focus on writing something for my aunt. Aunt Blair worked for a *much* bigger outfit than the *Phoenix* out of Phoenicia – had to love the alliteration there.

Aunt Blair worked for *Coterie*, one of the biggest women's magazines in the nation.

Coterie's readers numbered into the millions, and they were all over the country – hell, they were all over the world. Thanks to the miracle of online readership, the few articles I'd actually gotten published by them had been read by people across the globe.

I had readers in *Australia*.

That was such a kick. People in Oz had read my work.

Not just people up in Buffalo or Phoenicia who'd picked up the *Phoenix* or another one of the local magazines I'd been lucky enough to get published in – but all across the world.

It was such a rush to think about it.

"How about you stop thinking about it and start actually writing another article?" Wiping the dopey grin off my face, I gave myself a kick in the pants so I actually would focus on it. Aunt Blair was happy to take a look at anything I put in front of her, but it had to be something that her reader base would want.

Sometimes my freelance pieces were hit-or-miss.

I couldn't help it though. I had never been a normal twenty-something. No matter how hard I tried, normal was just not what I was.

I liked to pretend it was the writer in me.

Pulling up the file, I clicked it open and started from the beginning, tightening up the writing as I read through to refresh my memory. It didn't matter that I had a Masters in this shit. When I got in the groove, my brain was firing too fast to worry about things like grammar and spelling. That was why *and* so often ended up as *amd* and *an* became *and*.

It was also why I needed an editor.

A half an hour later, my groove was strong, and I was somewhat thrown when the phone rang.

Actually, *thrown* wasn't the word.

I was *irritated*. I hated it when I had a good groove going and somebody or something interrupted me.

This was why I didn't have a cat.

This was why I didn't have a roommate.

"This is why you don't have a boyfriend," I muttered.

Although that was actually a lie. It was one I told to comfort myself when I felt lonely, but it was bullshit.

Answering the phone, I tried not to sound like I was ready to bite the person's head off through the handset.

"Make it fast," I snapped.

Aunt Blair laughed. "Wow. You're either writing something brilliant or you stayed up way too late watching Netflix. Which one is it?"

Having to recalibrate my attitude and my mood on the fly wasn't easy, but I managed.

"Both?" I offered. Realizing I was going to be on the phone for several minutes at least, I pushed back from my desk and got up to go get some coffee. Coffee made everything better.

That was just a fact of life.

And when you found the coffee pot empty that just made life worse. Groaning, I rinsed out the damn pot and started a fresh batch while Aunt Blair rightly guessed, "Are you out of coffee already?"

"I'm starting to think you have cameras planted in my office."

"No, I just know you. Tell me something, love, are you ever going to wake up in a good mood because you've had fantastic sex all night?"

If only.

"Sure," I quipped, keeping my voice light to hide the wistfulness inside me. "Who did you have in mind?"

"I can't help you figure that out, sweetheart." There was something in her voice, though, that made me think I wasn't fooling her. She didn't push. One more reason I loved her above all other aunts, uncles, and cousins. "So, listen, sweetie...I've got some news."

"Do you?" Interest twitched inside me. When Aunt Blair usually called this early in the morning with *news*, it was because she had work for me. Especially when she started off the conversation like that.

I thought about everything I had on my plate and decided most of it could be done fast enough and none of it was important enough that I couldn't work my aunt in. Especially if it had to do with *Coterie*.

"Oh, yes," she said, heaving out a sigh that was torn between fervent and beleaguered. "I'm in a bind, sweetheart, and you're a bit inexperienced, but seriously, you're one of the best writers I know and that's what I need. If you do a good job on this, which I'm sure you will, this could be a big break for you."

I held my breath as she paused, knowing better than to ask a question or interrupt.

"It was an article that Gina Goddard was going to write. She pitched it to me months ago and we've got the space, everything all lined up. We've already pitched it to our reader base. They're expecting it, but Gina was in a wreck. We're *so* fucked. Gina can't write for the next month, minimum."

At first, all I heard was...Gina Goddard.

Gina was like my guru. I read *all* of her pieces. I scoured the internet looking for her older articles, and I studied her interview techniques. She'd been in a wreck?

My heart fluttered. "Oh my goodness, is she okay?"

"She will be." Aunt Blair gave another strained sigh. "I don't know why she insists on driving that insane little car of hers."

"Aunt Blair...it's a Porsche. And more, it's a rather unique one. They only produced ten of that particular model the year it was made." Rolling my eyes, I fought the urge to tell her how car-illiterate she was. *I* was car illiterate, but I looked like an *A* student next to her.

"And she should have left that Porsche sitting in the garage next to her apartment," Aunt Blair replied. "Somebody hit on her Fifth and the car folded around her like a candy shell. She's now in the hospital with a broken leg, a punctured lung, and she's battered and bruised to Kingdom Come."

Aunt Blair's voice was taut with worry, and I immediately felt bad.

"I'm sure she's going to be okay, Aunt Blair. Gina is tough."

Tough barely described Gina.

The woman was beyond tough. She was also a dedicated reporter and freelance writer. The thought that my aunt was trusting me enough to write a piece that had been meant for

Gina was more than just a compliment. To be honest, it was slightly unnerving.

And if I thought about it for too long, I'd get too nervous and too panicky.

"What's the piece?" I asked, determined to get my nerves settled.

"Well, in line with our earlier topic of discussion..." Aunt Blair laughed lustily. "It's all about how to have multiple orgasms, sweetheart. This oughta be enlightening for you."

The only thing I really heard was multiple orgasms.

"So, are you interested?"

The greedy, determined writer in me said "*Yes,*" before the common sense part of me could even figure out a response.

It was probably a good thing.

The common sense part of me was too busy thinking...

But I've never had multiple orgasms.

The common sense part of me was thinking...

Tell her no, you can't do this.

The common sense part of me was thinking...

How in the hell do you research something like that?

But the greedy writer had already taken control.

"Aunt Blair, that sounds fascinating and delightful. When do I start? She has research?"

Aunt Blair sounded delighted. "Oh, *wonderful,* honey. Just *wonderful.*"

"Her research?" I asked hopefully.

"Not so much," Blair said. "She hadn't quite yet started. And you're going to have to rush this because this was supposed to run in the Valentine issue. Gina was running behind, but we trusted her to get it done as always. So, I need your best, and I need it fast."

'But you said she hadn't started it?" Oh, shit.

Now the other shoe dropped.

"Honey, you'll be fine. You've got a lot of what you're going to need already lined up. She has an interview set up with a man she told me has been called the king of multiple orgasms." Another deep, dirty laugh. "Honey, you're going to be interviewing a gigolo."

"What?" I demanded.

"You heard me. I'll send you the information via email shortly. You might want to get a haircut, a manicure. Nobody wants to see a male prostitute when their nails are looking all ragged." She clicked her tongue a few times. "Use the business credit card I gave you."

Blair sounded positively cheerful about all of it.

"I know how you are on deadline."

2

MICHELLE

MICHELLE

"This is insane." I understood he needed to be able to pick me out of a crowd, but this was *still* insane. Huddling inside my coat as I hurried up the steps, I tried to understand what was the point of going someplace in this kind of weather wearing a mini skirt and high heels sans stockings.

No tights. Nothing. No stockings at all.

Boots apparently had been out of the question.

Fortunately, my coat went all the way to my ankles. Not only was it warm, it was lined and heavy enough that the wind didn't send it flapping all around me. Still, I shivered inside it as I hurried through the doors.

I turned it over to the man just inside and fluffed my hair.

It was packed inside, and I tried to see if the seat I was supposed to find was open as the instructions in the email had insisted it would be.

Aaaaannnnddd...it was.

Sure enough, the second seat from the end at the bar was empty. It was insanely crowded in here, but those two seats sat vacant. Shaking my head, I gave my hair one last fluff and then made my way over toward the bar. A couple started to approach the two seats, and I froze. Maybe I was wrong.

"Excuse me," a churlish voice came up from behind me, and I sidestepped, realizing I was standing right in the middle of the one clear path available.

A waiter eyed me with cool appraisal as I stood there.

"I'm sorry," I said, easing a little farther out of the way.

The waiter cut around me without any reply, and when I looked back at the bar I realized the couple had abandoned their attempts to take the seats. "Okay. Let's try again," I told myself. I resumed my walk and nobody else got between me and those seats.

When I got to the bar, I waited for the bartender to look at me. Feeling foolish as I stood there, I toyed with the strap of my purse until he finally glanced my way. When he did, he raked me up, then down with a quick look before simply nodding at the seat.

"Ah, I believe one of these seats are mine."

He put a drink down in front of somebody and gestured to the stool I'd been eying.

Well. A man of many words.

I sat down and looked around, but the only solo guy I saw was an older man who looked to be in his sixties. *Please tell me that's not him.*

It wasn't that he was a bad looking older guy, but he looked like he was somebody's grandpa, not The King of Multiple Orgasms. How could I talk sex with somebody who looked like a grandpa?

I had to fight back the urge to giggle and ended up ordering a glass of wine so I could do something other than laugh nervously or stare.

Several minutes ticked by as I waited, but the older man didn't approach.

Neither did anybody else.

The King of Multiple Orgasms was running *late*.

When the bartender put down my glass of wine, he laid down a piece of paper with it.

I'M HERE. Don't look up and please stop looking around. My job requires absolute discretion and looking around attracts attention.

If you understand, please nod your head.

MY HEART STARTED TO RACE. Wow. This felt kind of cloak-and-dagger-ish. But I picked up the wine and right before I took a sip, I nodded. Some part of me was waiting for Gina and Blair to pop out and yell surprise.

It didn't happen, and less than a minute later, a man slid onto the stool next to mine.

I started to turn my head in his direction.

"Don't look at me. Discretion, remember?"

His voice was low and smooth, accented slightly. He sounded like he was from someplace out west. Texas, maybe.

That low, easy twang did something weird to all the girly parts inside me – or maybe it was the deep, smooth sound of his voice. I had no idea.

My reaction was surprising enough that I took a drink of wine before replying. "Hello." I fought to keep my voice level and at the same low tone of his.

Somebody labeled *The King of Multiple Orgasms* probably paid a lot of attention to the female persuasion. It only made sense, otherwise how could he be the king of *one* orgasm much less the king of *multiple* ones?

"I'm happy to talk to you, but you can't look at me," he said in the same low voice that somehow carried to me despite the noise. "Confidentiality is key in my line of business so you can't use my name. Anything I tell you must be kept between us. Are you okay with that?"

I wasn't sure how I was supposed to do this without naming a source, but I'd find a way. I needed this break. After another sip of wine, I went to look at him, only to get another stern reminder.

"*Don't* look at me." He sounded mildly exasperated now.

I toyed with my glass, thinking this through. I guess I could still use his information without naming the source and in his line of work I didn't blame him for wanting to stay anonymous.

"You do understand that this is confidential? I need to be able to trust you on this."

I gave another single nod. Then, hoping I used the proper amount of amusement and professionalism, I asked, "Am I okay to record this? I'll take notes, but I do better having my recordings as back up."

He was quiet a moment, then I sensed him shrugging. "Maybe. But...no peeking. And it might help if you say please."

"Good grief," I muttered, unsure why I felt so unsettled just then – or turned on. But I tossed out a flippant, "Please."

"Alright, then." He stroked one finger up my bare arm, making me shiver.

"I get it, you know," I told him, trying to cover my uneasy arousal. "You want to be an international man of mystery. But why not just let me interview you over the phone if privacy was so essential?"

He laughed, and the sound of it was even sexier than his voice. "Because I can't read you over the phone. Can't see if you follow the rules, do as I say."

"So this is a test?"

"Of course."

Trying to distract myself, I flipped my notebook open, but I wasn't sure how to start this. How did one interview a male prostitute? I should have written down some questions, but I'd been interviewing people for several years now and had come to accept that I never felt right asking the staid, boring, typical questions. Winging it always produced better results.

But the only thing in my mind right now was...

Awful.

Blood rushed to my face. Hoping to hide the blush until it faded, I propped my chin in my hand. "I hope you don't mind answering some of these questions. Some might sound kind of silly, or intrusive. Or both," I hedged, waiting for even a *silly* question to come to mind.

So far, all I had was...*do you really sleep with women for money?*

"If I wasn't open to answering questions, I wouldn't have agreed to the interview." He sounded amused, and I had a difficult time not turning to look at his face.

Finally, another question popped into my head, and it made it to my lips too.

"How much do you charge?"

"Well, you just get right to it, don't you?" He reached over, trailing a finger down the hand that still propped my chin up and shielded my face. "You'll have a hard time taking notes like that. You are right handed, I believe."

"I am. I just..." Babbling made me sound *so* professional. "I'm still trying to figure out the right approach to this, to be honest. This is a little different from most of my articles."

There. That sounded honest enough, didn't it?

"How so?"

"Well, my last one was about all the hot, happening places in Phoenicia, New York. I'm pretty sure if I'd turned in a piece that had anything to do with male prostitutes, I'd lose the chance to get another job with them." Immediately after, I regretted the directness of my reply.

But he didn't seem to mind. "Not everybody has an open mind about sex. That's just life. But it's a basic need – like food, water, companionship."

I'd lowered my hand, and from the corner of my eye, I could see that he'd leaned in closer. The light gilded his hair now, and I had the impression that it was pale gold.

"I imagine you can understand that, can't you?" he murmured, his voice closer to my ear now. "By the way, speaking of companionship, I didn't catch my companion's name."

"Ah..." I swallowed, feeling like there was a knot in my throat the size of a fist. "I'm...ah...Michelle. I imagine you were expecting Gina, but there were circumstances. I assure you, there are good reasons–"

"Drink your wine, Michelle. I know about Gina's wreck. Her assistant emailed me to let me know somebody else would likely handle the interview...perhaps even the article. Are you nervous?" He nudged the wine closer.

Did it *show* that I was nervous?

Crap. I hoped not.

Determined to get back on track, I focused my brain and jotted down some questions that seemed legit. "How did you...get started? I assume this isn't something you planned on doing from the time you were a young boy of five or six," I added dryly, relying on humor to help cover my discomfort.

His laugh was just as sexy now as it had been the first time I heard it. He shifted on the stool, and I caught another glimpse of his profile. It was definitely a *nice* profile. Nice enough that my heart fluttered a bit, and I wanted to turn and look him full in the face. But I stuck to the agreement.

"It's a long story. Does the answer help you write your article?"

"I...well, I don't know."

He leaned in and whispered, "I don't think it does. How did you end up becoming a writer? Do you enjoy it?"

"You do realize I'm supposed to be interviewing you, right?" Tapping my pen on the notepad, I scrawled something in the shorthand only I would understand. "You've got something of a reputation. A nickname to go with it too." Blood rushed to my cheeks, and I swallowed hard before I continued, "A very descriptive nickname."

"And just what nickname is that?" he asked, clearly teasing me. But he didn't push for an answer, continuing to talk without waiting for me to reply. "It's true though that I take pride in my work. If you're going to do something, you might as well do it well."

"I'm going to assume you're..." I stopped, nibbling on my lower lip as I wondered how in the world Gina did this. She'd interviewed dominatrixes and submissives before, swingers and others who led...interesting sex lives. A sex pro would probably be a piece of cake. And I was stumbling trying to think up a few questions.

"Who came up with the nickname? You or a client?"

"A client." He laughed, a rich, full laugh that made me wish I hadn't asked. "It would be a bit arrogant for me to use that, don't you think? It's not like I have it written on a business card. Word just...gets around, we'll say."

"Do you have a business card?"

"No. Do you?"

"I..." Hesitating, I started to look at him, but stopped. "Of course. But this isn't about me."

"But it might come in handy," he replied. "In case I think up something I should tell you later on."

He put a hand out.

It was the first direct contact we'd had, and I found myself staring at the long-fingered hand and wondering what it would feel like to have the King of Multiple Orgasms touching me.

Immediately, I blushed. In order to hide it, I busied myself digging out a card from my small purse.

"Here..." I thrust it in his direction. "Now, can we please focus and talk about you?"

"We're trying to, but you keep getting distracted. How long have you lived in New York City?"

"I'm..." Flabbergasted. I blew out a breath. "I'm not *getting* distracted. You're *distracting* me. And I've lived here a few years. What about *you*?" Maybe that was how I should play it. Answer his questions, then turn it around on him.

"About the same. Where did you live before here?"

This was like pulling teeth.

Huffing out a breath, I replied, "Chicago. What about you? Where did you live before you came to New York? Did you come here for work?"

"In a way," he replied. "I had a feeling you were from Chicago.

It's in your voice."

"You've got a good ear." Most people couldn't pick up on it after the years I'd spent going to college in Iowa, then the time here in the city. "I suppose you must enjoy the female persuasion, considering your line of work." I decided not to make it a question. He'd probably ask *me* if I enjoyed women in return.

Instead of answering right away, he reached over, picking up my glass of wine. I heard him swallow and then he put it back down in front of me. He had just drank my wine. I couldn't decide if I was irritated by the fact that he hadn't asked or...inexplicably aroused.

Why would I feel pleased by the fact that he was drinking from the same glass?

What was the sense in that?

Take a drink, a teasing voice inside my head whispered. *Maybe you'll taste him on the glass.*

My mouth went dry at the thought, and the only thing I had *to* drink was the wine, and I reached for it, desperate to wet my throat. To my credit, I deliberately made sure to keep from turning the glass so my lips wouldn't touch where his had.

"I didn't realize we were working up such a thirst," he murmured. His voice was so close.

I gasped as he traced a finger down my arm.

How in the hell did Gina do this?

"I'm going to assume you're..." Great. I was babbling now. Feeling his watchful eyes on me, I kept mine focused on the glass. "I mean, I guess you're good at this. Otherwise you wouldn't very well have earned the name the King of..." My cheeks flamed, and I couldn't finish. "You know."

"I assume I'm good, but I have to take my partner's word for it. Her word...her reaction. That's the key, you know. How she reacts. Paying attention to her." The finger that had trailed up my shoulder returned, this time skipping up my neck, then down. "Seeing if she likes having her neck touched, or she's too ticklish to enjoy it. I don't think that's the case with you."

It sure as hell wasn't. I had to fight not to let my head fall to the side in open invitation.

"You know, I think I'm glad Gina couldn't come. Pity about the wreck and all, but I think I like you."

My skin flamed, going tight in response to those simple words.

"There's not much to like."

"Oh...we disagree there." He leaned in, his face so close I could feel the heat of his breath through my hair. Focusing straight ahead, I caught a glimpse of our reflections in the wine glass as I lifted it. He was practically nuzzling my hair. If I concentrated, I could hear him breathing in too. Like he was...

Oh, hell.

He was checking me out. It was like he was deciding if he liked the way I looked, the way I smelled. I'd already decided I liked the way *he* smelled and maybe I was crazy, but there was something decidedly erotic about what he was doing.

How would his scent change if it was rubbed all over me?

If it clung to *me*?

I didn't know, but I was suddenly enamored with the idea of finding out.

And that thought terrified me.

"You..." Skin going cold, I grabbed my wine and tossed it back. "We really should get to work on this interview," I said, my voice shaking a little as the adrenaline that had filled me for the past few minutes started to crash, then wane. "I've hardly asked you a single question."

"I'm all ears. Just what would you like to know?" As if he'd sensed the tenor of my questions had abruptly changed, he straightened in his seat, and I lost the reflection again. He flagged down the bartender. After he'd ordered some ice water, I felt the intensity of his stare settle back on me.

I managed to force out all of two questions before a whole new sort of distraction dropped into my lap.

The furor started up behind me, quiet at first, then spreading through the room until I couldn't hold back my curiosity anymore. I shifted around to toss a look back at the door, expecting another D+ list celebrity or one of the socialites who kept appearing in the papers.

Instead, I was treated to the full glory of the current Hollywood heartthrob who'd just racked up three Golden Globes – and his date.

She looked bored.

But he had a smile on his face that made him look as open and endearing as he'd been when he'd accepted one award after another. Something that might have been excitement crashed inside me.

"Son of a bitch," I whispered, wishing I'd brought one of the photographers with me. "That's...oh, man. Do you see who that is?"

"Yes." He sounded bored.

I started to shoot him a quick glance, but froze half way in place and he caught me with a hand between my shoulder blades. "Remember the rules, sugar."

Instead of looking at him straight on, I focused on the ground in front of me – and the cowboy boots he was wearing. Black, tooled leather, a pair of faded jeans, what looked like an incredible pair of thighs, muscled and lean and long...

My heart was racing when I finally swung my head back around to look at the heartthrob of the month. "You think they are really a thing, the way the tabloids say they are?"

"No," he said softly.

"Why not?" Watching as the movie star leaned in to kiss his date in a way that was decidedly intimate, I studied them with more clinical interest than I liked.

"Because she's bisexual and expects all her partners to share...male, female, doesn't matter. He doesn't play that game. He couldn't care less about her sexual preferences, but when he's all in, he expects the same from his partner. This is convenience, nothing more."

My jaw fell open. "What...how do you know that?" I demanded.

"Tricks of the trade. It would ruin her if anybody knew, considering how she sells herself." There was something cool and measuring in his words.

A split second later, I understood.

He was trying to determine if he could trust me or not. Waiting to see if I'd push for more details, or maybe even trying to decide if I'd go public with the information.

Fat chance.

She wasn't my story.

He was.

I said nothing though. Keeping my attention on the couple who had just walked inside, I said softly, "That has to be lonely, picking your dating choices based on who will notice you."

A bright light flashed, and I flinched, lifting my hand to block it instinctively, not quite reacting in time.

Brilliant lights flashed in front of me, alternating with little black dots, and I blinked, trying to clear my eyes. "Whoa," I muttered, trying to clear my head. "Paparazzi. Stage left."

The noise level multiplied by the second, and the flashes became so common, they developed a strobe-like effect.

"There goes the neighborhood," I muttered.

I turned back, and my mouth dropped open. He'd left.

Panic welled inside me, but I battled it down. I was panicking – I had to be. He hadn't given me *anything*. So...he wasn't gone. He'd gone to the restroom or something. Surely, he'd said something, and I just hadn't noticed over the chaos.

He'd be back in a few minutes.

But then I noticed the slip on the bar.

The tab.

Swallowing, I picked it up, ignoring the bills that fluttered off the side. He was a generous tipper, that was pretty clear. He'd paid for my wine and left a tip that cost as much as the single glass – and he'd scrawled a note at the bottom for me.

I'll be in touch.

"Yeah," I muttered, growing more disgusted by the minute. "Sure you will."

❄

JUST OVER AN HOUR LATER, clad in super soft pajamas and smelling of my custom blend of lavender and vanilla body lotion, I stood at the window, staring outside.

I'd been had.

Or conned.

Something.

Okay, so it wasn't like he ended up stiffing me with a bill for an expensive meal – or even a drink since he paid for my *wine*. But I hadn't gotten anything useful out of him.

Sure, I was no Gina Goddard, but I knew how to interview people.

I had dozens of interviews under my belt – close to a hundred by now, probably. But as I played that interview back through my mind, I knew there was nothing at all usable in the information I'd gotten from him. Or rather, the information I *hadn't* gotten from it.

Getting more aggravated by the second, I went back to my purse and pulled out my phone, tapping on icons until the digital recording app opened. I hit play and listened as it started to play.

"Shit!" Twenty minutes later, I threw the phone down on the couch, ready to rip my hair out.

There was nothing worth putting in an interview unless I planned to write a piece about *myself*. And even that would be about as boring as could possibly be.

There was nothing at all usable.

Burying my face in my hands, I muttered, "My aunt is going

to kill me." A split second later a worst thought occurred to me. No, Gina is going to kill me. She had turned over a *prime* source, and instead of getting anything from him, I had wasted the entire meeting, letting him distract me.

"How could you be so stupid?" With a groan, I tried to figure out if there was any way I could sell this stuff, but there was nothing I *could* do except own up to the mistake.

Forcing myself to accept that, I moved over to the computer and clicked on the icon to open my email. With my eyes closed, I sat there for a good five minutes, trying to think through the best way to approach the email I had to write.

Aunt Blair wouldn't wash her hands of me, I knew that. But it would be awhile before she would trust me with a job like this again.

And I would have disappointed her too. She had trusted me to do this, and I hated disappointing people, especially those who had put their faith in me.

Finally, unable to figure out anything I could say except the honest truth – *he had a sexy voice and he flustered me and I fucked up* – I opened my eyes and focused on writing what I had to write.

Then I just sat there, staring.

I had an email.

Actually, there were several.

But the most recent one was from a *J. King* and the subject had my heart pounding.

For your article

Nervous as hell, I clicked on it and started to read.

Then, once I was done, I sat there for a full minute, hardly able to believe what I'd read.

My heart was racing.

My head was spinning.

I didn't know what part of me was more excited.

The writer...or the man.

Who in the world would have guessed that just reading an email could be so erotic? Everything I needed was in that email...including his name, which I'd forgotten to ask.

He'd signed it simply.

Jake.

3

JAKE

She wasn't beautiful, but she was pretty and the blushes that kept coloring her cheeks were pretty damn cute.

One thing was certain – she wasn't what I'd been expecting.

But then again, I wasn't sure what I'd been expecting. When a woman contacted me out of the blue about an article she wanted to do with Jake King, the King of Multiple Orgasms – shit, what a name – I'd been tempted to say no.

But I'd been tempted to say no to a lot of things in the past decade of my life, and I hadn't. All for one reason. If it could serve as a mean to an end, then I wasn't saying no.

And while I wasn't sure if somebody who wrote for a woman's magazine like *Coterie* was considered a reporter or a writer – was there a difference? – one thing was certain. Anybody who worked for an outfit that big would have connections. I'd spent my entire adult life cultivating any and every connection I could get.

Why stop now?

I'd been right though.

The woman who'd requested the interview was Gina Goddard, one of *Coterie's* top writers.

The woman sitting next to me had nervously given me her name – Michelle.

They were two different people. There was no doubt in my mind. Different styles, different approaches. I didn't even have to ask. Gina Goddard wasn't a woman who'd blush about asking a man how he'd gotten his start at fucking women for money.

The woman next to me with her pretty blushes and her uncertain glances was a different matter entirely. And those blushes were proving to be far more enticing than I'd imagined possible, and I wanted to see just how far down they went.

Finally figuring out the right way to approach all of that, I studied the interior of the tequila bar where we'd agreed to meet and decided that the ideal way to handle this – *her* – was to tell her we needed more privacy.

That plan got dashed to all hell less than five seconds after I hatched it.

The last thing I needed was to see a movie star come in.

No, the last thing I needed was to get intrigued by the cute little redhead conducting the interview. But that was what happened. And it had been followed by the second to the last thing I needed to happen – the entrance of a movie star followed by paparazzi.

Now I was stuck in this damn bar with a writer, paparazzi, and the problem of how to get out. I never should have agreed to this damn interview. Women didn't need to read articles on how to achieve multiple orgasms. They needed a really good vibrator, or better yet, a really good partner.

That's where I came in.

With the right dollar amount, I would give a woman as many orgasms as she wanted.

Sometimes, I didn't even need the dollars thrown in there.

I dated, had sex off the job. A busman's holiday, maybe. I didn't need to get paid to get off. It was just...what I did. It was what I was good at. And it was a means to an end.

Michelle wasn't exactly the sort of woman I would have

sought out on my own, but having her dropped into my life was...well, who turned down such a sweet surprise?

Granted, there was nothing about sitting there with Michelle that was helping me accomplish that end I'd set for myself a long time ago, teasing and flirting with the sexy redhead who had actually come out in the freezing weather wearing a strapless dress under a coat that had almost convinced me she wasn't the woman I was looking for. Right up until she shrugged out of the coat to reveal that dress, and that body.

All those curves had been perched on a pair of fuck-me heels, done in a shade of blistering red – the high heels sans pantyhose and a pink miniskirt. It was possible there could be a woman wearing that same get-up but nobody else but the woman I needed to meet would be likely to be alone as she approached the seat my bartender buddy always kept open for me on the nights I told him I had a meet.

Now, here I was with a woman I wouldn't mind being alone with, but the one thing I didn't have time for was convincing her of that – not when the camera flashes were getting as consistent as lightning during a summer thunderstorm.

Michelle crossed her legs, murmuring something under her breath, and I was acutely aware of the way one shoe dangled off the tip of her toes.

I had to get the hell out of here, or I wouldn't care enough to do it later.

Buck, my faithful bartender sidekick, glanced my way and I gestured toward her glass, already knowing how much the wine would cost – and calculating how much of a tip I should leave to cover his trouble.

He glanced at Michelle, but gave a single nod.

I had the money out before he even reached me and took the pen from the little leather folder as he laid it on the counter.

Scrawling her a note, I left the bills, making sure I took the business card she'd fished out of her purse earlier.

I hadn't seen the last of Miz Michelle.

But I wasn't seeing her here.

That was for certain.

❄

BACK AT MY APARTMENT, simple, sparse and spartan, I looked up Miz Michelle Nestor.

I had more interest in her rather than finding out why she'd been at the restaurant rather than Gina, but I did take a few minutes to research the popular writer from the women's magazine.

Her accident had actually made a couple of the local news outlets, so it was pretty easy to understand why she had somebody else filling in for her.

Finding out information about Michelle wasn't quite so easy.

She had a Facebook page, but it was locked down tight.

She had a LinkedIn page, but it was locked down even tighter.

No Twitter that I could see.

The only online presence that held any really hint of *her* was a brief online website for freelancers, and all I could see from that without having an account was a headshot and a few reviews and references.

"You're not making this easy are you, sweetheart?"

I studied the headshot, taking in the smile that was both polite and warm, but distant somehow. I didn't like it.

It wasn't really her.

"I guess I'm not going to find out much about you online, am I, sugar?" I touched a finger to the curve of her cheek and leaned back, head cocked as I continued to ponder her face.

Plucking the card from the pocket of my jeans, I eyed her email, then opened the email app on my laptop.

"I wonder if I can make you blush from just a message."

❄

AN HOUR LATER, I locked the door behind me, leaving the warmth of the apartment behind yet again. I had an appointment in Manhattan at a boutique hotel where anonymity was just as much a selling point as the lush, 1920s art-deco style rooms.

My client was waiting for me, lying in bed naked, sipping from a glass of wine and checking her email.

"Can't you take a night off, darlin'?" I asked.

She glanced at me. "I am. That's why I'm here...darling." She gave me a slow smile and dropped the phone on the nightstand before taking a sip of her wine, smiling at me over the rim as she swallowed.

Alicia was one of my favorite clients. I'd almost even call her a friend, if I allowed myself to have friends.

But friends weren't exactly something I liked to put my trust in. I'd done that before, and it had fucked me over good and proper. I wouldn't let myself get in that position again.

Still, I liked Alicia.

She was easy to talk with, easy to please, she was a good bed partner, and she paid well.

What wasn't to like?

"Are you in the mood for anything specific?" I asked, moving to the foot of the bed.

"Just you." She gave another smile and crooked her finger at me.

I approached, and she offered me her glass of wine. I put it on the table for her instead of drinking and bent down low, kissing her soft lips. She tasted of the chardonnay she'd been drinking, and I had a brief moment to wonder...*how would the zinfandel Michelle had been drinking taste on her lips*?

Then I jerked my attention back to the job.

Alicia moaned as I covered her body with mine, deliberately dragging my chest against her breasts so that the cotton of my sweater rubbed over her nipples.

"I changed my mind," she said against my lips. "I do want something specific. Hard and fast."

"As you wish."

I flipped her over onto her belly and brought her up onto her knees. As she braced herself on her palms, I pulled a rubber from my pocket – it would be the first of three we'd use, although I carried a couple extra just in case.

By the time she had herself steadied on her hands and knees, I had my cock sheathed in latex, and I grabbed her hips again, hauling her back and half lifting her slim form. I had another flash – rounder hips, because Michelle was a powerhouse of curves and lines, her pale flesh glowing like a pearl against my darker, rougher skin.

Groaning, I thrust deep.

Alicia cried out my name, and I forced myself to think, to focus. "Rough?" I asked.

"Please...yes. Hell, yes."

I caught the thick weight of her hair in my hand and made a rope of it, pulling her back until her spine arched as I rode her. "Come for me, you sexy little bitch," I said as I palmed her breast with my free hand, tweaking her nipple.

Alicia whimpered and pushed against me, butt and breast, and I shoved all thoughts of everything else from my mind.

After all, I had a reputation to uphold.

4

MICHELLE

"*I will be allowed to speak, correct?"*

"Maybe...if you say please."

With my feet kicked up on the desk, I pondered the stamped tin ceiling tiles overhead and replayed those few moments over and over through my mind.

Was it me or had there been something sexually charged in that?

Was he into bondage?

The master and slave stuff?

That idea freaked me the hell out, and not in a good way, but there was something about his teasing voice when he'd said it.

Maybe...if you say please. The memory made me shiver.

There was some unfamiliar part of me that was already willing to say *please* to Jake in a number of ways. For a number of things. It was embarrassing to acknowledge it, but more than once, I found myself wondering how one might handle approaching a man in his position.

Not that I enjoyed sex really.

I actually kind of sucked at it.

I could get myself off with a vibrator just fine, but if I had a guy with me, once we got past the petting stage, things got really, really boring. And awkward.

That being the case, I didn't understand why I kept thinking about all the petting...and the *more* stuff. The stuff that usually made my brain freeze up.

His hands sliding my clothes off.

His hands sliding up and down my body, between my thighs, or cupping my breasts...his fingers...

I gasped when I felt the brush of my own fingers against my clitoris, not aware until that moment that I'd been stroking myself. Biting my lip, I moved my legs until they were farther apart and shifted in the chair a bit. The skirt I wore fell open around me. I trailed my free hand up over the thigh high, thick woolen socks I'd pulled on under the skirt I'd put on earlier.

It's all about gauging her reaction...following the cues her body gives you, he'd written in the email. *When you touch her thigh, does she sigh or shiver?*

Smoothing my fingers up my skin, I decided if he'd been the one doing this, I'd probably be sighing *and* shivering.

Does she need a bit more time to warm up? Tease her a bit. Touch her through her clothes, but it's just to tease and you keep the touches light.

I brushed my fingers against my clitoris again, the nub of flesh hard and stiff. I was wet already, and I rubbed harder, enjoying the friction of the material against me.

A smart man knows when she's ready for more. I like to think I'm a smart man.

I dipped my fingers inside my panties and gasped at the heat I discovered there.

When she's ready, a woman will all but bring herself to that first climax if you're not careful – and sometimes, that's just fine. I don't mind going along and enjoying the ride.

I thrust my fingers in, panting. In, out. I'd never ever felt this wet, this aroused. The chair wobbled under me and some latent sense of self-preservation had me lowering my feet to the floor.

That change in position thrust my fingers deeper, and I cried out. Flinging a hand against the desk for leverage, I started to rock against my touch, riding my own hand now.

Once she's close, I'll sometimes pull her back and draw out the pleasure.

Fuck that idea.

I'd never felt a climax quite like this.

I broke, right there in my chair, in front of my computer. Climaxing so hard it ripped a cry from my throat, I sagged bonelessly forward, my head dropping onto the keyboard as my body started to shut down on me.

Multiple orgasms are all about the timing, you know.

Hell. All I'd done was think about him, and this one had all but wiped me out. I wasn't sure I could handle the *timing,* and the thought of *multiples* almost melted my brain.

❄

THIRTY MINUTES LATER, reenergized by a shower, a sandwich, and coffee, I settled back down at my desk. Somewhat bemused by what I'd done, I brought up his email and read it again.

It wouldn't happen again, surely. Reading through it wouldn't cause that same erotic buzz that I'd been feeling all week, ever since I met him, compounded and complicated by his written words. It had just been a while since I'd broken out my vibrator. A couple of months, probably. I'd just been on edge, and I'd needed the release.

But the second I started reading and thinking about Jake, the hotter and heavier my body felt.

Sometimes, a lady I'm with will be done after just one session. But sometimes, she'll need more. I'm always happy to oblige. I just watch her and see what her body is telling me.

If he was here right now, my body would be screaming...*do me*!

Of course, five seconds after he made a move toward me, it might scream something else entirely.

"Son of a bitch," I muttered, closing the email, and scrolling up to catch up on messages from last night and this morning.

There were three from Aunt Blair, two last night and one from this morning. The last from twenty-five minutes ago. *Call me or I'm calling you.*

Blushing, I thought about what I'd been doing twenty-five minutes ago, and I wondered if she would have guessed just what I'd been up to by the sound of my voice.

With a nervous laugh, I picked up my coffee. "I'll call in a few, Aunt Blair," I murmured, toasting the picture of the two of us near one of the bridges in Central Park. "Just let me get a little more–"

The phone rang mid-sentence, and I had no doubt as to who was calling. Well, shit. With a mental groan, I picked up the phone.

"Good morning, sunshine!" Aunt Blair said, her voice ringing out. She sounded like she'd been awake for hours and already downed about a gallon of coffee. She probably *had* been awake for hours, but she didn't *drink* coffee. I didn't understand her. "How are you doing, sweetheart?"

"I'm fine. You sound too awake for me," I said, hoping she'd attribute any sluggish moments to me being tired or...something.

"You don't rest enough, eat right or exercise enough. Do all those things and call me in the morning."

"Ha, ha."

"You also don't get laid enough," Aunt Blair continued blithely. "What you need is to hook up with some guy who will eff your brains out once or twice a week."

I could have choked on the coffee I'd just taken a sip of. "Thanks," I said after a few awkward seconds. "I'll keep that in mind."

"Do that. So...listen. I've got news." Tension hummed

between us before she continued. "The powers that be *loved* your article. It's running in the next issue *and*...they want more."

Excitement exploded inside me. More? They liked it? Would I write them? Would I be able to see Jake again?

A million questions started to fire inside my head.

But she squashed them flat in the next second.

"Gina's recovering pretty well. She can sit up in a chair for longer periods of time, and she's already at work editing some of her other pieces. We think she'll be able to handle the series the higher-ups want, but thank you for doing such a bang-up job, sweetheart. We will *definitely* be using you for more pieces."

Disappointment had turned the excitement to ashes, and I had to fight to make my voice brisk and professional as I responded, "I'm very glad you all enjoyed it, Aunt Blair. Please give my best to Gina. I've got to go. I've got lunch cooking and it's about to burn."

I hung up before she could say anything else.

I couldn't fake the brisk tone for more than a few seconds, and I didn't want her to hear my dismay.

Granted, I couldn't even lie to her properly. Was I more upset about the fact that I wasn't finishing the series? Or the fact that I wouldn't have a reason to see Jake again?

I had no idea.

5

JAKE

The latest issue of *Coterie* lay open on the basic wooden coffee table in the middle of my living room, turned to the first page of the interview.

Michelle was one hell of a writer.

Those were *my* words she'd taken and used, but she had made them her own. I knew all about what she'd written, because I'd told it to her.

So why the hell did I still have a fucking hard-on ten minutes after reading it?

Maybe it was because something about *her* words had made me think that when she'd been writing it, *she* had been as filled with erotic anticipation as I was now.

Most of my clients were jaded about sex, even the ones who ended up with me because they'd lost interest in the act and expected me to change that.

A few of them, like Alicia, had healthy sexual appetites, and for one reason or another, it was just easier to have an arrangement with me rather than pursue some other, *normal* relationship with a regular, average nice guy.

Normal.

Nice.

Maybe that was the problem.

Michelle seemed like she was just the girl next door...normal, sweet, nice...she blushed when I pushed her about intimacy, but she pushed back if I went too hard.

It was different from what I was used to and that was enough to drive me a little crazy. It was also enough to make me think about her too often during the day.

Three times, I'd sat down to email her, the words I'd used already laid out in my mind.

I'd ask if I'd proven to be helpful.

If there was anything more she'd like to know.

Maybe we could meet for coffee, and I could answer some of the questions I'd left open the first time we met.

I knew how to catch a woman's interest, and Michelle's weakness was her curiosity. But still, my fingers lingered over the keyboard, unsure.

My cellphone rang, and when I checked the display, my heart skipped a beat. The caller ID read *COT UNLTD.*

Coterie.

Gina and I had spoken several times from a phone that belonged to the magazine. Maybe this was Michelle.

Still, I didn't answer on the first, or even immediately on the second tone. Sure, I was desperate to hear her voice, but I didn't need to let her know that.

"Hello?"

"Heya, gorgeous," a familiar, sexy voice said.

The voice was *not* Michelle's.

"Gina. Hi. I heard you were in an accident," I said, trying not to let my disappointment show in my voice. It was second nature to hide that sort of thing though. Most of my life had been filled with disappointment.

"I was. Tell you what, if it wasn't for sexy male nurses..." She ended with a lusty sigh that wasn't too different from how she sounded when she asked me if I *really* fucked women for a living. "They made the Nurse Ratchet I had to deal with at night a little more tolerable. But you don't want to hear about all of that. I wanted to talk to you about the article."

"The one Michelle wrote."

"Yes. She did *fantastic*. I was all but fanning myself when I was done, and since I've got one arm in a cast, my other hand was getting tired." She laughed impishly.

I had to smile myself. Gina was cocky, confident, and incorrigible.

I still wished it was Michelle on the phone.

"We're lighting up with responses from our readers on social media, email boxes are *full*. They want more, Jake. They want more of *you*. The bosses here want a series of articles. What do you say?"

My instinct was to correct her and say that they wanted more of Michelle. After all, it had been her way with my words that had written the article that had lit up social media and filled inboxes.

But...

"I might be interested," I said slowly, turning to look at the magazine.

"Fantastic. What will make that *might* into a *one hundred percent*?"

"I want Michelle to handle it."

Gina was quiet, but only for a split second. It had been my estimation that very little slowed her or swayed her for long. I was right. It didn't take her long to say, "I'm totally cool with that. My editor and I came up with the idea, but Michelle handled the interview and her article is going over like gangbangers. But I can't make any promises. My editor has to give the final okay. Are you cool with that?"

"Cool enough to wait and see what they say."

Because if they didn't say yes, I wasn't doing it.

"Excellent. You'll hear from me or Michelle soon." She hesitated, then added, "Jake?"

"Yeah?"

"Michelle...she's a nice girl." She didn't add anything else, but she didn't need to.

"I noticed, Gina. Don't worry. I don't make a habit of eating nice girls alive and leaving nothing but a quivering, broken heart."

I ended the call and pushed my phone back into my pocket, then went over and picked up the magazine, skimming the article one more time.

It wasn't good, I told myself, that she was filling my head as much as she was, taking over my thoughts.

I'd been honest with Gina when I said I didn't make a habit of messing around with nice girls. I didn't have time, and honestly, the kind of *nice* girls she meant when she talked about Michelle – nervous, shy, a little uncertain about her own sexuality – they didn't often come looking to pay a man for sex. Maybe they dreamed about it, thought about it...? I had no idea.

But they steered clear of men like me.

I tossed the magazine back down on the table, running my hands through my hair. I hadn't always been a whore.

There had been a time when I probably qualified as nice and normal myself. Looking up, I stared at my reflection in the mirror, the tattoos covering some older, rougher – *uglier* – work, studied the muscle that had been developed over months and years of a hard life. There was no sign of the nice, *normal* boy I must have been once upon a time.

Maybe that was why I wanted to spend time with Michelle.

She hadn't instantly gone from *hi* to *let's go fuck*.

Although one thing was sure...*let's go fuck* was pretty high on my list of things to do.

Continue reading in the full novel. Go to http://mybook.to/SexCoachPB to order the paperback.

ALSO BY M. S. PARKER

The Billionaire's Muse

Bound

One Night Only

Damage Control

Take Me, Sir

Make Me Yours

The Billionaire's Sub

The Billionaire's Mistress

Con Man Box Set

HERO Box Set

A Legal Affair Box Set

The Client

Indecent Encounter

Dom X Box Set

Unlawful Attraction Box Set

Chasing Perfection Box Set

Blindfold Box Set

Club Prive Box Set

The Pleasure Series Box Set

Exotic Desires Box Set

Pure Lust Box Set

Casual Encounter Box Set

Sinful Desires Box Set

Twisted Affair Box Set

Serving HIM Box Set

ABOUT THE AUTHOR

M. S. Parker is a USA Today Bestselling author and the author of the Erotic Romance series, Club Privè and Chasing Perfection.

Living in Las Vegas, she enjoys sitting by the pool with her laptop writing on her next spicy romance.

Growing up all she wanted to be was a dancer, actor or author. So far only the latter has come true but M. S. Parker hasn't retired her dancing shoes just yet. She is still waiting for the call for her to appear on Dancing With The Stars.

When M. S. isn't writing, she can usually be found reading–oops, scratch that! She is always writing.

For more information:

www.msparker.com
msparkerbooks@gmail.com

ACKNOWLEDGMENTS

First, I would like to thank all of my readers. Without you, my books would not exist. I truly appreciate each and every one of you.

A big "thanks" goes out to all the Facebook fans, street team, beta readers, and advanced reviewers. You are a HUGE part of the success of all my series.

I have to thank my PA, Shannon Hunt. Without you my life would be a complete and utter mess. Also a big thank you goes out to my editor Lynette and my wonderful cover designer, Sinisa. You make my ideas and writing look so good.

Made in the USA
Monee, IL
25 March 2021

63829853R00177